THE CONTRIBUTORS

HARLAN ELLISON . . . Winner of the Hugo, Nebula, Bram Stoker, and Edgar Awards

NEIL GAIMAN . . . World Fantasy Award winner and best-selling author

KATHERINE KURTZ . . . Bestselling author of the *Deryni* and *Adept* series

BRIAN LUMLEY . . . Bestselling author of the *Necroscope* series

JANE YOLEN . . . World Fantasy Award winner and National Book Award finalist

CHARLES L. GRANT . . . Winner of the British Fantasy Society Award for Lifetime Achievement

JOHN MASON SKIPP . . . One of the original "splatter-punks"

NANCY HOLDER . . . Winner of four Bram Stoker Awards

ALAN RODGERS . . . Bram Stoker Award winner and World Fantasy Award nominee

LUCY TAYLOR . . . Bram Stoker Award winner for superior achievement in a first novel

JO CLAYTON . . . Author of the acclaimed *Diadem* series

DON DÍAMMASSA . . . Acclaimed author and reviewer for *Science Fiction Chronicle*

P9-CRF-631

CHRISTA FAUST . . . Provocative storyteller, model, and tattoo enthusiast

ROBERT J. HARRIS . . . Story writer and author of several well-known role-playing games

BRIAN HODGE . . . Author of *Prototype* and *The Darker Saints*; he has appeared in almost 70 magazines and anthologies

CAITLÍN R. KIERNAN . . . Author of the Bram Stoker Award–nominated novel, *Silk*

MARC LEVINTHAL . . . Musician, writer, and composer of film scores and a hit single

MELANIE TEM . . . Prolific and acclaimed author of novels and short fiction

WENDY WEBB . . . Author and editor who also collects and photographs gargoyles

CHARLES DE LINT . . . Author of dozens of novels, and musician specializing in Celtic music

In the
Shadow of the
Gargoyle

Edited by

Nancy Kilpatrick and

Thomas S. Roche

ACE BOOKS, NEW YORK

IN THE SHADOW OF THE GARGOYLE

An Ace Book / published by arrangement with
the editors

PRINTING HISTORY
Ace trade paper edition / October 1998
Ace mass-market edition / October 1999

All rights reserved.
Copyright © 1998 by Nancy Kilpatrick and Thomas S. Roche.
Cover art by Victor Stabin.
This book may not be reproduced in whole or in part,
by mimeograph or any other means, without permission.
For information address: The Berkley Publishing Group,
a division of Penguin Putnam Inc.,
375 Hudson Street, New York, New York 10014.

The Penguin Putnam Inc. World Wide Web site address is
http://www.penguinputnam.com

Check out the ACE Science Fiction & Fantasy newsletter
and much more on the Internet at Club PPI!

ISBN: 0-441-00700-7

ACE®
Ace Books are published
by The Berkley Publishing Group,
a division of Penguin Putnam Inc.,
375 Hudson Street, New York, New York 10014.
ACE and the "A" design are trademarks
belonging to Penguin Putnam Inc.

PRINTED IN THE UNITED STATES OF AMERICA

10 9 8 7 6 5 4 3 2 1

ACKNOWLEDGMENTS

Thanks to all my wonderful friends, who make life worth living, and without whom this book, not to mention this editor, would not exist: Philippe Bourque, Rob Brautigam, Eric Kauppinen, Mike Kilpatrick, Sephera Giron, Hugues Leblanc, Michael Rowe, Caro Soles, and Mari Anne Werier. Tammy Glasby—you are missed. And thanks to my stalwart collaborator Thomas Roche, for keeping me laughing and screaming! And a special note of gratitude to Ginjer Buchanan, for her help and guidance, and her mutual obsession with these enchanting grotesqueries.

Nancy Kilpatrick

This book is dedicated to my family, whose enthusiastic support has been invaluable to me. Thanks to the following for their friendship and support on this project: M. Christian, Mike Ford, Paula Guran, Katharine Kerr, and Michael Rowe. Appreciation and respect also goes to Ginjer Buchanan for her dedication to and interest in the fields of fantasy and dark fantasy, and her willingness to take a chance. Nancy Kilpatrick gets major thanks for making this collaboration an unmitigated pleasure. It is a testament to Nancy's talent and diplomacy that no gargoyles were harmed during the making of this anthology. The contributors receive my gratitude for offering Nancy and me the pleasure and privilege of publishing some fantastic stories. Finally, thanks to all the scary gargoyles in my life, standing guard with stony-faced silence and infinite loyalty and beyond-infinite patience, black leather jackets and combat boots and attitude that just don't quit, wards and watchers of all that is holy.

The editors want to thank each of the authors in this volume for producing superior stories. We are especially honored to be able to publish one of Jo Clayton's last stories.

Thomas S. Roche

Contents

INTRODUCTION

＊＊＊

THE FRENCH CALLED THEM *gargouille,* meaning: to gurgle. From their humble beginnings as fancy rain spouts on European churches and castles, gargoyles branched out to become prized adornments on buildings of all types. These dark angels, often chiselled in stone, can also be hammered in brick, carved in wood, formed with metal, fashioned out of ceramic, clay and leather, and adorned with feathers, beads, jewels, stones, paint, and fabric.

Medieval sensibilities had more in mind than utilitarian esthetics when they created sculptures, often grotesque, above doorways to sacred places. Joseph Campbell and Jungian analyst Marion Woodman have talked of the need to protect the sacred, and for that, the demons of hell are perfect. If you can face them without being devoured, you can enter the realm of transformation. Gargoyles have the power to see into your heart.

Currently in vogue, gargoyles are for sale in department and specialty stores in various forms: indoor and outdoor statuary, candle holders, windchimes, calendars, greeting cards, refrigerator magnets . . . Gargoyle tattoos are fashionable with the young. And the even younger are enamoured with the popular cartoon program *Gargoyles*.

So, why are we attracted to these often-hideous representations? One reason seems to be that they act as a bridge between two worlds. At first glance it's a dog, or a snake, but the second glance—the longer look—reveals not an ordinary animal, but something not quite of this earth, yet startlingly familiar. It's a paradox. These beings that stand between two realities both attract and repel us. If their draw wasn't powerful, we wouldn't keep them around.

But why now? As the turn of a millennium approaches, gargoyles may serve many functions. They express realms beyond what our senses can detect. They remind us that there are moral choices to be made every minute of the day, and that such choices involve consequences. And they show us the beauty of a slower era, when human beings took time to reflect on the many layers of existence, and the overall meaning.

The wonderful stories in this volume present the gargoyle in all its manifestations. Beautiful and ugly, helpful and harmful, old world and new world. Let the stories entertain, thrill or unnerve you, but most of all, let the gargoyles act in the complex capacity for which they were intended—to mirror the soul.

Nancy Kilpatrick

THE SIGHT OF A gargoyle marks a place: a place of power. All creatures bound in stone, all sentient architectural aberrations, show themselves as warnings and invitations—but also as markers of locations sacred and profane.

In medieval Europe, the gargoyle fulfilled two purposes: It served as a protective ward on sacred places, and it reminded the faithful of the torments of Hell. Gargoyles therefore are horrors which defend from horrors, monsters which protect from monsters, visual nightmares which terrify in order to instruct. They form a sort of permanent demonic underclass, perhaps unjustly modeled after the psychic hobgoblins of those it protects. The gargoyle can be both a nurturing and a threatening force: Its existence is dictated by the need to protect, but its protection, however reliable, is on some level tentative. For the gargoyle is in service, and no service is ever immutable. Those protected would do well to respect the power which protects them.

By this token, the stories in this collection are meant to terrify in order to instruct, to nurture and threaten, to show us the twisted faces of those forces which protect us that we may better appreciate their protection. They mark the sacred places within us, and reflect the horrors of the damned as well as the pleasures of art. Admire them, and their grotesque visages become beautiful. Respect their power, and they will protect you as passionately as you honor them.

                                                      Thomas S. Roche

Charles L. Grant

The Soft Sound of Wings

THE SOFT SOUND of wings on a late September morning, a flutter and pause that barely disturbs the leaves in the old maple in the yard. The sky a hard blue never seen in summer, not unpleasant to look at but a warning just the same, that winter is a lot closer now than it was last week. The temperature cool but not yet crisp; time to air out the sweaters and bring the jackets from the closet, check the furnace, unfold the quilts. The grass still growing, but slower now. Much slower. And not as green, not as thick.

Like the flowers in the garden, the lawn's just waiting to die and too stubborn to go.

The voice of the neighborhood on a late September morning, kids and cars and mowers and breeze. So familiar it's almost silent. Comfortable. Comforting.

And it would all be just fine, if it wasn't for those damn wings.

I stood at the kitchen sink, finishing the dishes that had piled up during the week. I don't believe in washing every night.

It's only me now, and it isn't worth it to run the water for just a plate, a glass or cup, and a couple of pieces of silverware.

It hasn't been worth it for quite a while.

As I rinsed the last bowl and set it out to drain, I listened again to the wings, and smiled.

By leaning forward just a little I could see through the open window to the nest in the maple's heavy lower branches. Mabel and Phil have been with me for a number of years, robins who had taken a liking to that old tree, and the bread crumbs I left behind whenever I left the house. They certainly weren't tame, but neither did they flee when I sat on the back steps and watched them go about their living. Not even when the eggs hatched.

That's probably because I did my best to make sure they survived the season.

They had enough to worry about, keeping the nestlings from falling out of the nest, teaching them to fly, feeding them, keeping them dry. So I chased the jays, and the occasional crow, and threw enough stones at prowling cats to teach the little buggers to stay away from the small yard. I never hit one, though. I didn't try to. They got the message just the same.

Blurs and rustling leaves; it looked as if the robins were getting ready for their southern trip. I envied them a little. But not all that much. It was a miracle of sorts that they came back at all. I didn't want to think what I'd do when they didn't.

A sigh, then, and I turned my attention to the kitchen, a room not large but large enough for me not to have to squeeze around the small round table that seated four.

It was clean.

So were the counters, the refrigerator, the stove, the microwave, the floor, the walls, every damn thing in the room.

I walked into the dining room, and it was clean too.

"You know," I said to the hutch that held Dorrie's china, "you really ought to get a hobby, old man. A guy could perform a damn operation in this place."

The paper was on the front porch. I brought it in, sat on the living room couch, and read it nearly cover to cover.

Even the horoscope, which told me I'd best take care with business associates today or they were going to screw me royally and leave me lying in the gutter.

What I looked for, I didn't find—a story that would tell me they had caught the murderer of a young thief found in the park three weeks ago, just after school began. Or the murderer, probably the same one, who had dumped the mutilated corpse of a fellow killer on the lawn of the grade school last spring.

It almost made me wish I were back on the force.

Almost.

I was getting older; I wasn't getting more stupid.

A town like this doesn't have much in the way of violent crime. A few break-ins now and then, a drunken fight on the occasional weekend, petty arson, but seldom anything as serious as dying. That didn't start until the people from the suburbs and the city decided they'd had enough of locking every door and window in sight, and moved out here. The problem was, the more who came out, the more trouble was brought with them.

Naturally, they were the ones who screamed loudest about police protection and quality of life and what kind of place is this to bring up a child.

My answer has always been the same: a pretty damn good one until you guys came along.

Which did not endear me to either them or my superiors.

If I hadn't quit on my own, I figure I would have been forced to retire just to keep the chief from strangling me.

But neither they nor the chief had anything to do with why I finally did.

It was the school, the damn school that killed my wife.

I closed my eyes and let the paper fall to the floor. Heat shimmered in my cheeks, and ice settled in my stomach. Once again I was letting the past get to me, letting memories false and real get me riled for no reason.

I took a few deeps breaths, and went back to the kitchen where I made myself a decent lunch, and cleaned up again, this time laughing aloud as I did, recognizing what I was doing.

Still, I cleaned. And watched the branches sway as Mabel and Phil and their two young ones darted around from twig to twig.

Until, at last, there was the soft sound of wings, and within a blink the nest was empty, a single half-gold leaf rocking its way to the ground.

I couldn't see them in the sky, I couldn't see them in the grass, but I could see them just the same, and I could still hear their wings, so I lifted a hand in a slow, farewell wave.

All of it was empty then—the tree, the yard, the kitchen, the house.

"All right, all right." I grinned as I dried my hands. "Don't start, you old fart, don't start."

A quick check of the house to be sure there was nothing left to do, and I hurried back to the living room and looked around. Habit more than expectation. Nothing changed in here. It seldom did.

Then I grabbed an old wool-lined windbreaker from the back of a chair, slipped it on as I opened the door, and said, "I'll be back soon," before stepping outside into the shadow of a cloud.

I checked the sky, saw no rain impending in spite of the cloud, and headed slowly down the block. Listening to the leaves, to my footsteps, to a child laughing by itself in someone's backyard, to a car racing along a street not too far away, to the muttering of a crow that picked at something flat and red on the tarmac.

There were times, like today, when living wasn't half bad, not at all. And there was still the beauty of autumn to come.

A little girl bundled in blue played with a scruffy dog in her front yard. She waved and called my name; I sort of waved back, but I didn't look over, and I didn't speak.

Three blocks later, humming quietly, I reached the park.

And saw the school.

I didn't know which was worse, then—the unwelcome sting in my eyes, or the way the fire took hold of my chest and made me want to grab something and smash it.

Deep breaths, I ordered as I stood on the corner; deep breaths, you're all right, deep breaths.

Every day.

Deep breaths.

For over ten years.

I could always keep walking, of course, and avoid all this nonsense. I could walk along the street, let the school and park pass by, and find something to do in the town center. I could see what was at the movie theater, I could waste time gossiping with friends who worked in some of the stores, I could even stop in at what used to be work and see how the guys were doing.

Sometimes I actually did.

But only if I took another route into town; only if I didn't see the school.

So who, I wondered, do you think you're kidding?

I jammed my hands into the jacket's pockets, and let the stinging pass, the fire retreat.

The park wasn't large. It stretched unbroken for two blocks to the right, surrounded by a stone wall waist-high on a normal man, one break on each side to let the kids and lovers in. Tall trees spotted now with color, bushes on the inside trimmed to prevent them from hanging over the stone. In the old days the place was perfectly safe night and day; now, a patrolman walked the paths and checked the bushes, and at night, from midnight to dawn, the entrance gates were locked. A futile gesture, since the wall was so low, but it was appearance more than actual deterrence that made the people happy.

I crossed the street.

I didn't have to look directly at the school that faced the park to know what it looked like. Dorrie had worked there for twenty years, and it hadn't changed. Not a bit.

Built before the time when someone had decided all schools had to be low to the ground and resemble brick-faced factories, it was three stories of imposing brownstone, with tall windows whose shades were perpetually pulled halfway down. Wings extending out at either end that were the width of two windows. Green grass in front thirty feet from building to sidewalk. A sign that told passers-by this was the proud home of the Eagles.

Three wide and gray marble steps up to a high marble-arched entrance, and three sets of glass doors. Marble trim around the windows; marble trim at the eaves. Protruding granite ledges that marked each story, and along the ledges a dozen drain spouts that poked through the twisted-grin beaks of marble creatures that were once, tradition had it, the faces of stooping eagles, until the weather had worn them down and made them look like no eagles this world had ever seen.

They had cousins, too. On either side of the base of the arch, and just under its peak, were ledges that held three more eagles, these with hunched shoulders and slightly raised wings, their faces glowering at whoever walked beneath them. They, too, had been badly treated by decades of harsh winters and boiling summer, but no one ever suggested they be replaced.

This, after all, was the proud home of the goddamn Eagles.

It was, I hated to admit, a handsome old building. One of a kind, and well-kept.

So naturally, as things go these days, there was a referendum every year or so to tear the thing down and build a new one; each time, the referendum failed; and every time since Dorrie died, I voted in favor of the bulldozers and dynamite.

"Hey, Chad!"

I started, rubbed a hasty hand over my face, and did my best not to show that I'd been daydreaming again.

Between the stone wall and the sidewalk on all sides of the park was a narrow patch of grass that refused to die no matter what the dogs and kids did. Redwood benches had been placed on either side of each entrance, used primarily by those whose legs couldn't carry them more than a few steps at a time.

One of them on the school side had been stolen a few years back and never, for some reason, replaced.

On the remaining bench sat the man who had called me. The leader of the Watch.

I walked slowly toward him. "How you doing, Mike?"

I wasn't a small man by any means. I still had plenty of meat, didn't stoop, and my hair, such as it was, even had a few hints of the brown it used to be.

Yet Mike Halpern made me feel small. High and wide, Dorrie used to say, and as wrinkled as an old sheet stuffed behind the hamper. Her students guessed he was older than God. His clothes looked it, too. I'd been trying forever to remember the last time that topcoat had been in style. Or those thick-toed shoes.

He gestured with a spotted hand. "Can't complain."

"Sure you can. All damn day."

This from a heavy-set woman sitting on the wall to the right of the entrance. A long floral skirt that reached her ankles, a long sweater that folded over her lap, long hair in a thick single braid white enough to be invisible when December decided to snow. A carpetbag rested on the wall beside her, overflowing with knitting needles and skeins of varicolored yarn.

She grinned at me. "All day he sits, bitches about his hemorrhoids, and eats peanuts." She waggled one heavy white eyebrow. "So, you wanna mess around today?"

I shook my head solemnly. "Not today, Francie."

Her expression sobered. "Can't be in mourning forever, Chad Parma. Bad for your health."

"Soon as I'm ready, you'll be the first to know."

"Soon as he's ready," another voice said sourly, "he'll be too old to know what the hell to do with what he thinks he's still got."

The bushes behind Halpern shook and parted, and a second woman climbed agilely over the wall, brushed leaves from her skirt, and hiked herself backward to sit on the stone. She appeared younger than the others, her hair still reasonably dark, her figure still apparent beneath fresh jeans and a plaid shirt; around her neck she'd tied the arms of her cardigan, mostly, I think, to hide the wattles.

Halpern didn't turn around. He snorted his disgust instead, muttered, "Hush, Trina," and waved a hand toward the school.

"Nothing to report, Chad."

I nodded.

"Pretty quiet."

I nodded again; I did not, however, laugh.

"You know," Trina said, lighting a cigarette, not blowing out the match until it nearly burned her fingers, "you really ought to get a life, Chad. No fooling."

"Hey," Francie scolded.

Halpern stiffened.

I ignored her. I hadn't liked Trina when I'd first met her, didn't like her now, and paid no attention to anything she said. The only reason I spoke to her was for Halpern's sake, and Francie's, and because talking to her was preferable to taking a bat to her skull. Not by much, though; not by much.

Besides, the Watch wasn't a bad thing, and I encouraged it all I could.

Even before Dorrie had died, the town had been changing. Growing too fast, too soon. Children were followed on their way home. One had been molested in the park, another severely beaten right on the school's front walk. In broad daylight.

Eventually the outrage had faded, as these things always do, but Halpern hadn't forgotten. As far as I knew, he had no family of his own, and had adopted the school instead. Every day, from an hour before the first teacher arrived to just after sunset, he and his friends sat on the bench and wall, and watched.

They learned the names of the children and the faces of the parents.

Noting the cars that drove by too often for coincidence; noting those adults who maybe stayed too long after the kids went in, who wandered by without evident purpose, who hung around for no apparent reason after the last bell had rung.

I had just recently slipped over the cliff edge into my sixties, but these three were easily a decade older. Probably more. You wouldn't know it, though; you sure wouldn't know it.

And the kids loved them.

There was always a large group around them every lunch hour, and before and after school.

"They catch that guy yet?" Francie asked, squinting as the afternoon sun worked its way overhead.

I recalled the article I'd read in the paper. "I don't know. I don't think so."

"Stupid cops," Trina muttered.

"You can't do much without any clues," I answered automatically, defensively, my left hand bunching into a fist in its pocket.

"Jesus," she said in disgust. "The poor sucker was sliced open. How can you not have any clues, for crying out loud? It's been months!"

"He doesn't work with them anymore," Halpern said wearily. Then he said, quietly, "Buick. Red. Check the plates."

I didn't look. I closed my eyes insted and waited, listening to one of them scratch something on a pad.

The thing is, I couldn't look. That would mean turning around. That would mean looking at the school.

"Got it," Trina said softly.

So solemn, those three; so serious.

The main reason I stopped by, once or twice a week, was to make sure they were all right. I dreaded thinking what would happen if they actually came up against one of the people they were supposed to be watching for.

I didn't want to admit it, but if they had adopted the school, I guess I had kind of adopted them.

A wave, then, and a caution, and I cut through the park to continue my walk. That way I wouldn't have to see the school. It was unreasonable, I know, and probably a therapist would be able to help me work things out, but there was no way I would ever look at that building again.

I hated it.

I wanted it gone.

• • •

Eventually I returned home, the school and the Watch out of sight and out of mind. I felt good, if a little tired, and ended my day the way most days ended—read the newspaper again, made some supper, watched some TV, and went to bed.

I stared at the invisible ceiling and did what I usually did instead of counting sheep—I tried to figure out some way to blow the school up without getting caught.

Over the years I had come up with some amazingly elaborate plans, not one of them feasible, some pretty damn silly, but every one a tonic.

The thing is, it was that school that eventually led my wife to her grave. Two decades in the classroom before the little bastards drove her away. No discipline, she said; no interest in learning, she said; parents refusing to help, whining instead about holding jobs and raising kids and why the hell didn't she do something about it?

They drove her into early retirement because the school board claimed she was too old-fashioned, too out of touch with the times. I'd been a sergeant then, but in a town this size that was a title without much compensation, and she had had to take a night job at the drugstore because we needed the money.

Never complaining, and weeping in her sleep.

Eleven years ago I buried her. The doctors said it was cancer; I knew it was a broken heart. Because the students didn't care anymore, and she was helpless to change them.

And I had been helpless to help her. I wanted her to fight, I wanted her to sue; every day I pressed, and every day she said no.

It cost me my job, that goddamned school; it cost me my life, too.

I was nearly asleep, when I heard the wings.

The window was open a little from the bottom, and a nightbird fluttered by and landed noisily on the roof. I smiled, thinking of Mabel and Phil, but I didn't get up. I didn't want to scare it, whatever it was. It was just nice to know it was there.

It rained the next day, and the day after.

I puttered around, watched TV, napped, cleaned, and once or twice came close to screaming from boredom. The third time it happened, I called an old buddy down at the station, just to see what was going on, maybe find out if those killings had been solved. They hadn't been, of course, so we gossiped until something came up and he had to go.

That's when it happened—when I stood there, the receiver still in my hand, and realized with a grimace that Trina, of all people, was right.

A simple hobby wouldn't do it; I had to get a life.

Dreaming and daydreaming about schools and demolition was hardly the way to live long, much less prosper; listening to gossip about people I no longer knew or cared about was something less than stimulating.

So what does a sixtyish man do with his life?

I didn't know, but I intended to find out as soon as I could.

Meanwhile, I chose to spend the rest of the afternoon protecting Mabel and Phil's nest from the coming winter. Burlap loosely wrapped around it, twine to keep it anchored. The neighbors undoubtedly thought I was nuts. I didn't care.

That night there were sirens, and I was out of bed and dressed almost as fast as if I were still in uniform. I threw on my jacket and stepped out, shivering in the damp cold. Trees whispered to each other. The shadow of a cat raced along the street.

From the sidewalk I could see flashing lights down by the park, and my first thought was of the Watch. That one of them had stayed late and had fallen victim. I wasn't much for exercising, but I hurried anyway, ignoring the pounding in my chest, and the light throbbing in my temples.

Blue lights swept across the park wall. Red lights flared across the black of the trees. There were lances of white as men with flashlights combed the interior. Two patrol cars were parked nose-in at the school, and sawhorse barriers had already been set up to block off the street in both directions. An ambulance, its rear doors open, idled at the curb.

Please, I thought; please don't let it be one of them.

I did see the lump on the grass, however, covered with a white sheet, and the detectives standing around it, shaking their heads and talking softly to one another.

Others had come out to see the excitement, but no one I recognized, so I made my way to the barrier, thinking I might be able to get one of my old patrol buddies to give me some details.

Not that I really needed them.

That close, I could see the red-turning-black splotches spreading across the sheet; I could see the dark puddles gleaming on the sidewalk, and the patches of black on the low-cut grass.

If I tried, really hard, I could probably smell the blood.

I shifted to the left, toward the barrier's edge, watching as a couple of patrolmen strung yellow crime scene tape to further cordon the area off. I tried to get their attention, but they ignored me. I tried to duck under the tape, and was ordered to get back or I'd be taken in for obstruction.

I didn't recognize any of them.

They were all strangers.

And I looked at the school.

Its windows glared each time a light danced across it. The entrance was lit by spotlights aimed at the doors from two places on the ground, a safety precaution that only served to make the place look larger, and darker, and made the roof vanish into the high reaches of the night. The ledge eagles sneered. The eagles around the arch puffed their wings and watched.

I turned my back and went on home.

But not before I saw a red Buick parked around the corner.

I slept hard that night, no rest at all. Each time I looked at the window moonlight cast faces on the screen. Open mouths and open eyes, shimmering as if underwater, pressed against the mesh as if trying to get in.

I thought I heard wings, but I didn't open my eyes.

I didn't go to the park the next day. Or the day after that. The newspaper told me all I needed to know, in that way papers have of saying a lot without saying a thing—that the victim had been badly cut up like the others, that he was indeed the owner of the red car, and that if it hadn't been for the public services of the Watch, the police would have had a difficult, if not impossible, time identifying the man as a bail-jumper from Pennsylvania, wanted for the alleged rape of a preteen girl.

No one seemed to care he was dead; there wasn't even comment from his family.

On the other hand, I was making progress. I had already contacted a couple of places looking for people with police experience. Not night watchmen, or guards, but companies needing someone to conduct discreet inquiries into things like petty theft and such. Nothing fancy, nothing glamorous. Certainly nothing dangerous. But it was something I knew how to do, and what the hell, it beat sitting around watching soap operas all day.

I had a feeling the Watch would be pleased.

When I saw them next, there was no preening, no self-congratulations, about their role that night at the school.

Halpern smiled a greeting, all those folds and wrinkles shifting and settling, his smile widening when I told them what I was up to. "I have a better idea, Chad," was all he said.

Trina wasn't there, something about having to visit the doctor. But Francie said from her perch on the wall, needles flashing, yarn dangling, "Good one, too."

"What?"

Halpern shifted his immense bulk, cleared his throat, and said, "Be one of us, Chad."

I frowned. "I'm sorry. What?"

Francie agreed. "Sure, why not? We could use your experience. Spotting the bad guys, you know? What do you call them? Perps?"

I laughed. I couldn't help it. The word sounded so bizarre coming from someone like her, it almost had no meaning. She blushed but didn't look away. The needles blurred.

"Well?" Halpern asked.

I shook my head. "No. Thanks, but no."

They didn't speak; they weren't insulted.

"Do you good," Francie said lightly. "A man as young as you, he ought to have something positive to fill his days."

I felt the school at my back. "Oh, I do, Francie, I do."

Halpern frowned, but said nothing.

Francie stared at me oddly, the needles slowing, but not by much.

"Besides," I added, "the referendum's up next month again. I have a feeling that this time you'll be the ones who'll have to find something to do."

The needles stopped.

"You sound almost happy."

I nodded without thinking. "Damn right."

That's when Halpern's face closed down, and the needles went back to speed, and the chill I felt on the back of my neck had nothing to do with the breeze that broke from the trees in the park.

I stood for a moment longer, trying to think of some way to explain that it wasn't them, honest, it was something else, but I knew it would be futile. I had hurt them. Hurt them badly. It wouldn't be easy to find something for me to do, but it would happen sooner or later, I knew it.

For them, it would be impossible.

I stammered a little, backed away, and finally hurried off. Wonderful, I thought; just . . . great.

I spent the next two days trying to figure out some way to make it up to them. I couldn't. Everything I came up with sounded either too lame or too condescending. They were proud, those three. Charity was something they neither wanted nor needed.

I stewed, I fretted, I wandered, I drove myself nuts, and

finally planted myself on the couch and turned on the television.

I grinned when I saw an actress hand an actor a statue made of gold.

"Yes," I whispered. "Damnit, yes."

They were there, all three, as I walked up with a large shopping bag in one hand.

Clouds hid the sky, and despite wavering patches of sunlight here and there on the ground, there was a light drizzle that shone on the street and the leaves and the increasingly bare branches. They had umbrellas, the Watch did, large and black, held not quite low enough to hide their faces.

School was out, and a half-dozen kids giggled at something Halpern told them. A dozen others shrieked into the park, calling to Francie and Trina as they passed. The street was packed with cars picking sons and daughters up. A school bus grumbled in wait at the corner. Tires hissed across the tarmac.

I stood there while the kids looked me over, not one of them smiling.

As always, I ignored them.

The Watch ignored me as well until the last child, a little girl bundled in blue, kissed Halpern on the cheek before racing away.

They did look at me then. Watching. No expression.

I had worked all day on a speech, contrition and explanation, and forgot it all when I realized they wouldn't listen.

So I said, "When I was a cop, they expected me to do my job. I did it. They thanked me. You guys have been here for practically ever. You do great stuff, like identifying that guy the other week, and I'll bet they thanked you for a job well done, and not much else, right?"

After a long moment, Francie barely nodded.

Trina stared at me. Hard.

I reached into the bag and pulled out a small trophy I had had made up at a local sports shop. It had their names on a plaque beneath the silver statue of a winged man raising two victorious fists to the sky.

I shrugged with one shoulder. "It's not much, but . . ."

They didn't move, not to smile, not to take it.

I put it on the ground in front of Halpern, suddenly angry. "You can share it," I said tightly. "It'll remind you every day that someone gives a damn about . . ." I gestured toward the school. "About what you do."

In gesturing, I had half-turned, forcing me to see the building.

Behind me I heard Trina say, "You hate them, don't you."

The school was empty now, at least out front. The clouds had merged, and the windows were dark and blind.

"She lives two doors from you," Halpern said.

I blinked. "Who?" But my voice sounded distant, not from me at all.

"Marcy Adams." Halpern's voice was flat. "The child who kissed me."

I blinked again.

Drizzle turned to rain.

"It isn't that school," Trina said with quiet rage. "It's the children you hate."

"You didn't even recognize her," Halpern said.

And Francie, over the click and clatter of her needles, her voice filled with regret and sorrow, said, "Oh, Chad."

I turned back quickly, ready to protest, ready to lie, ready to ask just one question . . . but I couldn't say a word.

The needles sounded like claws scraping across old stone, and the umbrellas black and slick looked too much like . . .

It's a good thing I do a lot of walking.

Otherwise I don't think I could have run the way I did.

Sometimes you live with someone for so long, you don't know who they are anymore. They're just there.

Maybe Dorrie really had been driven from what she loved, from her life, but it hadn't been the children or the school board or the damn school that had driven her into what I had believed was an early grave.

It was me.

The bitterness, and the anger, and my constant, incessant insistence on revenge. She couldn't fight both her loss, and me. At the end she was too weak; and at the end she was gone.

Sometimes you live with something for so long, you don't know what it looks like anymore. It's just . . . there. Like a shadow you don't notice, not even when it's gone.

That day, standing in the rain, listening to Trina and Mike and Francie, listening to those needles click and clatter, click and clatter, I saw the school for the first time in years. Saw it, not just looked at it.

I saw the Proud Eagle sign, and the contorted faces of the stone birds as they spat out the rain.

The rain-streaked windows, and the locked doors, and the three empty ledges tucked inside the arch.

I don't really believe it, you know.

I am not a stupid man, and certainly not a man who gives in to his imagination or old-age fancies.

But it's autumn now, deep autumn. The leaves have long since fallen and blown away, and the lawn has finally died, and frost turns the brown grass pale and brittle every morning.

I don't go out anymore, except to take the long way to the store, and I only do that when I absolutely have to. And only in the morning.

Because every day since that last afternoon, a group of children, different children every time, stand on the sidewalk after school and stare at the house as if it's haunted.

And I know who sends them.

For every night I beg Dorrie to forgive me, for what I had done, for what I had become, for what I was.

Every night I hear the click and clatter of talons making their way across the roof, and the sound of slow ripping, and the rhythm of something breathing just beyond the reach of my dim bedroom light.

Hovering.

Watching.

Waiting.

While I listen to the unmistakable soft sound of wings.

NEIL GAIMAN

How Do You Think It Feels?

I AM IN BED, now. I can feel the linen sheets beneath me, warmed to body temperature, slightly rumpled. There is no one in bed with me. My chest no longer hurts. I feel nothing at all. I feel just fine.

My dreams are vanishing as I wake, overexposed by the glare of the morning sun through my bedroom window, and are being replaced, slowly, by memories; and now, with only a purple flower, and the scent of her still on the pillow, my memories are all of Becky, and fifteen years drift away like confetti, or falling blossom, through my hands.

She was just twenty. I was by far the older man, almost twenty-seven, with a wife, and a career, and twin little girls. And I was ready to give them all up for her.

We met at a conference, in Hamburg, Germany. I had seen her performing in a presentation on "The Future of Interactive Entertainment," and had found her attractive and amusing. Her hair was long and dark, her eyes were a greenish blue. At first, I was certain that she reminded me of someone I knew, and then I realized that I had never actually met the person she reminded me of: It was Emma Peel, Diana Rigg's character in *The Avengers* television series. I had loved her and longed for her, in black and white, before I ever reached my tenth birthday.

That evening, passing Becky in a corridor on my way to some software vendor's party, I congratulated her on her performance. She told me that she was an actress, hired for the presentation ("After all, we can't all be in the West End can we?") and that her name was Rebecca.

Later, I kissed her in a doorway, and she sighed as she pressed against me.

Becky slept in my hotel room for the rest of the conference. I was head-over-heels in love, and so, I liked to think, was she. Our affair continued when we returned to England: fizzy, funny, utterly delightful. It was love, I knew, and it tasted like champagne in my mind.

I spent all my free time with her, told my wife I was working late, needed in London, busy. Instead I was in Becky's Battersea flat.

I took joy in her body, the golden litheness of her skin, her blue-green eyes. She found it hard to relax during sex—she seemed to like the idea of it, but to be less impressed by the physical practicalities. She found oral sex faintly disgusting, giving or receiving it, and liked the sexual act best when it was over fastest. I hardly cared: The way she looked was enough for me, and the speed of her wit. I liked the way she made little doll faces out of modelling clay, and the way the plasticine crept under her fingernails. She had a beautiful voice, and sometimes, spontaneously, would begin to sing—popular songs, folk songs, snatches of opera, television jingles.

Colors seemed brighter because Becky was there. I began to notice parts of life I had never seen before: I saw the elegant intricacy of flowers, because Becky loved flowers; I became a fan of silent movies, because Becky loved silent movies; I began to accumulate CDs and tapes, because Becky loved music, and I loved her, and I loved what she loved. I had never heard music before; never understood the black-and-white grace of a silent clown before; never touched, or smelled, or properly looked at a flower, before I met her.

She told me that she needed to stop acting and to do something that would make her more money, and would bring that money in regularly. I put her in touch with a friend in the music business, and she became his personal assistant. I wondered, sometimes, if they were sleeping together, but I said nothing about it—I did not dare, although I brooded on it. I did not want to endanger what we had together, and I knew that I had no cause to reproach her.

"How do you think I feel?" she asked, "Knowing that you are going back to your wife, every night? How do you think it feels for me?"

I knew she was right. I did not want to hurt anyone, yet I felt as if I were tearing myself apart. My work suffered. I began to nerve myself to tell my wife that I was leaving. I envisioned Becky's joy at learning that I was to be only hers. It would be hard and hurtful, but it would have to be done.

Each time I played with the twins, took them to the park, tucked them in at night, it hurt me inside. But I knew what I had to do; that the pain I was feeling would soon be replaced with the utter joy that living with Becky, loving Becky, spending every waking moment with Becky, would bring me.

I took her out to dinner, and told her that I would be leaving my wife and children for her. I expected to see a smile on her face, but she said nothing, and she did not smile.

In her flat, that night, she refused to sleep with me. Instead, she told me it was over between us. I drank too much, cried for the last time as an adult, begged her and pleaded with her.

"You aren't any fun anymore," she said, simply and flatly, as I sat, sadly, on the floor of her living room, my back resting against the side of her battered sofa. "You used to be fun, and funny. Now you just mope around all the time."

"I'm sorry," I said, pathetically. "Really, I'm sorry. I can change."

"See?" she said. "No fun at all."

Then she opened the door to her bedroom, and went inside, closing it and locking it, finally, behind her; and I sat on the floor, and finished a bottle of whiskey all on my own, and then, maudlin drunk, I wandered about her flat, touching her things and snivelling. I read her diary. I went into the bathroom, and pulled her soiled panties from the laundry basket, and buried my face in them, breathing her scents.

I made the gargoyle for myself in the small hours of the morning, out of gray plasticine. I remember doing it. I was naked. I thumbed and kneaded it until it was soft and pliable, then, in a place of drunken, horny, angry madness, I masturbated into it, and kneaded my milky seed into the gray shapeless mess.

I have never been a sculptor, but it took shape beneath my fingers then, blocky hands and grinning head, stumpy wings and twisted legs: I made it of my lust and self-pity and hatred, then I baptized it with the last drops of Johnny Walker Black Label and placed it over my heart, to protect me from beautiful women with blue-green eyes and from ever feeling anything again.

I lay on the floor, with the gargoyle upon my chest; and, in moments, I slept.

When I woke up a few hours later, her door was still locked, and it was still dark. I crawled to the bathroom, and threw up all over the toilet bowl, and the floor, and the scattered mess I had left of her underwear. And then I went home.

I do not remember what I told my wife when I got home. Perhaps there were things she did not wish to know. Don't ask, don't tell, all that. I can barely remember.

I did not ever return to the flat in Battersea.

I saw Becky every couple of years, in passing, on the Tube, or in the City, never comfortably. She seemed brittle and awkward. We would say hello, and she would congratulate me on whatever my latest achievements were, for I had taken my energies and channeled them into my work, building something that was, if not an entertainment empire, then at least a small principality of music and drama and interactive adventure.

Sometimes I would meet girls, smart, beautiful, wonder-

ful girls and, as time went on, women, for whom I could
have fallen; people I could have loved. But I did not love
them. I did not love anybody.

Heads and hearts: and in my head I tried not to think
about Becky, told myself I did not love her, did not need her,
did not think about her. But when I did think of her there
was a pain in my rib cage, a perceptible, actual hurt inside
me, as if something were squeezing my heart.

And it was at these times that I imagined that I could feel
the little gargoyle in my chest. It would wrap itself, stone-
cold, about my heart, protecting me, until I felt nothing at
all; and I would return to my work.

Years passed: The twins grew up, and they left home to go
to college, and I left home too, leaving it with my wife, and I
moved into a large flat in Chelsea and lived on my own, and
was, if not happy, then, at least, content.

And then it was yesterday afternoon. Becky saw me first,
in Hyde Park, where I was sitting on a bench, reading a pa-
perback book in the springtime sun, and she ran over to me,
and touched my hand.

"Don't you remember your old friends?" she asked.

I looked up. "Hello, Becky."

"You haven't changed."

"Neither have you," I told her. I had gray in my beard, and
she was a trim woman in her mid-thirties. I was not lying,
though, and neither was she.

"You are doing very well," she said. "I read about you in
the papers."

"Just means that my publicity people are earning their
keep. What are you doing these days?"

She was running the press office of an independant television network. She wished, she said, that she had stuck
with acting, certain that she would, by now, have been on
the West End stage. She ran her hand through her long, dark
hair, and smiled like Emma Peel, and I would have followed
her anywhere. I closed my book, and put it into the pocket of
my jacket.

We walked through the park. The daffodils nodded their
heads at us, yellow and orange and white, as we passed.

"Like Worsdworth," I told her. "Daffodils."

"Those are *narcissi*," she said. "Daffodils are a kind of *narcissus*."

It was spring in Hyde Park, and one was almost able to forget the city surrounding us.

"Was there someone else?" I asked her, eventually. "Someone you left me for?"

She shook her head. "You were getting too serious," she said. "That was all. And I wasn't a homewrecker."

Later that night, much later, she repeated it. "I wasn't a homewrecker," she said, and she stretched, langourously, and added, "—then. Now, I don't care."

I had not told her that I was divorced. We had eaten sushi and sashimi in a restaurant in Greek Street, drunk enough saki to warm us and to cast a rice-wine glow over the evening. We took a taxi back to my flat in Chelsea.

The wine was warm in my chest. This was only a few hours ago, but I cannot remember her taking off her clothes. I remember her breasts, though, still beautiful, although they had lost the firmness and shape they had when she was little more than a girl: Her nipples were deep red, and pronounced.

I had put on some weight. She had not.

"Will you go down on me?" she whispered, when we reached my bed, and I did. Her labia were engorged, purple, full and long, and they opened like a flower to my mouth as I began to lick her. A red clitoris swelled beneath my tongue, and the salty taste of her filled my world, and I licked and teased and sucked and nibbled at her sex for what felt like hours.

She came, once, spasmodically, under my tongue, and then she pulled me up, and we kissed some more, and then, finally, I pushed inside her.

"Was your cock that big fifteen years ago?" she asked.

"I think so," I told her.

"Mmm."

After a while she said, "I want you to come in my mouth." And, soon after, I did.

We lay in silence, side by side, and she said, "Do you hate me?"

"No," I said, sleepily. "I used to. I hated you for years. And I loved you, too."

"And now?"

"No, I don't hate you anymore. It's gone away. Floated off into the night, like a balloon." I realized as I said it that it was true.

She snuggled closer to me, pressed her warm skin against my skin. "I can't believe I ever let you go. I won't make that mistake twice. I do love you."

"Thank you."

"Not, 'thank you,' idiot. Try 'I love you too.'"

"I love you too," I echoed, and kissed her still-sticky lips, sleepily.

And then I slept.

In my dream, I felt something uncurling inside me, something moving and changing. The cold of stone, a lifetime of darkness. A rending, and a ripping, as if my heart were breaking; a moment of utter pain.

I must have dreamed the gray dawn as well. I opened my eyes, moving away from one dream but not entirely coming awake. My chest was open, a dark split that ran from my navel to my neck, and a huge, misshapen hand, plasticine-gray, was pulling back into my chest. There was long dark hair caught between the stone fingers. It retreated into my chest as I watched, as an insect vanishes into a crack when the lights are turned on. The split in my chest healed, knit and mended, and the cold hand had vanished. I felt my eyes closing once more. I was tired, and I swam back into the comforting, saki-flavored dark.

I slept once more, and those dreams are now lost to me.

I awoke, completely, a few moments ago, the morning sun full on my face. There was nothing beside me in the bed but a purple flower. I am holding it now. It reminds me of an orchid, although I know little enough of flowers, and its scent is strange, salty and female.

Becky must have placed it here for me to find, when she left, while I slept.

Pretty soon now I shall have to get up.

I wonder if I shall ever see her again, and I realize that I scarcely care. I can feel the sheets beneath me, and the cold air on my chest. I feel fine. I feel absolutely fine.

I feel nothing at all.

KATHERINE KURTZ

The Gargoyle's Shadow

━━━◆━━━

IN THE BITTER COLD of a windy December night, the gargoyle's dark gaze scanned restlessly over the deserted streets of Dublin. Not far below, as the tattered clouds briefly gave way to brilliant moonlight, the clock in the tower of St. Patrick's Cathedral began to strike midnight. The sound of the bell reverberated on the crystalline air, skittering among the city's chimneys and steep slate roofs. Soon the rhythm was picked up by other clocks elsewhere in the sleeping city.

Revelling in the music that spelled freedom, the gargoyle stretched stubby wings and gave a snort of satisfaction. From his perch behind the crenellated Irish battlements of the cathedral's bell tower, invisible from street level, he had guarded this part of the city for centuries, released but once a month on the night of the full moon, to descend from the tower and prowl among the shadows.

The clock in the bell tower finished striking midnight, and the gargoyle flexed his wings again, took a deep gargoyle breath, and exhaled. As he did so, the shadow that

27

gargoyles cast only in full moonlight—darkling manifes-
tation of a gargoyle's true essence—sighed from the
stone-carved jaws and plummeted toward the pavement
below, only slowing with an abrupt *whoosh* of suddenly
extended wings as he touched down gently instead of
splatting on the pavement. In less than a blink of an eye he
was hidden in the sharp-edged shadow of a buttress, cast-
ing a glance around to see whether anyone had witnessed
his descent.

The street was empty and silent, just the way he liked it.
Furling his leathery wings, he turned to skulk along the side
of the cathedral, ghosting from shadow to shadow. Catching
his shadow-reflection in a frosty window, he briefly bared
his teeth in an expression of ferocity.

The shadows were fewer in the old churchyard, but it was
also deserted at this midnight hour. Vigilant nonetheless, the
gargoyle glided along one moonlit footpath in a blur of
speed and plunged into the murky darkness of St. Patrick's
Well, scaly wings bumping and scraping against the ancient
stone as he fell.

The chamber in which he landed was redolent of rat
droppings and the foul, dank smell of stagnant water, lit-
tered with rubble and the refuse generated by mortals—
empty soda cans and cider bottles and paper trash.
Ignoring this evidence of mortal sloth, the gargoyle
squeezed through a series of drains and ancient water con-
duits to emerge in the underground tunnel system that still
connected St. Patrick's with Christ Church Cathedral,
Dublin Castle, and St. Michan's, on the other side of the
Liffey.

Down the close, musty passageway he sped on his midnight errand, sparks flying every time the close-furled wings
brushed against the low ceiling, talons scuffling hollowly
against the stone underfoot. A creature of the night, he could
see well enough in the inky darkness, but as he passed beneath Dublin Castle and approached his destination, the
light-limned outline of a door beckoned, and a distant murmuring sound grew gradually more distinct.

He pushed open the door to a barrage of agitated voices

and the fierce, ruby-glowing gaze of more than a dozen other gargoyles milling in the vaulted chamber beyond.

"Hey, Paddy, we were beginning to worry you'd be late," one of them called, to murmurs of greeting and agreement from several others, as they began to take their places.

Late, indeed! As Paddy settled between the venerable Christ Church gargoyle and their colleague from St. Audoen's, another very ancient church, he reflected that in all the centuries he'd been guarding St. Patrick's, he'd never once been late to the monthly conclaves that all duty gargoyles were obliged to attend on the night of the full moon.

Beside him, the St. Audoen's gargoyle resumed harping on his usual complaint—though it was certainly justified. The church he'd guarded for centuries had been turned into a Viking heritage center a few years back. The old synod hall at Christ Church had suffered a similar fate, now housing some tourist venue called "Dublinia." The gargoyle of St. Audoen's hadn't yet been turned out of his living, because the building was still standing, but guarding tourist attractions was hardly in the same category as guarding sacred buildings. All the gargoyles were still outraged about the conversions.

"It just ain't right, it ain't right," the St. Audoen's gargoyle was muttering under his breath. " 'Lo, Paddy. I just don't understand the big fuss about Vikings. The Vikings were terrible people. They raped and pillaged—especially, they pillaged!"

"I never liked Vikings much, either," the Christ Church gargoyle agreed. "Back in the old days, we used to give 'em what-for! Remember the time I turned a Viking into a puddle of putrid flesh?"

"You did?" a youngster from the Custom House restoration said eagerly, as several of his elders rumbled acknowledgement.

"Before your time, kid," a Trinity gargoyle quipped. "You civic gargoyles'll never see the kind of action we used to see in the old days. I say the rot set in when the Georgians stopped putting gargoyles on churches!"

"It was before that," said the gargoyle from St. Werburgh's. "I blame it on the Reformation—Luther and Calvin and that crowd. No proper sense of how things ought to be, and no sense of humor!"

"Yeah, but at least the Protestants still remember it's supposed to be the Church Militant," said the gargoyle from University Church, a Roman Catholic edifice over on St. Stephen's Green. "My building's all right, but you look at most of these modern Catholic churches—not one goddamn gargoyle! No bell towers, either. How do they expect to defend the faith?"

"Damn right!" one of the Church of Ireland gargoyles agreed. "People think those little pointy spires on our bell towers are just for decoration. Boy, would *they* be surprised if they knew the things were surface-to-air missiles!"

"But will *He* let us use them? No!" the Christ Church gargoyle pouted. "I liked things better when He was an Old Testament God, and we were His avenging angels. Why even bother to call us the Church Militant anymore?"

"Yeah, and most of these new churches don't even *have* bell towers, much less missiles," said another. "Or, if they do have towers, they've got *electronic bells!*"

"Not at Saint Patrick's, we don't!" Paddy said proudly. "We've got a full peal of *real* bells—*and* missiles! Back when they were making all that fuss about the city's millennium, my bell team rang a marathon of *one thousand* changes! Now, *that's* ringing."

As several other gargoyles agreed that the feat was, indeed, something to be proud of, two more gargoyles pushed through the door, engaged in an angry and animated disquisition.

"It's this modern generation: They got no respect!" one of them was saying. "Somebody said the cherubs in the churchyard saw the whole thing—but these days, nobody's gonna pay any attention to a bunch of naked *putti!*"

"Yeah, but what're ya gonna do?" his companion replied—a tough old gargoyle from north of the Liffey. "Street punks! Lager louts! They litter the streets with empty cider cans and cigarette butts, and scribble graffiti on the walls—*illiterate* graffiti—and throw up on the sidewalks, and piddle in doorways—"

"I know what *I'd* do!" the first one grumbled. "In the old days, we would've set their piss on fire! St. Michan's used to be a damned decent place."

"What're you talking about?" one of the Dublin Castle gargoyles demanded. "Has something happened at St. Michan's?"

"Where've *you* been?" one of the new arrivals asked disdainfully, as he took his place.

"At my post!"

"Let's don't *us* fight," the second newcomer said. "You know the vaults under St. Michan's?"

"Of course."

"Vandals broke in and trashed the place a couple of nights ago."

A horrified chorus of "No!" greeted this revelation.

"Yeah, got pissed on cider, smashed a lot of the coffins, set a couple of fires—*really* busted up that crusader mummy who made it back from the Holy Land."

"But, that's outrageous!" said one of the Trinity gargoyles. "That's where Bram Stoker got his idea for the crypts in *Dracula*! I remember when he was writing that. He used to walk across the Trinity yard, mumbling under his breath about vampires. 'Course, everybody knew he was a little strange. . . ."

"Well, what are we going to do about it?" asked the very practical gargoyle from the Unitarian church on St. Stephen's Green. "Has anyone seen anything suspicious?"

"Who can tell, with tourists all over the place?" another grumbled. "Over at St. Andrew's, they've turned the place into a damned tourist information center. I spend my days having my picture snapped by hordes of Spanish tourists! Or French, or Italian, or—God help us—Germans. At least the Brits and Americans speak the language—sort of."

"At least you haven't got people running around dressed like Vikings!" the St. Audoen's gargoyle muttered darkly.

"Let's get back to the point," said the somewhat offi-
cious gargoyle from the Lord Mayor's residence at Man-
sion House. "We've all had to adapt to the times. At least
some of us are able to continue doing our jobs. And the city
planners—*despite* their many faults," he emphasized, glaring at the others to silence the incipient grumbles. "The
city planners do continue to reinstate some of us when they
perform restoration on major public buildings." He nodded
toward the young Custom House gargoyle. "That's a big
plus."

"So, who wasn't doing his job that night at St.
Michan's?" a crusty old gargoyle from Collins Barracks demanded.

"Well, we *are* spread very thin," said the exceedingly
proper gargoyle from the Catholic Pro-Cathedral in Marl-
borough Street, a stately classical building whose design re-
quired that no trace of its gargoyle be visible from the
street. "St. Michan's lost its gargoyle years ago, when the
Georgians tore down the old church and built the present
one on the old foundations. It's hard to have proper gargoyle security on a mostly classical Georgian building. As
a consequence, more of us are Recalled every year."

A gargoyle from atop Leinster House, seat of the parlia-
mentary chambers of the Daíl and the Seanad, gave an ex-
asperated sigh. "We aren't going to get anything done if
we don't stop bickering among ourselves and making
excuses."

"Yeah, just like the government," another muttered, to
snickers from the National Gallery gargoyle and the stone
monkeys from the front of the old Kildare Street Club, who
shook their pool cues in the air and made rude noises.

The meeting continued for a while longer, still plagued
by periodic interruptions, but eventually a stepped-up neigh-
borhood-watch plan was agreed upon and the gargoyles dis-
persed.

Paddy spent the rest of the night prowling the streets of
Dublin, for only in their shadow-forms did gargoyles have
this mobility, and then only for the twenty-four hours immediately following the monthly conclaves. He ranged among

the shadowy back streets and alleys of the city until nearly dawn, watching for evildoers and occasionally spotting another gargoyle on similar patrol, but the snow was keeping most people indoors. The clock on St. Patrick's was striking seven as he approached—and saw the flashing blue lights of an ambulance and several garda cars pulled to the curb outside the south door, which was standing open.

Keeping to the shadows—fortunately still plentiful at this time of year, even at seven o'clock—Paddy eased his way closer into the shelter of a buttress to get a better look at the people clustered at the back of the ambulance. Young Jack Kelly, one of Paddy's favorite vergers, was sitting on the back bumper and holding a compress to his forehead, while a uniformed garda wrote things down in a small notebook and an ambulance attendant applied a bandage to Kelly's hand. There was blood down the front of Kelly's cassock of St. Patrick's blue, and one eye was swollen shut.

"They took an alms basin from the high altar," Kelly was saying. "Probably would've gotten more, but I interrupted them. It was one of the really big, heavy ones: Georgian hallmarks—irreplaceable. And they'll probably melt it down for the silver."

"Anything else missing?" the garda asked.

"I don't know. I didn't have time to notice. They were here when I came to open up for Morning Prayer—two guys. The dean is on his way."

"Do you know which way they went?"

"Yeah, right up Patrick Street, heading for the North Side. Car was an old red banger."

That was all Paddy needed to know. He was really furious that punks had dared to mug young Kelly—and in the church, no less! And how *dare* they steal things from *his* cathedral?!

Restraining his indignation, he streaked up Patrick Street toward Christ Church, determined to find the red car and its occupants before it got too light to move around freely. The sky was brightening already, despite the snow, so he only had a few hours. And if he'd had no luck by midnight, it would be a full month before he could look again. By then, the thieves would be long gone.

He met the Bank of Ireland gargoyle coming out of Christchurch Place, and slipped into the shadowed ruin of the old Corn Exchange to brief him about the break-in at St. Patrick's before heading on through Temple Bar. The Bank of Ireland gargoyle might be a fussy old busybody, but from his rooftop post atop the graceful building that formerly had housed the Irish Parliament, overlooking College Green and the entrance to Trinity College, he saw and heard just about everything that went on in the center of Dublin. He would have the word out to the other gargoyles as quickly as anyone.

Across the Ha'penny Bridge and eastward along the quays Paddy sped, stopping briefly to confer with the river-god heads who graced the arches on the O'Connell Bridge, who grumbled at being disturbed, then heading into O'Connell Street itself. There, on a sudden whim, he paused to inquire of the Anna Livia statue reclining in her fountain—the "floozy in the jacuzzi," as the irreverent were wont to call her, for she looked more like a good-time girl than the noble goddess of the Liffey, more interested in good *craic* and a bit of a knees-up than in stringing together two thoughts in a row.

But she'd been civil enough the few times Paddy had spoken to her—not a gargoyle, of course, and no more mobile than the orators' statues lined up along the center island of O'Connell Street, or the classical statues adorning the Four Courts complex; but they were only meant to watch, after all.

To his delight, little Annie had seen something.

"Yah, there was an old banger came zipping past me and then off toward the station," she said. "Ran the traffic signals and nearly hit a milk truck."

"What color was it?" he demanded.

"Red, maybe? Yah, I think it was red."

With a nod of thanks, Paddy headed off in the direction of Connolly Station, threading his way through the warren of elderly buildings that once had been a very fashionable part of old Dublin. The dawn was fast approaching, the shadows fading. He would have to go home soon, or go to ground.

He had been brought up short by a dead end in an alley, and was turning to head back out, when something caught his eye through a chink in the bricks of an old, dingy building with a padlocked garage door. He did a double take and leaned closer to peer through the chink.

It was a gargoyle he had never seen before, silvery and still in the dim light, crouched on the radiator cap of a shiny black car of antique vintage. It had little webbed wings swept back from its scaly shoulders, and it was holding a heraldic shield in front of it. The shield was enamelled in red and white.

Vintage cars were hardly anything new to Paddy, of course. He had witnessed the evolution of the motor car from the very first horseless carriages, and still saw ones like this at weddings and such, at the cathedral. But almost all the others he'd seen with a double-R radiator badge like this one bore hood ornaments of graceful females trailing diaphanous garments behind them like wings.

The sound of footsteps on the pavement beyond the building sent Paddy zipping through the chink like a squeeze of liquid shadow, to peer warily back through the opening as a white-haired old gentleman in a black waxed jacket and tweed cap came tap-tapping up to the padlocked garage doors, using an umbrella as a walking stick. Above rosy cheeks and white moustaches, blue eyes twinkled with spry humor from behind old-fashioned wire-rimmed spectacles. He looked a lot like the Father Christmas in the window of the Brown Thomas store in Grafton Street. His breath plumed in the cold air as he hooked the umbrella over one gloved wrist and fumbled in his pocket for a key, then bent to unlock the doors.

Quickly Paddy retreated to the sheltering shadows behind a leaning stack of old shutters, as one of the doors screeched open far enough for the old man to enter. He made not a sound as the old man turned on lights, lit a gas heater, then set about making a cup of tea.

While the man was puttering, his back to the old car, Paddy tried to get a better look at the little gargoyle. But the man soon returned his attention to the car, humming contentedly under his breath as he removed his gloves and unzipped the front of his jacket. When he began wiping down the car's bright-work with a soft yellow flannel, starting with the little gargoyle, Paddy could contain his impatience no longer.

"Where'd you get that gargoyle?" he demanded, ducking as the old man whirled to look for the source of the voice.

"Who's there?"

"I said, where did you get the gargoyle? I need to borrow it."

"What?"

"I need the gargoyle," Paddy repeated.

"Who *is* that?" said the man, reaching for a huge spanner. "Damned kids!" he muttered under his breath. "You come out *now,* or I'm calling the guards!"

"No, don't do that!" Paddy said in alarm. "I can't come out. I'm a gargoyle."

"You're a *what*?"

"I'm a gargoyle."

"Right. You come out right now, where I can see you!"

"Sorry, can't do that."

"I'm warning you—"

"You don't want to see me."

"Why not?"

"You wouldn't believe what you saw. You'd be terrified. We're ferocious. Did you hear about the guy who saw one of us and his hair turned white, and he died three days later?"

"No," came the cautious reply, after a beat.

"Well, that was a couple of hundred years ago, but that's what happened. Believe me, you really don't want to see me."

"Who is that, *really*?" the old man ventured. "Seamus, if this is another of your practical jokes—"

"It isn't a joke. I need your help. I only want to borrow your gargoyle."

"What for?"

"I told you, I'm a gargoyle," Paddy repeated patiently. "We guard buildings—churches, mostly. It isn't easy, especially these days. Did you hear about what happened at St. Michan's a couple of nights ago?"

"I seem to remember something about it," the old man allowed, slowly lowering his spanner. "Didn't they break into the old vaults?"

"Yeah, and they busted up some of the mummies, set some fires, left the place a mess. Cider bottles and cigarette butts everywhere. You a Templar?"

"A what?"

"The shield on the gargoyle," Paddy said. "Isn't that a Templar cross?"

"No, Knights of Malta," the old man said, lifting his head proudly. "I'm a Knight of Malta. And that's a gryphon, not a gargoyle. But my name *is* Templeton," he conceded.

"Malta, Templars, St. John, St. Lazarus—they were all crusaders," Paddy said. "Who can keep track? One of those mummies that got busted up at St. Michan's was a crusader. You say you're a knight. How'd you like to put your knighthood to the test right now? Your own crusade: Help me right a wrong."

"What kind of a wrong?" Templeton asked, a wary edge to his voice.

"There was a break-in where I work, over at St. Patrick's. Sure, that's Church of Ireland, and you're R.C., if you're a Knight of Malta, but I'm not particular where I get help. Thieves stole an old alms basin—Georgian stuff. But what really has me steamed is that they roughed up a friend of mine. Got away in an old red banger. An informant tells me they headed in this direction."

"An old red banger, you say?" Templeton echoed.

"Yeah, you know of any in this area?"

"Actually, I do."

"Then, help me find them," Paddy said. "Make it your ecumenical gesture for the week. I'll put in a good word with the gargoyle over at the Pro-Cathedral. Heck, he can probably get the gargoyle at the Papal Nuncio's place to put a bug in the Nuncio's ear, have the good Cardinal sing your praises to the Holy Father, next time he's in Rome."

"Are you mocking the Church?" Templeton asked, drawing himself up stiffly.

"Of course not!" Paddy retorted. "Where would I be without the Church? Out of a job—that's where! Mind you, it isn't like it was in the old days."

"That's for sure," the old man agreed with a snort. "Too many changes, if you ask me. I don't miss the Friday fish, or hats on the women, or even the Latin—but when it comes to long-haired priests wearing hippie beads, and guitars instead of organs, and young people dancing barefoot in the church—

"And you Protestants have got *married priests*!" he added, flapping his yellow duster in the direction of Paddy's hiding place. "And *women* priests! What do you think of *that*?"

"Well, I'd agree about the fish, but I kind of liked the Latin, and the hats," Paddy allowed. "I used to see a lot of nice hats at St. Patrick's. And maybe women priests aren't a bad idea. Women know about setting tables, and serving a nice meal—and they're into vestments. I like vestments."

"Well, they can *sew* the vestments," Templeton muttered, "or iron them. Just keep 'em off the altar."

"But they make good ceremonies," Paddy pointed out. "They're really good at that. Especially weddings. How many weddings've you been to?"

"Oh, thirty or forty, I suppose."

"Well, I've seen thousands. Believe me, if it were up to men, there wouldn't even *be* weddings. They'd be out gathering the nuts and berries, or whatever it is they do these days, while the women keep things ticking over at home.

"But the women want ceremonies. They want the big dress, and the flowers, and the music, and bells and smells, and everybody dressed up in their Sunday-best, including the priest. So, all in all, women priests ought to have a better handle on stuff like that, right?"

"Well—"

"They should let the priests get married, too. How're they supposed to help married people sort out their troubles if they don't know what they're talking about? They can't, that's how. Get the women into the act!"

"I suppose you could have a point," Templeton allowed. "But the Church's teaching—"

"Hey, I don't have time for theological debates; I get those from the Trinity gargoyles all the time. Can you take that little guy off the car?"

"Yes, but—"

"Would you please just do it? It's getting late."

"Late for what?"

"I've only got until midnight, and I can't go out in the daytime."

"Why, are you a vampire or something?"

"Of course not. I told you, I'm a gargoyle. I'd scare people."

"So, why have you only got until midnight, and why—"

Paddy's snort of exasperation caused the shutters sheltering him to rattle softly. "Will you quit with the questions? You sound like those kids in the choir, always asking why! I told you, I've got to find the punks who broke into my church and mugged my friend—and if I can't find them today, I'll have to wait a whole month before I can try again."

"But—"

"You're impeding a gargoyle in the performance of his duties," Paddy said stiffly. "Would you *please* give it to me?"

He thrust a taloned forearm into the light in unmistakable demand, its iridescent scales shimmering flame-dark within matte-black shadow, fire glinting from talons as long as a man's hand. The old man gasped and backed up hard against the side of the car, crossing himself.

But when the talons only clicked together several times in obvious impatience—though that, in itself, was scary enough—Templeton groped his way warily to the front of the Rolls Royce and carefully unscrewed the car's mascot.

As he nervously polished the red and white shield with his yellow duster, he turned back toward the shadowed shutters.

The taloned arm was joined by a second one, both up-turned to receive the little gargoyle.

"I want to see you," Templeton said. "You come out where I can see you, or I'm not handing it over."

"You'll be scared," Paddy warned.

"So, I'll be scared. I've been scared before. These things are expensive."

With a resigned flash of his ruby-glowing eyes, Paddy moved into the light. The old man gasped and half turned away, shielding his eyes with the hand holding the gargoyle mascot while he crossed himself again with the other, his rosy cheeks draining of their color.

"See? You think I'm frightening," Paddy said.

"Well, of course! I've never seen a gargoyle before."

"And you still haven't. That takes a black mirror. We were avenging angels, in the Old Testament. Then the New Testament came along, and we got reassigned. These days, we mostly guard churches. But with congregations getting smaller, our job is getting harder. People don't pray enough anymore."

The old man dared a glance back at his visitor, still cringing, but he was starting to recover a little of his color. "That's what they're always telling us at Mass. The Holy Father says we should pray more. I guess maybe you and I agree on *that*, at least."

"Yeah, the old boy gets it right most of the time." Paddy lifted his talons toward the little gargoyle again. "Can I please have it?"

Templeton came just close enough to hand it over, jerking his hand back nervously as the talons closed lightly around the silvery form. But as he skittered back to a safer distance, closer to the car, he did a double take.

Reflected in the car's polished black door was not a darkly menacing shadow-shape laced with fire, but the stern, majestic figure of an armored warrior, with dark pinions sweeping from powerful shoulders to trail rainbows behind, and a diadem of stars bound across its noble brow. And what its strong hands were cradling against its armored breast was not a car mascot but a tiny winged cherub.

"Oh, yeah, I guess your car's a black mirror," Paddy said, as Templeton blinked wonderingly between the contradictory images, slack-jawed with awe. "That's the only way mortals can see us in our true form—unless, of course, they've really pissed us off. Then, you don't wanta know. Like I said, we used to be avenging angels. But nowadays, we don't get to kick ass like we did in the old days. The Boss has gotten a little soft on sinners."

When Templeton only stared at him, goggle-eyed, Paddy returned his attention to the little gargoyle in his talons.

"This is really neat. It's like holding your own child for the first time. I never thought I'd be a father."

"A father?" Templeton said blankly.

"Well, sort of," Paddy said. "Just wait. And watch."

Concentrating, he cupped his talons tenderly around the little gargoyle, willing into it some of the magic that had accompanied his recommissioning, when the stonemasons set his stone shell into place atop St. Patrick's so many centuries before. After a few seconds, he gently opened his claws. The little gargoyle was glowing a dull red and slowly blinked one tiny ruby eye.

"Better put your gloves back on before I give this back," Paddy said, at the old man's look of awestruck wonder.

"Why? Is it alive?"

"No, it's hot. To make it alive, I'd need help from Upstairs. You know—'through Him, with Him, in Him.' Now, put on your gloves. We're wasting time. It'll burn your fingers until it cools down."

"Right, sure, whatever you say," the old man murmured, though he did as he was told. "Uh, would it be presumptuous to ask if you have a name? Doesn't seem right to call you 'Hey, gargoyle.'"

"Then call me Paddy. And don't drop Junior! Now, put him back on the car."

Five minutes later, with the baby gargoyle now affixed to the radiator once more, Templeton had the old Rolls idling quietly before the garage doors. As he pushed them open, stepping outside to secure them so he could pull out, the dark shadow of the gargoyle of St. Patrick's moved—faster than the blink of an eye—in through the open driver's door, up and over the front seats, and into the back, to hunker down on the floor and pull a red tartan blanket over himself from the back seat, for it now was full daylight outside.

As the old man came back in from the alley, he glanced uncertainly around the garage.

"Uh, Paddy?" he called.

"In here."

Templeton whirled toward the source of the voice and took an involuntary step back at the sight of the tartan lump on the floor of the back seat.

"Get in, get in," Paddy ordered. "We haven't got all day. Or—actually, we do, but you know what I mean. Let's *please* get going."

Templeton got in. After pulling into the alley, he got out briefly to close the doors, then resumed his position in the big car's high front seat and put the car in gear. The tartan lump bulged a little higher behind the slit between the two front seats, but Templeton tried to pretend it wasn't quite so close, and concentrated on his driving.

They had to contend with rush-hour traffic as soon as they left the alley. The sun had come out, glittering on the residue of the previous night's frost. As they approached the very first cross street, Templeton had to stop to let a pedestrian cross, and he glanced impatiently in either direction as he waited, looking for an old red car. As he shifted his gaze forward again, he caught just a glimpse of the little gargoyle also turning its head to look.

He blinked and looked again, but the little gargoyle was staring straight ahead.

"Paddy?" Templeton said uncertainly, as he eased the car forward again, starting to signal for a right turn down the next alley.

"What?"

"Your kid moved."

"Of course he moved—though it's hard to see if you look

straight at him," Paddy said from underneath the blanket. "Just drive. Think of him as something like the needle of a compass. He's going to help us look for the bad guys."

"Right," Templeton muttered, making the turn. "Uh, can I ask you something?"

"Yeah, what?"

"Uh, is your name *really* Paddy?"

"No, but you probably couldn't pronounce the real one," came the slightly amused reply. "Besides, we're not supposed to tell. If you'd prefer Pádraig, that's fine with me. We usually go by the names of the places we guard. That makes it a little tough on some of the newer guys—damned new-fangled place-names."

Templeton chuckled despite his nervousness, grunting as he cranked down his window and reached out to free up one of the lighted trafficator arms that served as turn indicators on the old car. Some of the new housing estates *did* have bizarre names.

"I guess that *could* make for some strange names," he agreed, rolling the window back up. "For that matter, some of the old place-names are pretty strange. Do—uh—gargoyles guard places like Phoenix Park? I think I've seen some carved faces up there."

"No, they're just Watchers. They can't come down, the way gargoyles can. There're some great Watchers in O'Connell Street. The ones on the Irish Permanent building are pretty dozy, but you should talk to the sphinxes on the Gresham Hotel. Now, *they're* smart! And they don't miss much that goes on."

"Ah. How about the Egyptian slaves out in front of the Shelbourne?"

"The ones that hold up the lamps?" Paddy asked.

"The very ones."

"Not those, my friend. Sorry, but sometimes a lamppost is only—well, a lamppost."

"Oh," Templeton said.

"Yeah, don't assume that every carved critter you see on a building is a Watcher, much less a gargoyle. We're all spread pretty thin. Like I told you, we gargoyles used to be avenging angels. Once God got past His divine vengeance phase, we got reassigned. It was the stonemasons' idea, when they started building churches. I expect we'll all get recalled, one of these days. But meanwhile, we guard buildings."

Paddy and his newfound friend continued to cruise the streets of Dublin all through the day, looking for some trace of the battered red car and its passengers. Junior got bored after a while, occasionally starting to fall asleep on the job, so Templeton had to keep waking him up by sounding the horn; that always turned the heads of pedestrians, who would gaze nostalgically after the elderly white-haired gentleman in his elderly Rolls Royce, who seemed occupied in an animated conversation with himself.

Meanwhile, Templeton listened to the tales Paddy told of old Dublin, and some of the things he had seen over the centuries. In return, recalling their earlier conversation regarding weddings, Templeton reminisced about bygone days when he used to drive the old Rolls as a wedding car, back when his wife would festoon the hood with broad white ribbons running from the hood ornament back to the front corners of the roof. Inside, she would even put nosegays of real flowers in the little crystal vases on the side-pillars, to make the occasion even more special for the bridal couple. On fine days, Templeton would crank back the sunroof so the young people could enjoy the sunshine and fresh air; the light breeze from the open sunroof didn't ruffle the brides' coiffures the way an open window would have done.

But as teatime approached, long about half-past four, and the evening shadows began to close in, no progress had been made on their quest. By the time the lamps in the huge cast-iron streetlights began to come on, competing with the strings of colored lights that decorated the city at this time of year, the old man had about decided that all they had managed to accomplish, besides spend a pleasant if odd day swapping yarns—and the Irish were good at that!—was to burn up nearly two tanks of petrol and confirm the impression in most observers' minds that dotty old

men who drove around in vintage cars were wont to talk to
themselves.

"Listen, Paddy, this has been really good *craic,* and I've
enjoyed your company," Templeton said, as he switched on
the car's big Marschal headlamps, "but I don't think we're
going to find your bad guys. That car could be behind any of
those garage doors we've passed. Or they could have scam-
pered right out of town."

The tartan lump that was Paddy stirred slightly behind
Templeton, suddenly aware that Junior had perked up and
was really interested in something not far away.

"Slow down," he said. "Junior's onto something."

"He *what*?"

"He smells the silver. So do I. I told you, we get attuned
to everything that belongs in the buildings we guard. Go
down that street! I think we're getting close."

Startled, Templeton looked at the little gargoyle perched
on his hood. It was bouncing up and down and squealing,
madly flapping its left wing like one of the old car's traffi-
cators. And at the far end of the indicated side street, a battered old red car had just nosed out of a car park, its
rust-eaten front bumper pointing in their direction. Beside
and slightly behind it, two rough-looking men wearing flat
caps and ratty, out-at-the-elbows jackets were rolling a
heavy chain-link gate back into place.

"That's them, that's them!" Paddy cried, one scaly arm
emerging from under the red tartan blanket to point emphati-
cally through the crack between the two front seats. "They
must've been hiding out all day! Turn left!"

"That's a one-way street," Templeton objected. "I can't go
down there."

"You want 'em to get away? Turn!"

"But there's a traffic warden watching!"

"*Turn now!*"

"You're going to get me a ticket!"

"They're going to get away, if we go around. *Turn!*"

Muttering under his breath, Templeton turned the big car
ponderously into the side street. It was very narrow—an
alley, really—and the old Rolls was very tall and very wide.

As the big car crept silently closer, headlamps probing twin cones of yellowy light into the alley's deeper shadows, the little gargoyle settled down to smouldering indignation on its perch on the radiator cap, glowering from behind its shield as one of the men did a double take at the sight of the approaching Rolls.

"Hey, you, back it out!" said the man, gesturing belligerently as the big car rolled to a gentle halt about a car-length away. "Can't you read? This is a fookin' one-way street."

"Tell *him* to back out!" Paddy whispered from between the two front seats.

"He'll kick out my headlamps," Templeton muttered under his breath.

"Just let him try!"

Warily the old man cranked back the sunroof and levered himself to a standing position; the alley was too narrow to really open either of the wide doors. The second man, behind the shouter, had a pillow sack over one shoulder, bulging with something just about the right size and shape for a big church offering plate.

"That's it, that's it!" Paddy whispered, as the little gargoyle began flapping its wings wildly, like an excited moth. "I can really smell it now! You've got to delay them until that traffic warden gets here! And get her to call the guards! Brazen it out!"

With a nervous swallow, Templeton shook his fist at the man.

"*You* back out, if you can!" he taunted. "I know it's a one-way street. And I also know what you've done, you—you *hooligan!*"

A look of guilt mingled with astonishment and panic flashed across the face of the first man, and the second threw his bundle into the back seat of the red car with a snarl and pulled out a hurley stick. The expressions on the two men's faces, coupled with the sack Templeton had seen, were enough to convince him that they had, indeed, found the right men.

"Get the hell out of here, old man!" the second man said defiantly. "I don't know what you're talking about."

"I'm talking about the break-in at St. Patrick's!" Templeton said boldly, noting that a delivery van had just pulled in behind the red car, and a very beefy driver was leaning out the window to see what the hold-up was.

"Get that pile of shite out of here before I kick out one of those expensive headlights!" the first man said.

"He'll be sorry if he tries," Paddy whispered.

"You'll be sorry if you try," Templeton repeated, though not with quite the same conviction.

"Oh, you gonna stop him?" the second man chimed in. "You and who else?"

As the two started forward with obvious intent, Paddy muttered, "Get down. You don't want to see this."

Templeton collapsed back into his seat with alacrity and ducked down behind the steering wheel, gasping as he felt something jostle past his shoulder in a flurry of powerful wings.

What happened in the next few seconds was never altogether clear. The first man did, indeed, launch a booted kick at one of the big headlamps, but it never connected. Instead, he found himself buffeted sharply backward with a forcible *whoof!* of suddenly exhaled breath, by a shadow-blur that pummelled him head over heels with repeated smacks of heavy, leathery wings.

The second attacker fared no better. He yelped as the hurley stick was invisibly wrenched from his hands in mid-swing and he, too, was jolted abruptly into the maelstrom, where both men seemed to tumble, legs and arms akimbo, in something approximating a localized tornado. Simultaneously, the horns of the Rolls, the red car, and the delivery van behind it started blaring.

Almost in the blink of an eye, it was over, with both men left dazed, bruised, and bleeding on the ground, whimpering with pain and fright as they tried to clutch at all the hurting parts of their bodies at once. Templeton had not moved, only clinging numbly to his steering wheel as the scenario unfolded, his eyes wide as saucers.

"Some days, I do *love* being a gargoyle!" Paddy declared, when his shadow-form had whooshed back through the sunroof to burrow under the tartan blanket again. "But I decided not to kill 'em. I'm feeling mellow today. Besides, you could have had a lot of explaining to do."

Which was no more than the truth. The blaring horns were drawing attention from both ends of the alley, including that of the traffic warden. The astonished driver of the van, after pounding in vain at his stuck horn button, got out of his vehicle and came striding past the red car to see what was going on—and pulled up short at the sight of the two men moaning on the ground.

As the traffic warden squeezed past the Rolls with a similar reaction, she glanced back at Templeton in question.

"I have no idea what happened," he said, standing again to poke his head through the sun-roof. "They just fell down. Drunk, I suppose. But I suggest you call the guards. Those two are the villains who robbed St. Pat's this morning."

With that, Templeton sank back into the driver's seat and reversed the big Rolls carefully out of the alley. Before he set the old car moving forward again, he reached up and flipped the rearview mirror to the night position.

"Where to?" he asked, as a tartan-shrouded lump eased carefully to a sitting position on the back seat. "St. Patrick's, I presume?"

"That will be just fine," Paddy said.

A quarter hour later, Paddy watched wistfully from the shadow of a buttress as the stately old Rolls Royce disappeared up St. Patrick's Close—not for the last time, he somehow suspected. The prospect pleased him. From inside the cathedral, he could hear the sweet treble voices of the boys from the Choir School lifting in pure praise, as Evensong ended and snow began to fall in the silver moonlight.

Well content, Paddy launched his shadow-essence up the side of the cathedral to his post behind the crenellated battlements of the old bell tower, to settle in for another month. Soon, in the bell chamber below, his bell team began ringing simple changes to warm up, practicing for New Year's Eve. As each new bell joined in, the increasingly joyous sound of their ringing floated out across the streets and rooftops of Dublin.

And as Paddy hunkered back into his watch-post, his ever-vigilant gaze ranging out over the city—*his* city—he decided that on a night like this, it really was great to be a gargoyle!

DON DíAMMASSA

Scylla and Charybdis

KIM DEFIED HER PARENTS for the very first time when they told her to stay away from Scylla and Charybdis. She'd noticed the two gargoyles on her way home from school one day, was convinced she'd learned rather than invented their names, and chose the two as her very best friends. Charybdis was a bat-winged lion with a blocky head, muscular body, and perpetual frown; Scylla had a vaguely human torso with twisted limbs curled up within the shelter of his wings, and unnaturally long fingers and toes. They would not have looked out of place in a painting by Bosch, but Kim didn't think they were scary at all.

She was nine years old, a precocious reader, invariably polite, friendly, and well-behaved. Her parents sensibly allowed her as much freedom as seemed safe, and so their present stance was disconcerting.

"But why can't I go see them?" She wasn't angry, even now, just puzzled. "I wasn't hurting anything."

The older Turners fumbled for an explanation. "They belong to Mrs. Trent, Kim." Her mother was always the first to answer difficult questions. "It's her house and she doesn't want kids playing there."

"But I wasn't playing. I was just sitting."

"It doesn't matter what you were doing, Kim. She has a perfect right to tell you to stay off her property."

Although she'd wanted to argue the matter further, Kim had already worked out the dynamics of her family. If she persisted, she could only make things worse.

"Okay, I won't bother her anymore."

For a second, her mother's eyes clouded, as though she sensed the duplicity, but her father was anxious for a quick, painless resolution.

"That's all we ask, Kim."

Later that same day, she confirmed her resistance to the new limit on her freedom of action.

"I'm going to Perry's." Her voice was casual but her eyes were wary.

Audrey Turner glanced out the front window. "It's starting to get late," she said doubtfully.

"It's only a few blocks. I'll be back before it gets really dark."

"Could you pick up a bag of chips, kiddo?" Her father fumbled for his wallet, pulled out some bills. "Get yourself an ice cream or something. Audrey, you want anything?"

"No . . . I guess not."

Strictly speaking, Sheffield House, owned by Mrs. Trent for the past ten years, was not on the way to Perry's Convenience Store. But Kim detoured through an empty lot onto Main Street and slowed cautiously as she approached the oversized brick and stone building. The only light was in the back kitchen.

Kim stopped at the gate.

Scylla and Charybdis flanked the front steps. Although they were clearly conceived of as a set, there were subtle differences. Scylla's eyes were mere slits, intense, staring as though directly into the heart, while Charybdis surveyed broader horizons, eyes wide and all-seeing. Scylla had sharper tusks and claws, but Charybdis boasted thicker muscles. Kim favored Scylla, whom she thought of as friend and protector, and for his sake she tolerated Charybdis, whose rage seemed all-encompassing.

"They're monsters," Billy Gale insisted. "My dad says they killed a man once. Tore him up and ate his heart."

Not true, according to her father. "They told that same story when I was a kid. A workman did get killed while they were uncrating the statues; one of them fell over and crushed him. It was just an accident."

"You wouldn't hurt me," she whispered into the growing darkness. "I know you wouldn't."

And for the next year, she visited the two gargoyles clandestinely, usually in the early evening, sometimes during the day when she was sure Mrs. Trent was out shopping or visiting one of the neighbors. With a quite unchildlike tenacity, Kim studied the woman's habits, learned how to predict her movements. The elderly woman never had reason to complain about her trespassing, probably never suspected it. But Kim visited her bizarre friends at least twice a week.

They were simultaneously comforting and unsettling, reassuring and frightening. Kim huddled against Scylla's side, concealed from passersby on Main Street, and felt his strength like the glow of the radiator in her bedroom. She would like to have read to him, small pay for the joy of his company, but it was usually too dark, and in any case she didn't want anyone to hear her. But she whispered softly, revealed her secrets to friends she knew would never betray her trust.

Then one summer, workmen started erecting a wrought iron fence around the property. It was as though someone had slipped a knife into her heart.

"It can't happen," she told herself, even as she watched them dig the holes for the upright posts.

That same night, Mrs. Trent was killed.

Most ten-year-olds don't read the newspapers, but Kim devoured them page by page, everything from editorials to letters to obituaries to wine reviews. Everything, in fact, except the comics page. "Too dumb even for kids."

And so she knew as much as her parents about the murder. Gladys Trent was not so much killed as smashed. "Massive trauma" was the official description. Apparently an intruder had forced open the front doors and bludgeoned her to death while she lay in bed, shattering every bone in her body.

The crime remained unsolved.

Mrs. Trent died intestate, her savings ended up in the pockets of two opposing law firms, and the house in Managansett was more a liability than an asset. None of the presumptive heirs could be sufficiently stirred to force a resolution. And so the property remained vacant.

But not unoccupied.

For her thirteenth birthday, Kim received a fifty dollar gift certificate good at the local bookstore. Her parents were immensely proud of her accomplishments. "She's a better reader than I am," her father bragged to his colleagues at work. "And the amount she retains is phenomenal." Her teachers had mixed feelings. Some worried about her social skills and Mrs. Amaral had accused her of plagiarism. "This paper could not have been written by a twelve-year-old, Mrs. Turner. It's far too sophisticated." Her peers were less kind. "Kim's a weirdo," Billy Gale insisted. "The only time she doesn't have her face in a book is when she's talking to the monsters at Sheffield House."

Kim left The Book Nook with a bag full of recent horror novels. A year earlier she'd discovered Stephen King and, to her parents' dismay, she'd been devouring stories about vampires, ghostly children, demonic possession, and satanic cults ever since.

"Don't you think you're overdoing the horror stuff a bit, Kim?"

"No," she'd replied after a thoughtful silence. She was always "Kiddo" to her father unless he was being serious about something, and she respected his intentions even when she disagreed.

It was a Saturday morning, late spring, the sun was bright, the sky clear, and Kim felt on top of the world. She carried her bag down Main Street to Sheffield House, pushed through the overgrown hedge that blocked the front entrance, and greeted her only two friends silently.

Scylla and Charybdis responded in kind.

Kim brushed the dirt away from a section of the front steps and sat down, trying to decide which of her books to read first. She no longer read aloud, understanding that it was not the words that were important to her visits but rather her intentions, the moments of sharing.

The intruders arrived just as the story was getting interesting.

There were six of them, Billy Gale and his friends, her primary tormentors at school. Billy's peers regarded him with either fear or loathing, but many were drawn as well by his undeniable charm. His ability to catalyze hatred toward the outsider was in its way as remarkable as Kim's reading skills. She thought he'd probably end up a politician.

"What do *you* want?" Kim hoped she sounded disinterested. It wouldn't do to let Billy know he was annoying her. It would only encourage him.

"Keep your shirt on, Kimmy. We're just looking around." He glanced up into Scylla's impassive face. "Ugly fucking bastard." Two of the boys tittered at the obscenity.

"Takes one to know one." The words escaped before Kim could catch them. Don't provoke him, she told herself. If he gets bored, he'll go away.

Billy just smiled, came a few steps closer, stopped just beyond her reach. His friends spread out to either side, one climbing up onto Charybdis, straddling the leonine back awkwardly because of the shrouding wings. Kim glanced that way, wanting to order him off, knowing that would only amuse them further.

"This is private property."

"Oh?" Billy glanced at his friends, reassuring himself he had an audience. "Did your parents buy it for your birthday or something?"

"No, but someday I'm going to buy it myself." Kim closed her book and shoved it back into the bag, angry with herself for having been provoked into revealing something she'd never told anyone before. She *would* buy Sheffield House one day; she knew it with absolute certainty.

"Well, then someday you can tell us to go away and we'll have to do it. But today I think we'll just stay for a while."

It was clear to Kim that Billy's purpose was to tease, and with that realization came the solution. If she left, there would be no reason for Billy and his friends to stay either. And she could come back later, once they'd found someone new to torment.

She stood abruptly. "Stay then, but I'm going."

Billy's face betrayed just a hint of anger as she stalked past, but before she reached the street, he'd recovered.

"I bet we could knock the heads off these things. They'd look great in my room."

Kim hesitated. Most likely it was an idle threat. But Billy had a violent reputation—the broken front window of the Managansett Inn, toppled gravestones in the cemetery, a fire started in the basement of one of the vacant low-income housing units.

Ignore him, she told herself. *He won't do it if you walk away.* And perhaps that was true, but one of his friends had already picked up a heavy stone and was using both hands to pound it against Charybdis's comparatively slender throat.

"Stop that!" She whirled around, dropped her birthday books, and stalked back. "I'll tell your mother, Kevin. You know I will."

Kevin hesitated, the stone poised for another blow. A thin, jagged crack stretched from one of Charybdis's knobby shoulders to the other.

"No one cares, Kimmy." Billy had picked up another stone, and was poised to attack Scylla in similar fashion. "No one but you."

And as the rest of the boys searched for weapons of their own, Kim realized that Billy was right, that the two gargoyles could be smashed into dust and no one but herself would care. But she did care. She cared very much.

She managed to draw blood from Billy's cheek before two of the other boys pulled her off. He glared at her furiously and raised his hand as if to strike her with the stone he'd been using on Scylla. Kim heard cries of triumph from the rest of his gang, who were industriously pounding away at Charybdis.

"Watch this, bitch!" With exaggerated care Billy climbed to Scylla's back, rose to his feet, spread his legs to achieve a precarious balance, and raised the stone two-handed above his head.

"Say goodbye, Kimmy."

She closed her eyes, refusing to accept what was about to happen, and time froze, even when she felt them release her arms, even when she heard the screaming and realized something had gone terribly wrong.

It was several seconds before she dared to look. Under other circumstances, she might have screamed along with the boys.

Billy Gale would never bother her again. Somehow he'd lost his balance and fallen forward across Scylla's head. One of the curled horns had taken him directly under the chin, striking up into the brain.

Kim wondered if she should feel pity, but in fact her only emotion was a fierce joy, a joy that passed only when she turned and saw that Charybdis had gone as well. His massive head had shattered against the stone steps when it fell to the pavement. The boys had scattered by now, headless in their own fashion.

When the police arrived, they thought she was crying about Billy.

Adolescence modifies behavior. At seventeen, Kim might have been very popular if she'd made an effort. She was smart, attractive, and accepted if not particularly liked. Most of her evenings were still spent reading, although horror fiction was now only the first among many of her interests, and she still visited Scylla at least twice a week. Although she dated occasionally, she'd never been particularly interested in boys.

Until Scott Nicholson moved to Managansett.

Scott was clearly from a different world. He was sophisticated beyond his years, good looking, athletic—although he didn't participate in school sports—intelligent, although he only read nonfiction, and self-assured. Kim knew he had dated Valerie Gohannon, Tanya Gorham, and Mary Zydecki, the three most sought-after girls in the school, and for the first time in her life, she envied them. So when Scott stopped by her locker to ask for a date, she was nearly incoherent.

The evening was magical. Scott's manners were impeccable and he seemed generally interested in whatever she had to say, so much so that she ended up saying a lot more than she intended.

"I'm jealous," he said at last. "I don't think I've ever played second best to a statue before."

Kim laughed, but it was slightly brittle. She worried that her confessions had been perhaps just a bit too weird, and that she might have revealed too much. "Don't worry. You're much better looking."

"Still, I'd like to meet this Scylla. Where'd you say this place was again?"

And so it was that they walked together beyond the well-lighted downtown of Managansett, out toward the cemetery and the overgrown acreage that contained Sheffield House.

"It's pretty dark in there; you won't be able to see anything. Maybe we could come back during the day some time."

They were standing on the sidewalk, just outside the gates.

"Come on. We walked all the way out here, didn't we?" And Scott tugged on her arm, pulling Kim through the unruly hedge.

"What happened to the other one?" Scott gestured toward Charybdis after examining Scylla in the moonlight.

"Kids. It happened a long time ago."

"No one lives here, huh?"

"Not for years and years. Can we go now?"

Scott ignored her. "What's it like inside, do you know? Can we get in somewhere?"

"I don't think anyone's been in the house since I was a kid."

Still holding her wrist, a bit more tightly than she would

have preferred, Scott led her around the side of the building. "If I can get one of these windows open . . ."

Kim hovered between panic and anger. "Scott, I want to go now. I mean it."

He yanked her arm unexpectedly so that she was turned to face him, and caught her other wrist before she could react. "Cool it, Kim. Look, if we can get inside, there's no way anyone can see what we're doing. It's a pretty night, I like you a lot and I thought you liked me too."

"I do." But she didn't sound that way, and wasn't sure she felt that way either. There was something wrong, something had changed in just the last few minutes.

"So what's the problem? I think this could be really special if we let it."

He released her wrists then, and for a second Kim thought she'd been overreacting, panicking simply because a good-looking boy enjoyed being alone with her in the dark. She had even opened her mouth to apologize when she felt his hands on her again, one catching the belt of her slacks, the other pressing insistently against her left breast.

"Cut it out!" She tried to pull away, but Scott tightened his grip at her waist and jerked her forward. His other hand tightened possessively.

"No more bullshit, Kimmy."

It was the hated diminutive of her name that spurred her to act even more than his unwelcome touch. Kim lifted her knee sharply, just as her father had taught her, and Scott fell away, gasping with pain. She whirled and rushed headlong into the darkness, scratching her cheek and snagging her clothing as she pushed through the bull briar and mock orange that had once bordered a well-kept garden.

Scott made no effort to pursue, not even after he'd regained his composure. But he did call, "You blew it, Kimmy! I really kind of liked you, you know. We could have had a great time together."

She crouched in the darkness, out of breath, unwilling to answer.

"You might even have had fun. I'm pretty good at making love. Lots of practice. Valerie and Mary and the others could tell you."

He moved away from the building, started back toward the front yard. But he paused and called out once more before leaving. "Guys talk, you know. Everyone's going to assume I had you, and I won't tell them otherwise. In fact, I think I'm remembering some details already, like how you weren't a virgin after all and insisted on giving me a blow job first."

Kim bit her lip and lowered her head, willing him just to go away. And he did. And an hour after that, so did she.

Her parents were both sitting at the kitchen table when she came out for breakfast the following morning, and she could tell right away that something was wrong.

"How did your date go last night?"

"OK." Kim avoided her father's eyes while she poured herself come coffee.

"We didn't hear Scott drop you off."

"No, I . . . we walked back. It was nice out."

"Kim, we heard some bad news this morning." Her mother's voice was crisp and matter-of-fact, the tone she always adopted when she had something difficult to say and wanted to get it over with. "There was an accident last night. Scott is dead."

Kim's head came up sharply. "Dead? But I don't . . ." She looked away, not wanting any hint of her immense sense of relief to be noticed. "How did it happen?"

"Hit and run," answered her father. "His car smashed into something up on Reservoir Road."

"Was anyone else hurt?"

"Apparently not. In fact, the other vehicle drove off and left him. But there must have been a lot of damage. They'll catch whoever's responsible."

But they never did.

Kim lost her parents during her sophomore year of college. Their airliner, struck by lightning, crashed shortly after takeoff. The estate was large enough to pay for the rest of Kim's education, with a little left over. But she dropped out instead, and used the money to buy Sheffield House.

There was enough left to cover living expenses until she found a job at a local company, Eblis Manufacturing, as an inventory clerk. By the time she was twenty-six, Kim was Production Control Supervisor, with a high enough salary to allow her to restore the ground floor of the house, though the upstairs remained closed up and largely unusable.

Her next project was Charybdis.

She visited the Rhode Island School of Design and paid to have several busts modeled. Although she had described what she was looking for in great detail, even provided sketches, Kim rejected each of the completed models. Some of the likenesses were quite close and many were extraordinarily well-done, but none contained the specific spark of identity she was looking for.

"No, I can't explain exactly what's wrong, but when I see the right one, when I see Charybdis, I'll know it." The students shook their heads and took her money, and some even tried again, but Kim began to lose hope.

And so Scylla maintained his silent vigil alone.

Kim had just rejected another group of busts the day Chet Muir summoned her to his office to discuss infrastructure. Muir had been hired only a month previously, replacing Alan Daniels as head of Production Planning. Although Kim tried not to make hasty judgments, she considered Muir a mental lightweight, wondered how he would ever make intelligent decisions about the complex systems used at Eblis.

"Hello, Evan." She nodded to the other man in the room, troubled by his presence. Evan Conner was an ambitious, ruthless mid-level manager. The bad feelings caused by his reorganization of the inventory control function still lingered.

"I wanted to talk to both of you together," Muir said quietly, "so that we'd all have the same understanding of what we need to do."

Kim glanced at Conner, wondering how much conversation had taken place before she'd arrived. There was a self-satisfied look on the young man's face that she instinctively distrusted.

"As you may know, I've never understood why inventory control and production control were two separate functions in this company. I've decided therefore to combine them into a single department, which Evan here will head."

Kim blinked, wondering if she'd heard correctly. "I don't understand," she said finally. "I can see merging the two departments, but what qualifies Evan to run them?" She turned briefly in his direction. "Nothing personal, Evan. You do an excellent job. But you don't have any experience with the CPix scheduling system, you've only worked with one of the product lines, and there's only six people in your department. I've supervised thirty people for the last two years and I know CPix inside out."

"Naturally I expect you to continue to administer those systems until you've brought Evan up to speed, Miss Turner. And I don't want you to think of this as a demotion. In fact, I've convinced top management to simply freeze your salary for a few years rather than reduce your wages. And this way you won't have to put up with me anymore." He laughed unconvincingly.

"That's not the point. I have wider experience and more seniority. If anything, Evan should be reporting to me, not the other way around."

"Well, I'm sorry you see it that way, Miss Turner, but you have to understand that as a manager I have to make these decisions based on lots of . . . intangibles, and I'm afraid my decision is made."

She wanted to quit, wanted to storm out of Muir's office in a rage, leave them to struggle through the intricacies of CPix on their own. But Kim knew how tight her budget was, and she had no reserves. She needed the job. So she resigned herself to being Evan Conner's assistant for as long as it took to find a new position.

Three days after the reorganization was announced, Evan Conner didn't show up at work. Calls to his house went unanswered. His ex-wife had no idea where he was but expressed the hope that it was someplace unpleasant.

The following morning Evan Conner's body washed up on the shore below the reservoir.

"The police think he fell off the dam," Muir explained to the assembled staff. "Apparently hit the rocks on the way down and broke his back. He was dead before he hit the water, mercifully."

Kim became "acting" department head with no change in pay, and while the modifier never left her job title, there was never any serious attempt to replace her.

Another set of models was rejected. Kim began to suspect that nothing would ever satisfy her, that she'd somehow conjured up some unrealizable standard that could never be met. Two or three of the models had been photographically perfect renditions of Charybdis as she remembered him, but that's all they were, images. The spirit of whatever had made Charybdis himself was missing.

When the weather permitted, she spent most evenings sitting a few feet away from Scylla, her chair angled so that she couldn't see his decapitated mate. Still a voracious reader, she'd sit until the dimming light made her squint, then set the book aside and just glory in the moonlight until finally slipping inside for the night.

Kim took a week of vacation in early spring, spent two solid days excavating what would eventually be a pair of gardens flanking the new patio she was having built.

Exhausted by early evening, one night she settled into her usual chair beside the front steps and attempted to read, but found herself nodding off almost immediately. Kim rose, stretched, and walked over to Scylla, pressing her cheek against the cold stone.

"See you in the morning, old friend. I'm beat."

The carriage path had been cleared and paved to make a driveway, where her Toyota looked like a cub nestling at the side of its mother, a dusty cement truck waiting for morning when it would pour her new patio. Chet Muir had been replaced, and her new boss had added labor reporting to her responsibilities, along with a healthy salary increase, so she'd accelerated her restoration plans.

She locked the door behind her, doused the lights, and climbed the stairs to her recently renovated bedroom. The heat was thick and oppressive so she opened the oversized windows, letting in the cool night air. Ten minutes later she was fast asleep.

It was pitch black and considerably cooler when she awakened, disoriented, listening intently for whatever sound had disturbed her slumber. She lay propped up on her elbows for several minutes, but the house was silent. Or rather, its noises were the old, familiar ones.

She was thirsty.

Halfway down the stairs, Kim realized something was wrong. Light from the living room spilled into the hallway and one of the ground floor windows was wide open. She'd locked them all before retiring for the night. Half asleep, her mind didn't process the information quickly and she continued down the steps.

The intruder had pressed himself up against the staircase, and now he leaped up and caught her by the hair. Kim tried to pull away, lost her balance, and fell down the last dozen steps, landing painfully on her hip.

He moved toward her menacingly.

The intruder was the ugliest man Kim had ever seen, his face distorted by a twisted nose, a huge wen that ran across his browridge, an asymmetric mouth that didn't quite conceal the uneven teeth within. His skin was pockmarked with the aftermath of triumphant acne and his hair was long and unkempt.

She twisted away when he tried to kick her and scrambled to her feet, but not quickly enough. Powerful arms wrapped themselves around her body and she was literally thrown against the wall. The impact drove the air from her lungs and she slid slowly to the floor, struggling to draw breath.

There was a thundering sound from the front of the house, someone pounding on the door.

"In here! Help!" Kim barely managed to get the words out.

The intruder turned and started toward the open window, but Kim impulsively lashed out with her right leg, hooking his ankle. For a second he hovered on the verge of balance, then fell to the floor.

Snarling, he rose into a crouch, one hand holding a knife. Kim tried to stand up but he was too fast, his free hand catching hold of her throat and smashing her head back against the wall. When she opened her eyes, her vision grew blurry.

"I will not faint," she told herself, trying to regain control of her body. The knife flashed before her eyes and she realized the man was smiling.

There was a scream of tearing metal, then a tremendous crash as the double front doors flew open. Kim turned her head toward what she hoped was a rescue and caught just a glimpse of a charging shape before her attacker smashed her head into the wall again.

She carried a vision of Scylla down into the darkness.

Kim woke to daylight, stared at the ceiling in confusion until the discomfort of lying on the floor convinced her to get up. The sun was well up in a cloudless sky. There was an unfamiliar rumbling from outside that she didn't recognize until she looked out the window and saw that the construction crew was pouring concrete for the patio.

She searched the house thoroughly even before getting dressed. There was no sign of any intruder. At first she wondered if her memories of the previous night were simply a particularly vivid dream during which she'd walked in her sleep. But then she noticed that her television and VCR had been moved to an alcove near the open window, and the front door locks were broken, the metal literally torn out of the wood.

Kim showered and dressed and walked out the kitchen door into the side yard.

"Morning, Miss Turner." Dade, the crew boss, tipped a

non-existent hat in her direction. "Hope we didn't wake you or anything. I rang the bell but no one answered."

"That's all right." She walked past him to get a better view of the work site. "How's it coming?"

"Right as rain. I see you changed your mind about the pathway." He sounded mildly disapproving.

Kim ignored him because she'd already noticed the same thing. To preserve her view of the handsome white birch trees in the rear of the property, she'd located the patio approximately ten feet from the rear of the building itself. There'd been two possible routes for a walkway and she'd finally chosen the one on the west side of the house.

During the night, someone had filled in the trench and dug a new one, on the east side.

"Hope you didn't do all that yourself, Miss Turner. We'd've been happy to fill it in for you with a backhoe."

She shook her head vaguely. "No, that's all right. A friend of mine helped me and I needed the exercise."

It occurred to her that the filled trench was just the right size to contain a human body.

With a cup of coffee in her hand, Kim examined the wreckage of the front-door locks. "Have to get these fixed," she told herself, then swung open the door and stepped outside. Scylla remained as impassive as ever, but she thought there was some very subtle change in his expression. Satisfaction, she thought.

Kim usually averted her eyes from Charybdis's truncated figure, but this time it was Scylla who made her feel uncomfortable, so she turned to the side.

Her coffee cup shattered against the stone steps, spraying hot coffee over her ankles. Kim didn't even notice.

Charybdis had a new head, molded in cement that still glistened wetly in the sunlight. It wasn't much like the original, but it fit somehow, the protruding forehead, unkempt mane, snaggletoothed mouth, raspy complexion.

Kim raised her hand to the smooth stone, swept it over a muscular haunch, across the arched back and massive shoulder, let her fingers just barely brush the underside of

Charybdis's new chin. She looked into the eyes and saw something there, something that she'd missed for many years.

"Welcome back, Charybdis," she said softly.

JANE YOLEN AND ROBERT J. HARRIS

Studies in Stone

———◆———

GRYX WAS FED UP. He had spent four hundred years perched on the same wall of the same Scottish university building with nothing to do all that time but leer wickedly and spout rainwater out of his twisted mouth on passersby. Uncurling a gray, stony arm, he scratched himself in an unmentionable place.

"Another day spitting," he complained in his dull grate of a voice. "I could go for a bit of something new."

"You are a gargoyle," said his neighbor Styx, several windows and a spout away. "I am a gargoyle. We are all gargoyles here. We spit out rainwater. That's what we do. It's been good enough for four hundred years. It's good enough now."

"With all the redundancies," Prax put in far to his left, "you should be glad to have a steady job. Scotland's not an easy place for employment, you know."

"Steady all right," Gryx complained. "Steady as a rock."

"Gryx, you made a joke!" Styx said.

"Some joke," argued Jax, down the right line of the building.

"He should be on the telly," Stonz said.

"And what do *you* know about tellies?" Gryx asked.

"I know what I see. Through the window over there." Stonz pointed across the narrow stretch of Chapel Street with a gray, knobby finger that had only one good knuckle left, the rest having been pounded flat by four centuries of winter storms.

Gryx could just make out a slight flickering in the window. The other gargoyles all had better views into the neighboring buildings than he did from his corner perch. *Something more to complain about,* he thought grimly. He scratched himself again, the sound like a nail on slate, and watched as Jax belched out a flood of water onto the head of a red-robed student hurrying to registration.

"Hey! What's the story here?" the student cried, looking up angrily. But all he saw was a stone gargoyle above him, immobile and grinning.

An upperclassman slapped the student on the back. "Just the Boyz at play," he said. "Don't pay them any attention. It's what gargoyles do."

"See!" crowed Styx to Gryx.

The wet student went muttering on his way, hardly mollified, and the gargoyles indulged in a round of coarse, low laughter that sounded a great deal like the rumble of trucks on Market Street. But Gryx did not join in.

"I suppose," he commented sourly, "that's going to be the highlight of the day for you lot."

"Oh, come on, Gryx," said Jax. "It's always a good laugh to see some weedy bookworm take a gobful all over his fancy gown."

"At least that weedy bookworm is trying to better himself," said Gryx. "Getting an education. Making himself some prospects. That's more than any of us lot do. All we're capable of is sit and spit, spit and sit."

"Don't forget the leering!" cried Prax.

Silence was Gryx's only response.

As he continued in his silence, Gryx fell into deep thought. He and his five companions on the wall were lookers not bookers, this he had known . . . well, forever. They had been doing the same sit-down thing ever since 1559 when Cardinal Broom had overseen the construction of the three-story building as his primary residence, importing the famed Flemish stonemason Frederick van der Krock to carve the five gargoyles for "that authentic Gothic touch." Gryx remembered the day he had wakened to gray sky and North Sea wind and heard for the first time the puerile grumblings of his companions on the left, Styx and Prax, already set free of the rock by van der Krock's mighty chisel. Then the rains had poured down, the workmen had all fled indoors, and Gryx had unloaded his very first mouthful of water on the man who had made him.

Van der Krock had laughed uproariously at that and done a funny little dance below. But not many folks since reacted with such delight when the gargoyles spat on them. Most swore and shook their fists at the rooftop, as if that would change things above them. Really, Gryx would have preferred an occasional dance to balance the years of cursing. But as his companions would no doubt note, curses were a way of life for gargoyles.

Still, it didn't stop Gryx wanting more. For example, he had already used his four centuries to learn something about his corner. One might even say he was an expert on that particular place. From his spot under the eaves, Gryx had watched the burning of the old chapel by a mob of overzealous Presbyterians, history passing below full of fire and reform. And he heard the old cardinal thunder from the window beneath him: "You will perish in hellfire if you do not cease this iconoclastic vandalism." And he remembered, with real regret, that the cardinal's words had struck such a chord with the mob, they turned around and burned the cardinal as well. The smell had taken three days to dissipate. Even Gryx's stone nostrils had finally had their fill of it. Of course, the general opinion the whole of the next month, spoken heartily in the street below Gryx, had been that the cardinal had roundly deserved his fate. He had been, after all, notorious for the heretics he had himself burned, a suspiciously high number of whom had perished during the bitter winter of 1565 when supplies of coal and peat had run low.

And of course there was the night, right after the disastrous Battle of Culloden, that misadventure that had had most of the town muttering under Gryx's perch. He had seen a broad-shouldered figure draped in a dress sneak into the door right below him, a most unconvincing young woman Gryx had thought at the time. When hours later soldiers hammered at the door, waking the Hebdomodar and demanding to be let in to search for the missing prince, Gryx was not in the least surprised. Prince Charlie might have been bonnie, even from three stories up. But even a gargoyle could see he lacked the proper bits for a girl. Still, Gryx was a royalist, having been made in the mocking image of one of the crowned heads of Germany. And he was a Scot from four centuries of occupation on the roof. So he had gleefully unloaded an entire evening's thunderstorm on the heads of the soldiery. How the Hebdomodar had laughed at that. He had looked up at Gryx and winked. The near drowning of those English soldiers had made Gryx feel—for a moment—as if he were truly a participant in the great march of history. But still he knew in his stone heart that it wasn't so. Spitting rainwater was just something gargoyles did. No bravery in that. Or history, come to think of it.

In truth, Gryx thought miserably, *all we gargoyles have ever done is spit on the passing years.*

While he had dribbled rain through his granite gullet, he had often heard passersby speak of exotic far-off places like India, China, Pittenweem. Yet all he could see from his spot on the eaves were two streets, one little more than a narrow lane. That was his life: one broad street, one narrow, and a mouth full of spit. Suddenly it was not enough. He wanted to study history rather more closely than from beneath a third-story eave.

So, straining hard, which distorted his features into an even more repellent face than the one van der Krock had carved, Gryx pulled away from the stone at his back till he felt his right elbow crack loose, sending down a flurry of stone flakes to the pavement below. Next he wrenched out one leg, then the other, effectively dangling himself from the overhang. All he had left to do was one more arm and his rear end and . . .

"Hey, what are you doing?" cried Styx. "You're shaking the eaves."

"I'm shaking more than that," Gryx said. "I'm shaking off the dust of centuries and going down there to join *them*." He waved a gnarled grey finger in the direction of four students who were approaching from the far end of North Road.

"You're daft!" Stonz called.

"You'll embarass us all," added Styx.

"This has never been done before," Jax said.

Gryx turned his head to the right and left, showing them all a gray grimace. "I'm tired of never-been-done-before and that's-what-we-do! You can stay up here forever and wallow in your ignorance for all I care," Gryx told them.

"Gargoyles don't wallow," said Prax. "We squat."

"Then you can *squat* up here in your ignorance," Gryx snapped back, and with one last pull, he got himself entirely loose from the stone. He had planned to clamber slowly down but the final effort had freed him so suddenly, he plunged to the street below, snapping off two pinkies when he landed. They lay on the pavement like petrified dog foulings.

"We will!" his erstwhile companions called down to him. And to add emphasis to their disgust with his sudden departure, they eructed simultaneously, splashing a small white cat, two pigeons and a tourist from Northampton, Massachusetts, who was already more than a little bewildered by Scottish ways.

Gryx loped in an ungainly fashion toward the four students, waving at them with a naked grey arm.

"Wait!" he rasped. "Please. I have a question." He had never actually spoken aloud to a human before and did not know if they would be able to understand his grumble of a voice. As it turned out, two were from Glasgow and two from Dundee, so they had no trouble with Gargoylian at all.

"Great costume," said a redheaded boy, "but a bit early

for Mad Meg's Parade, don't you think. That's in the spring."

Adjusting his spectacles, a second boy, particularly weedy, with hair like dandelion fluff, pursed his lips. "Gargoyle. Early sixteenth century. Probably Flemish school."

The third, full of pimples and pusillanimity, giggled.

"Stop showing off, Angus," said the one girl.

Angus, the one with the dandelion hair, took off his glasses and wiped them on his red gown. He shook his head. "But he really *is* a gargoyle, Mairi. Look at the chiseling, the articulation of the fingers and toes. Absolutely brilliant!"

Mairi bent over Gryx and he was surprised at how nice she smelled. The only living things he'd ever smelled before were the doves who had nested each spring on the back of his neck and they didn't smell half this good. Oh—and the cardinal when he was burning. But of course the cardinal hadn't been living then. He'd been quite, quite dead at the time. So that probably didn't count.

Mairi touched Gryx tentatively on the arm, then looked up.

"Angus, you're right," she said. "He's made of stone."

"So nice of you to confirm my findings. But I'm always right."

"Are not."

"Are, too."

"And were you right that time in Turner's class when you said that ontogeny was . . ."

"Well I am *almost* always right," Angus interrupted quickly. "About the important things. And this really *is* a gargoyle."

Mairi smiled at Gryx and he smiled back. It was not a pretty sight.

"Really!" she said, "you filthy little grey man. Stop leering at me like that or I shall have to report you."

"He's a gargoyle," Angus said. "It's what they do. Leering."

"Begging your pardon," Gryx said, "it's what I *used* to do. But I want to improve myself. No more sitting or spitting . . ."

"Or leering," Mairi said.

"Or leering," Gryx agreed, though he actually hated having to give that up. Still, if it was something students didn't like, especially students who smelled as nice as Mairi, he though he might be persuaded.

"How can we help you?" Mairi asked. "You said you had a question."

"Yes, my question: I want to enroll in the university," Gryx answered. "As a student. Can you tell me where to go?"

"As a *mature* student, I suppose," said Mairi.

The boys all laughed and Angus added, "Four centuries mature, I shouldn't wonder."

And without any more pother, they took him right to the Admissions Office on Whitefriars Street, which is how Gryx's academic career began.

There were complications of course. There always are. And of course, being in Scotland, the question of fees came up at once.

"What's that?" Gryx asked.

"Money," said Mairi.

"Payment," said Angus.

And when Gryx still looked puzzled, never having paid any kind of fee in his life, the redheaded boy, whose name was Jamie, put in: "Bags of gold, you twit."

Suddenly Gryx understood. "Ah—highway robbery!" He had seen more than a bit of that, the narrow street overseen by his perch being a dark and dangerous venue until the present era when street lamps had made such a difference. "I know about that. I'll have your fees in the morning."

That night he went to a small house in Chapel Street across from his old eave. Two centuries earlier he had watched as Hamish Applemuir, the pale draper who lived there, had hidden a barrel of loot in the garden. Hamish had led a strange double life as the fearless Highwayman Ruthless McCutcheon. But he had never dared spend any of his ill-gotten wealth and had died miserable and poor without ever digging it up again. In the years that had followed no one had ever found the gold, and only Gryx knew of its whereabouts. So, heedless of the sassing he heard from his erstwhile rooftop companions, he sneaked into the garden that very night. No longer a draper's meager vegetable patch, the garden was now a carefully cultivated rose bed tended once a week by a hired gardener. It stretched behind the little house that was now a Listed property owned by Americans who came over only for the summer months. The barrel was just where Gryx remembered and it was filled not with gold but with period coins.

He dragged it into the street and heard the gruff voice of Jax shouting "Thief! Pillager!" And Styx adding "Ruffian! Stealthmonger!" But their voices sounded like the grumble of thunder far out over the North Sea, and so no one stopped Gryx as he rolled the barrel down the street.

With the help of his new friends, Gryx was able to sell the lot and thus pay his university fees, with plenty left over to take them all out for a night of drinking. They ended the evening at the Whey Pat Tavern, this being a place the students thought especially appealing, though Gryx found it dark and grim and cold, like midwinter on the eaves after a North Sea storm. They drank large draughts of lager until closing and then Gryx taught them all to spit into the gutter. The pimply boy, Harry, did it best, though Mairi explained that Harry wasn't exactly spitting but honking up the beer, which didn't really count.

Gryx thought he had never been happier.

The second complication had to do with gender/race/nationality. There was nowhere in the Admission Department's computer forms for the answer *Gargoyle* to be set down without throwing an awful spanner in the university's works.

However, Mairi had an idea about that. "Why not donate some of your Highway Robbery Funds"—which is what they had taken to calling Gryx's money, never dreaming how close they were to the truth—"and promise them you will fund a chair."

"But," Gryx said, truly puzzled this time, "they already have more than enough chairs. At least they do in Mayfield

Hall. I used to count them through the windows from my perch."

Mairi looked at him oddly. "Things must have been awfully slow up in the eaves."

"Sit and spit," Gryx reminded her, "for four centuries."

"An endowed chair. Brilliant!" said Angus. "Mairi—that's as good as anything I could have come up with."

Jamie clapped his hands. "Better!" he said and blushed when Mairi rewarded him with a smile.

Gryx wished she had smiled at him like that and for a moment his face was a misery. But as it was so like his usual grimace, no one seemed to notice the difference, and so the moment passed.

But Mairi's suggestion really had been brilliant. With just the promise of money for an endowed chair, the term *Gargoyle* suddenly showed up as a choice in the Admissions procedure. Gryx put a large check next to it and, with his friends' help, quickly finished the rest of the form. Interestingly, not a week later three other students claimed that they, too, were Gargoyles and were allowed to register as such, much to Gryx's disgust since it was absolutely clear that only one of them knew a thing about spitting and none of them was made of stone.

Less than twelve hours later, Gryx was seated opposite his Advisor of Studies, Dr. Geoffrey Willingham, in a small office at the rear of a nondescript grey building, having tea.

Tea, Gryx thought, *isn't at all like lager. More like dirty rainwater, actually.* He resisted the urge to spit, for the office didn't have anything like a gutter and he really hadn't had enough tea for a proper eruction anyway. His head felt awful and he didn't know why, never having been sick a day in his life.

Dr. Willingham cleared his throat and the sound went through Gryx like a sword. "There are some more papers here for us to fill out, my—um—boy."

Ponderously, Gryx nodded his head. For the first time in four centuries his stone temples throbbed and he reached up to rub at the sore spot. That didn't seem to help at all.

Dr. Willingham rustled through his papers; somehow the sound of that was louder than Gryx had expected. It made his head hurt even more.

"Now," Willingham said, tapping at the paper with his forefinger, each tap on the same beat as the throbs in Gryx's head, "you have not entered anything under family. Have you none?"

Gryx looked up painfully. "None?"

"Ah," Willingham suddenly smiled. "Now I understand. You've been out celebrating with the locals. At the Whey Pat, I expect." He nodded solemnly. "It often takes first-years like this. Don't be embarassed. Just learn from the experience." He pushed a couple of white pills across his desk at Gryx. "These will help."

Gryx looked at the pills.

"Swallow them, son," Willingham said, pouring more tea into Gryx's cup. "Haven't you ever seen a headache pill before?"

Gryx shook his head, a gesture Willingham ignored as he couldn't believe the truth of it. But the pills helped Gryx's head almost at once, and he tried a small smile of gratitude.

"I'd watch that leer if I were you," Willingham said. "There's many a young lady here who'd report you for less these days. Now—about this family thing."

"I believe," Gryx said slowly, "that I am distantly related to the Jacobite Monument on Grackus Moor."

Mr. and Mrs. J. Monument, Grackus Moor, Willingham scribbled onto the page.

"We never see one another," Gryx added.

"Ah well, some families are like that," Willingham said, something close to sympathy in his voice. "And now about a course of study. Admissions have noted here that architecture might be something you would enjoy. Or geology."

"Actually," said Gryx, scratching himself below the table, the sound much louder indoors than it had ever seemed up on his eave, "I know a bit about history. And . . ." He remembered the many years monks from the cathedral had passed under his perch, whispering in a language he had come to love, a language that sounded as liquid as the doves over his neck, rather than the rougher, rockier Scottish tongue. "Latin."

"Latin?" Willingham looked a bit bemused. "But why?"

"The monks spoke it softly," Gryx said. "Sung it, too. And the priests thundered it out on the street corner. Though that," he grimaced, "was not so nice. All about heretics and schisms and noncomformists and such."

"Heretics and schisms and nonconformists . . . oh, my!" Willingham took a long drink from his tea cup.

"Usually ended in a burning," Gryx said thoughtfully.

"I'm sure it did," said Willingham, whose field was mathematics, and suddenly he was completely delighted that it was so.

"I didn't like the burnings," Gryx added.

"No reason you should," Willingham said. "Now—I believe we can arrange your studies to suit. History. And Latin." He rose and, only a bit reluctantly, shook the proffered stone hand.

Gryx's actual scholarly career commenced even more successfully. For one, he had no need of sleep. So, unlike his fellow scholars, he could always succeed in dragging himself to even those lectures that had been unthinkingly scheduled for the forenoon. Often he found himself the only student in the lecture hall, or at least the only one actually awake.

For another, being an *extremely* mature student, he was highly motivated to learn. His work—though unimaginative, even, some might say, dull—was thorough, so much so that some of his tutors speculated that there might eventually be a place for him in the university's administration.

He found his small room in St. Utter's Hall comfortable in the extreme, though four hundred years stuck to the side of a building in all kind of weather was hardly a basis for comparison. Still, he was often heard to say, "What luxury this is!" And anyone near him who had been about to complain of the short bed frames or the lack of wardrobes or the windows that would never open in summer or stay closed all winter, found themselves understandably falling silent. In

the face of Gryx's continuing paeans to his place, such pans
were unseemly at best, unScottish at the very worst.

Due to his mineral nature, Gryx never actually got drunk,
though he did develop a fondness for cask-conditioned ale.
So he was popular as a drinking companion as he could always be counted on to drive home. And he was an absolute
whiz at card games, becoming known for his stamina and
his pot-winning poker face. Stone, of course, gives nothing
away.

And so his first university year sped along to a satisfying
conclusion.

But at the beginning of the second year, Gryx began to be
subjected to periods of sluggishness. He even began to ar-
rive late for lectures and tutorials. A transfer student from
America's Yale University called it "sophomore slump."
And Willingham would have concurred except that during
one visit to his room, Gryx suddenly stopped in mid-sentence, lapsed into silence, and remained for almost half an
hour still as stone.

"Gryx!" Willingham called. "Are you all right?"

Gryx did not stir for another few minutes, then at last
slowly rallied. "I seem to be losing the ability to move," he
whispered in his gravelled voice.

Without hesitation, Willingham sent for a doctor but the
woman only shook her head as she folded the stethoscope
back into her black bag. "If he were human, I might diag-
nose Fatigue Syndrome. It's a useful catchall for all kinds of
immune system breakdowns. But, I wonder—does he have
an immune system at all? I am afraid I don't know stone,"
she said. "Perhaps you need a geologist."

So Willingham put in another call, this time to the head
of the Geology Department, Dr. Clemson Carling, a wiry little man with a bristly red moustache, known by his students
as Climber.

Eagerly, Climber came at once, having long wanted to
have a closer look at Gryx but, being English and never having been properly introduced to the gargoyle, had not ever
gotten the chance before.

"For once a doctor's got it right," Carling said. "Stone

can become fatigued, just like people. Stress fractures result. And this seems to be a stress fracture of the mind. If you are not careful, young man, you will end up *completely* immobile. I expect you miss the mass of stone at your back. Why not take a year off. Or five. Go back to your perch and regroup. I could take a ladder every few weeks and see how you were getting on."

"I *can't* go back there," Gryx said. If he had not been stone, he would have cried.

"Well a bit difficult, I know, but I'm sure we could get the loan of a crane," Climber said.

"Not . . . that." Gryx could scarcely get the words out, then relapsed back into a stony stillness.

For once his advisor understood something. "He means the ridicule of his peers, the disappointment in his own heart." Having said such a thing aloud, Willingham was embarassed into silence, and Climber with him.

Which is how Mairi found them, an hour later, when she came for her own appointment with Willingham: three stone men sitting by a cold fire. The silence in the room was complete.

"What is this?" Mairi asked. "No one at home?" She tapped her fingers to her head.

Climber shook off the malaise first. A pretty young woman can have that effect on males, even professors. "Just leaving," he said, touching a hand to a nonexistent hat and escaping the room.

Willingham was next, but as the room was his own he could not very well leave. But he stood, trembling, and offered Mairi a chair.

However Gryx remained like granite, staring into the dead embers of the late fire.

"Oh, Gryx—not again!" cried Mairi, putting her hand to her breast and sighing. By this Willingham understood that Gryx's friends already knew of the problem. Which, he thought, could make things better—or worse.

"Dr. Willingham, we must *do* something!" Mairi cried.

"Climber . . . er, Dr. Carling is a stone expert and he says poor Gryx here is stressed. Needs a mass."

"Stressed?" said Mairi. "He's a student! Of *course* he's stressed. We're all stressed. It just takes us differently. But why does Gryx need to go to church?"

"Not a Mass, a mass. A mass of rock at his back," Willingham explained patiently.

"Not his old eaves," Mairi said. "He'd never agree to that."

Willingham nodded. "I know."

Mairi leaned over Gryx and rubbed his stone brow. "Come on, you old gargoyle, time to get you back to your room. I'll make you a cup of tea and find us some scones in the buttery. You always like that."

Her warm touch and the sweet smell of her soap-clean skin roused Gryx just enough. He managed to get out of the chair and follow her slowly back to St. Utter's where he once again lost mobility on the front steps of the hall. And nothing, it seemed, could move him from there.

One street over, at his old building, Styx had been watching Gryx sink down into immobility onto the stone stair.

"Pssst," Styx whispered to the gargoyles down the right and then left lines of the eaves. He pointed at Gryx with a sharp, unforgiving chin. Both lines of gargoyles commenced to jeer loudly, calling Gryx names like "Rock-baby" and "Granite-groin," "Simple Stone Man," and "Fool." The sound of their voices was like a murder of crows.

No one but Gryx understood them, of course, and he—poor bugger—was too far gone to care.

And so he might have stayed, a granite clump, grey and unappealing, on St. Utter's steps for the rest of time, had not his fellow students at the university taken matters into their own hands. No one passed by St. Utter's without giving Gryx a quick rub on the top of his head or whispering into his pointed stone ears. Tourists were encouraged to give him a swipe as well. And this offering of human warmth and friendship, small as it was, still kept him alive—marginally—till one day in late March when Mairi and Angus came galloping down the stairs.

"Look! Look!" Mairi said, shaking a newspaper in front of Gryx's stone eyes. When she saw he was not reading, she sat right down by his side, sheltering out of the wind, and whispered into his one ear, "Listen then. To the headline. It's from *Le Monde*. That's French. I'll translate: IRREPLACEABLE STATUE DESTROYED BY LIGHTNING. Gryx—are you listening?"

He was listening, but could only manage a small groan, not unlike the sound a building makes when it settles a bit on its foundation.

Angus sat down next to Mairi and put his arms around her, as if he were trying to keep her other side from the wind.

"Listen, you old sod, this is it!" Angus said. "It's brilliant!"

Mairi continued to read. "One of twelve gargoyles at the Church of St Dagmar's in Paris has been struck by lightning and knocked from its perch. The impact with the ground damaged the sixteenth century stone piece beyond repair, much to the despair of the townsfolk who regarded the statues as symbols of good fortune."

"*Good* fortune, you bugger!" It was Jamie, coming down the stairs. He crowded next to Gryx on the other side.

"And," crowed Harry from an upper step, "guess who carved them all?"

Something deep inside Gryx responded. Something warm. Something not very stonelike at all. He could feel an answer rumbling up, rather like an eructation, and he was glad he could not stop it.

"Van . . . der . . . Krock . . ." he cried at last, a great grumble of heartfelt sound.

"We're going to pack your bags," said Angus.

"And drive you through the Chunnel and over to France," added Jamie.

Harry threw his cap in the air. "Hurrah for Gryx! Hurrah for Gryx!"

"And good news for the good people of Paris!" whispered Mairi. "You can recover there and have masses and Masses at the same time! Think what the new surroundings will do for you! You will have wonderful fresh histories to write about when you are ready to return back home. And lots of new people to watch."

Gryx slowly, ever so slowly, turned his vast, ugly head till he was eye to eye with Mairi. And then slowly, with a great deal of love, he leered.

"Leering, too," she said, patting him affectionately on the top of his stone head. "I understand they adore that sort of thing in Paris!"

MELANIE TEM

Hagoday

—━━◅❦▻━━—

THIS TIME THE PURSUERS had tree branches coming out of their mouths. Eric wasn't even particularly surprised. They'd been a lot weirder than that. Sometimes they'd been nothing but heads, or half-men, half-lions. Once they'd been, he swore, severed penises high as his belt buckle and big around as his arm, small for a person but gigantic for a dick; he'd almost laughed out loud until he'd reminded himself they meant him harm and in some detail imagined the method they could use.

One of them had said something to him. A talking penis was about as bizarre as you could get. And among all the other crap Eric refused to consider was what this might mean about his sanity. But one of them had sort of sidled up to him and looked him straight in the eye—with what? He was not so far gone that he thought dicks had eyes—and said in a voice that was more or less what you'd expect if you thought dicks had voices, except that it was female, "You're afraid of the wrong thing, asshole. We're not what you should be afraid of."

That was bullshit, of course. They chased him. He had no idea what they wanted, but it couldn't be anything good. He never could predict when they were going to show up or what disgusting form they'd take. Who wouldn't be afraid?

This time he saw them crouched here and there along the side of the mountain road. If he hadn't learned to be always on the lookout for them, they'd have been easy to miss in the changing light as the sun worked its way up above the cliffs. They didn't do anything, just watched him pass with the same twisted face repeated over and over or with no face at all, but it gave him the creeps.

One or two or three of them jumped out in front of him, where he couldn't help running them over. He knew that was a trick of the scattered darkness and of his mind, also dark, full of pointlessly horrible things he'd so far managed to keep out of sight. But he braced himself for another impact and it was all he could do not to swerve or slam on the brakes. Every time he sped by them, the sweep of his headlights would pick up more detail than he should have been able to see: big flat feet in the sparse grass, knees bent up high so they were hard to distinguish from shoulders, bulging eyes with staring unblinking pupils like holes drilled deep, long tangled hair all of a piece with long tangled moustaches and beards, big hands stretching back the corners of mouths already bigger than any normal mouths, and foliage sprouting from deep in their throats.

Long fingers with long nails grabbed his door handle. He knew enough to keep his doors locked, but he still heard plainly what the thing yelled. "Yo, Eric! We're your friends! Trust me! Slow down, man!"

A length of soggy vine from the creature's throat poked through the crack where the window didn't seal, wetly breaking off and sliming down onto the seat. Eric gagged, pressed on the accelerator, and outran them again.

He was shaking, but these days that was nothing unusual. He had driven straight through, but since he hardly slept anymore anyway that was no big deal either. He didn't know what was the matter with him.

It might have helped if he'd had a traveling companion,

somebody to talk to about anything other than where he was going and why. Ridiculously, he missed Rosie. He was better off without her, and she never would have come along on a trip like this anyway. But the place in his life throbbed where she used to be before the accident, before he'd killed somebody but it wasn't his fault. Sometimes the ache was worse than others, like his thigh with the metal rod in it, like his need to get high which didn't ease no matter how high he got. Right now he was pretty high, on beer and reefer, and he had plenty more of both with him, and still he wasn't anywhere near high enough.

Another car was behind him, too close. He hadn't noticed it until it was right on his tail. Its horn blatted and its brights glared in his mirror. He couldn't see the driver, but he could guess. He clutched the wheel.

The angle of the lights must have changed, or the slant of the several layers of glass between them, because suddenly Eric had a clear view of the other driver. Actually, he saw only one of its features, and he thought, though it didn't make sense, that maybe that was the only one it had: a huge mouth, wider than the steering wheel, and in it someone's head.

Trying to think what to do, he was tempted to brake and let the creep crash into him; at least that would stop the chase. He did slow down, and, to his surprise, the other car drifted past.

Against his will, Eric glanced left and saw that the head in the thing's grinning, gaping, toothed mouth was his own. He recognized his ponytail, his black hair thinning at the temples, the tattooed R he now wished wasn't on the right side of his neck.

The creature laughed, and the jiggling of its teeth made Eric cough. "You think *we're* ugly, bro? You ain't seen nothin' yet!"

Gasping, hardly able to see in the night suddenly blacker and wetter, Eric had to focus all his attention on keeping his car on the road, and when he dared to ease up and glance around again, the other car was gone. No point wasting time trying to figure out how it could have disappeared like that.

He'd been chased practically since the accident, by grotesque creatures that came and went as they damn well pleased and never did him any harm but threatened, always threatened, and said stupid things that made a crazy kind of sense.

Eric didn't like books much, and he liked libraries even less, but just before this trip he'd gone to one. Figuring out the computers enough to look up "Monsters," he'd found books with pictures of vampires and werewolves and zombies and mummies, but none of those were the things that were chasing him. But gargoyles were.

Gargoyles. People must have carved those things, but nobody knew who. They were supposed to keep away evil spirits because they were so ugly; nothing would keep away evil spirits, Eric snorted. The ones with exaggerated sex organs were supposed to help you make babies. Just what he needed. Sometimes, like on churches, there'd be these bizarre door handles called hagodays with gargoyles all over them, and if you had the balls to open the door and go in, whatever was chasing you couldn't follow. Sure. Sometimes drain pipes were carved into gargoyles, so they heaved or pissed waste water into the streets. Great sanitary engineering.

Eric had found pictures of gargoyles he hadn't met up with yet and pictures of those he had. But he couldn't stand the library very long, and he had to get on the road, so he'd left without getting a clue as to why gargoyles were pursuing him. Just lucky, he guessed.

Now he took a swig from the bottle in the cup holder, barely felt the whiskey going down or any effect from it once it had. He set his teeth, flexed his stiff hands so he could clutch the wheel again, and drove.

He really didn't think about the accident anymore. There was no point; what was done was done, and he didn't see how it had been his fault, even though the law said it was and Jesse's family had demanded what they called justice. Like locking him up would bring back Jesse. They'd both been drunk and stoned. He'd just happened to be the one behind the wheel when they missed the curve and went off the mountain road. This road, as a matter of fact, although nothing about it was familiar and he knew it was the same road only because the map said so.

He used to wonder whether Jesse had felt the incredible rush of those few airborne seconds before the crash. He used to wonder whether Jesse had come to, as he had, in a silence filled with echoes of things breaking and dying, darkness filled with things that never touched him but meant to do him harm. He used to wonder if Jesse hurt, and if he knew he was going to die.

He'd stopped wondering a long time ago, probably in prison where he'd done his best to stop wondering about everything. It was over. He'd done his time. Since he wasn't dead, he'd had to get on with his life.

But nothing had worked out right. Which was why he was on this trip, and why he *could* take this trip; there was no job, no family, nothing he was leaving behind.

Ahead, there was a glow off to the right where the road spiraled sharply upward. Eric squinted at it, reluctantly remembering what it was. It stayed blurry for quite a while, but gradually it showed itself to be a restaurant and bar, the little dive they'd stopped at that night. They'd already been pretty well sloshed; the bartender shouldn't have served them. For a while Eric had thought for sure Jesse's parents would go after the bar, and that if they did it would somehow go easier on him.

He was hungry and thirsty and needed a bathroom. He pulled in, barely making the turn. When he got out of the car his legs wobbled, and he felt sick to his stomach. The narrow parking area in front of the dilapidated building, thinly graveled and hardly graded at all, seemed to buckle and twist under his feet.

It wasn't the first time he'd stumbled like this, and he just kept going.

Vastly irritated, he shoved open the door too hard for the sprung hinges and it banged back against the wall. The girl behind the counter looked up, scowling, and he saw that she didn't have a body. Her arms and legs grew directly out of her huge egg-shaped head. "Help you?" She made it clear that helping him was way low on her list.

Eric couldn't look at her, couldn't keep from staring. The girl who'd served him and Jesse that night had been friendly and not bad-looking. He'd thought about coming back to see her later. Jesse probably had, too. But Jesse had died that night. Eric muttered, "You got a bathroom?"

"For paying customers," she informed him.

"I'll have a beer. Whatever you got on tap."

"Can't serve alcohol this time of night."

"Coffee and pie then."

"All I got left is cherry."

"Cherry. Fine."

"We can talk," she said, grimly.

Oh, Jesus. "Sure. Yeah."

"I got things to tell you you need to hear."

"I gotta take a piss."

"Around back." She handed him the key on a long wooden slab. Eric hurried out, unable to stop himself from glancing over his shoulder at her wiping off the table where obviously he was supposed to sit and eat his cherry pie, in her company since they were the only ones in the place. Her arms came out right under her ears. Her legs were attached to the base of her neck so that when she bent over to wipe the far edge of the table her curly hair lifted up to expose the backs of her thighs. Eric couldn't believe he was fantasizing about her, but it had been a long time since he'd been with a woman.

Slowed by booze and weed and fatigue and long hours of driving, he was zipping up before it came to him that she wasn't a woman in any ordinary sense of the word. She was one of them. A pursuer. A gargoyle, for Chrissake. Disgusted and shaken, he got a little revenge by locking the key inside the bathroom. His tires spat gravel as he whipped the car back onto the road.

Nobody had chased him in prison, which, in a cold sort of way, had surprised him. He'd expected the joint to be practically nothing but people out to get you, but he'd actually felt safer there than after he got out. Not that he wanted to go back. The sound of cell doors clanging shut every night was still with him.

The first time he'd noticed one, before he'd known what to call them, had been on the Greyhound going home. Half-asleep, he'd been trying to get used to being out and to the fact that it didn't feel any weirder to be out than it had to be in, or any freer, either. He'd sort of been thinking about Rosie. He had definitely not been thinking about Jesse.

Then he'd found himself staring into the pupil-less eyes of the passenger across the aisle. A woman—female, anyway; undeniably, grotesquely female—she'd locked his gaze with hers and drawn it downward. Huge tits, huge belly, exposed thighs, and her long fingers spreading herself apart, right there in the gloom of the half-full bus heading north.

Then one of those long, smelly hands had reached out toward him. "Ooh, big boy," she'd crooned, ludicrously but with a certain kinky sex appeal. "Come here. Come *here*." Knowing full well she could see his hard-on through the thin prison-issue pants, he'd stared out the filthy bus window and pretended to ignore her. She'd made a noise that could have been a laugh or could have meant she was about to hawk a noogie. "Oh, you will. Sooner or later."

"Like hell," he'd snarled, wished he hadn't. In prison he'd learned not to go looking for trouble but not to back down from a fight, either.

"Then we'll just chase you forever." She laughed so hard he thought he was getting slimy from it, and the dirty, musky odor of her puffed up around him and settled back down on his skin.

Eric had been seriously grossed out, but he'd also been tempted, by what and to do what he still wasn't sure. In order not to go to her, he'd gotten off at the next stop, way before he'd meant to, and then had to stay and work in that little dump to buy a ticket the rest of the way home. Where nothing had been waiting for him except more pursuers.

As if he hadn't paid. As if he could never pay enough. It wasn't fair. He hadn't meant to kill anybody. He'd hardly known Jesse; it wasn't like they'd been friends or anything.

They'd just been a couple of young guys out for a good time. No point feeling guilty for the rest of his life. No point losing sleep over it.

Eric rolled and lit a joint with one hand and toked rapidly, holding the bitter smoke in his lungs until his throat burned and his eyes watered. Nothing much happened. The weed was crap.

His ears popped as the car climbed. He was getting a headache. Banked on his left by sheer rock striped different shades of gray and on the right by the continuation of that same cliff straight down, the road bent more sharply and more often now, and there weren't a lot of guardrails. It would be really easy to miss any one of these curves and switchbacks, just to go sailing off into any one of these canyons, which were getting steeper and deeper by the minute. But he had to wait for the right time and place and frame of mind. He might be a coward and a murderer, but he had to wait. He didn't think he could wait much longer. The car kept straining toward the edge. He gave it more gas. He'd done the same thing the night of the accident; he remembered speed.

Somebody was in the car with him. Eric took his eyes off the flying road long enough to glance at the figure in the passenger seat and get an impression of more heads than there ought to be, three heads on one squat body, three pairs of beady eyes, three mouths hanging open, three sets of teeth.

The three-headed monster didn't make any move toward him, and it was as silent as carved stone. But Eric didn't miss its evil intentions, and the car went off the cliff. There was that few-seconds rush of being airborne again, and he was yelling and swearing and laughing again, and there was the same enormous crash so loud and so hard he still couldn't believe it had ever stopped. In fact, the noise and the pain didn't go on for very long at all, or the screaming. Then there was silence.

Eric sat there, too drunk and stoned to figure out what to do, not enough to pass out and be done with it. He was fumbling under the seat for the bottle, which must have broken because the floormat was wet and he thought he felt a cut open in his hand, when the driver's door opened and he was thrown out. He'd been thrown out of the car then, too, and so had Jesse, so he'd known not to wear a seatbelt this time either.

He lay on the ground for a long time. Pine needles worked themselves inside his clothes and rocks against his shoulder blades, the small of his back. He was bleeding, but only, it appeared, from the flesh wound the broken bottle had made across the heel of his hand. Appalled to discover himself now totally sober, he yearned for a drink or a toke.

It could just as easily have been Jesse behind the wheel that night and Eric dead with a broken neck.

It wasn't.

Darkness skimmed the pine trees over his head and sent a thin chill onto his face. He waited for something to happen. He hadn't thought beyond this point—hadn't thought *to* this point, actually; hadn't thought ahead much at all lately. He had no idea what to do next, why he should go to the trouble to get up and find out if the car was driveable and make a decision which way to turn on the highway at the top of the cliff.

He did, though, get himself up on his haunches, then—hastily, clumsily because his thigh hurt—stood up. He'd heard something. He heard it again now, distinctly, grunting and thudding, something coming after him up the steep tumbled slope.

Now it didn't make any sense to Eric that he was afraid. What could happen to him worse than what already had? But he turned awkwardly upslope meaning to run to his car, lost his footing and caught himself on his hands, his pinned leg and cut hand stabbing, felt around for handholds and footholds and tried to pull himself along. The pursuer was closing in.

He stumbled over all kinds of obstacles, hard as rocks and soft as torn flesh. Patches of the uneven ground seemed to be slicked with a clotting liquid that cost him his balance time and again. Now there were more pursuers behind him, filling in the valley below and behind him and oozing up on both sides.

They were talking to each other, about him. Their noise was hollow and hard, wind blowing through carved canyons, eyes and mouths of rock opening wide and slamming shut, hands and feet with long stone nails scrabbling, stone cocks erect and stone pussies sucking.

"Ha! Ha! We'll get him now!"

"Now it's time to pay the piper! We've done our job. He owes us."

"He thinks he can outrun us. He thinks he can get rid of us. Ha!"

"We stop chasing him, he'll *really* see ugly!"

Because of his bad leg, Eric wasn't exactly running up the slope. What he was doing was crawling, and, while he didn't much like the thought of that, there was also something gratifying about it. Fitting. He didn't know why he didn't just collapse and let the pursuers take him, but he had such a strong dread of them and of something worse that might be behind them that he scrabbled in the dirt, which broke off in his hands. Bushes he grabbed dislodged themselves at their roots. His knees and toes tried to wedge into depressions that filled in under his weight. The slope was a lot longer than he'd first thought, and steeper. The horde of pursuers rose behind him like a flood.

He was making some progress, though; he could tell that he was higher up the incline than when he'd started. But so were they. One of them—maybe more than one—grabbed at his ankle with a cold appendage, not necessarily a hand although it felt more or less like a hand with long fingers. Eric managed to jerk his foot free of it, but the creature had his shoe and shrieked in triumph like crazed birdsong. He could feel the pin in his leg jerk against flesh and bone and nerve.

Suddenly he was seeing over the rim of the cliff. The car sat right in front of him and he didn't think it was very far away. If he could get to it and lock himself inside, maybe they wouldn't be able to get to him fast enough to stop him from driving away.

His shaky arms gave out after just a few seconds and he sank. But the brief view of possible escape gave him a spurt of new energy, and, grunting, he pulled himself up again, this time to stare right into the hideous face of a pursuer not six inches from his own. This one looked as much like a bird as a person, with a beak and what might have been feathers, but it yelled, "Fool!" in a very human voice. "We're guardians! We protect you!"

Eric managed to fling back, "Great. I get guardian gargoyles."

The thing grabbed him by the collar and pulled him close to its beak. Its eyes, one set deep in each feathered temple, were focused off to the sides, but he felt fixed in its stare. "Get rid of us, you little piece of shit, and you know who you'll get then? *Jesse,* that's who. You want that? You want to face Jesse?"

Eric lost his precarious grip and slid some distance down the slope, scraping his chin and banging his bad leg more than a few times. Something like a saw blade came down on the back of his left calf, and something tugged at his right pant leg, tearing it, wrenching the pin. He yelled and scrabbled away, barreling into the bird thing with his lowered head and knocking it aside. It was a lot more solid than he'd expected, like stone, and his vision blackened from the impact, his hearing buzzed.

When his senses cleared, he was crawling across more or less level ground, trying desperately but without much success to keep his injured hand and his bad leg from coming into contact with anything rough or hard, not thinking about Jesse being dead. The hardpack was strewn with little nubs bigger and sharper than gravel. Eric squinted down at one that thrust itself into the cut on the heel of his hand, which was still bleeding, and recoiled when he recognized a leering little stone face with a wide, flat nose and protruding tongue; it was the hard, sharp tongue that hurt where it stuck into his wound. The heads were everywhere. He couldn't move without dislodging half a dozen of them, and they rolled on their own power under his hands and knees. They were all talking, murmuring, whispering.

Desperate to distance himself from the little severed heads, Eric struggled to his feet. He was unsteady, but he could walk, could even sort of run, and he ran toward the car. He actually had a hand on the fender, caked with dirt and gouged and pocked, when cold liquid suddenly cascaded down his back. He cried out and pivoted awkwardly, looked up to see a huge creature with a long mouth like an alligator spewing something that might have been nothing more than water but smelled like sewage. With the rank liquid came words: "You don't want to do that."

Eric backed up against the car and felt behind him for the door handle. His injured hand, which now felt swollen and stiff, bumped painfully into something hard sticking out of the door, and Eric thought it must be the handle although it didn't seem to be the right size or shape or in the right position. He found it again and tried to pull, but he couldn't get his hand around it right and the huge creature, like the corner of a wall, spat down at him again.

Drenched and stinking, Eric couldn't see in the pitch dark, but somehow he was aware of things transforming all around him, or showing what their true natures had been all along. Rough bark pressed into his flesh until it raised and indented in ugly patterns. It roughened further in some places and grotesquely smoothed in others, revealing long thin faces, beards to the roots, hollow eyes extending well above Eric's head to branches which were hair, which were claws coming out of the sides of the heads. Heart-shaped aspen leaves fluttered to face him, evil heads on bloodied stems. Things out of the ground started crawling up his legs. Things out of the sky started wrapping around his neck.

Panicked, Eric bent, then squatted to find the door handle, thinking maybe the car had been damaged on this side, the handle torn off. But something was where the handle should have been on the edge of the door, and he squinted at it, couldn't quite make out what it was. Something flat and hard, metal, like some kind of foreign coin. Revulsion made him clench his fists, but at the same time his hand itched to touch the thing and his wrist wanted to turn.

Bracing himself, he reached out gingerly and laid his palm flat on it. The lever had somehow been replaced by a metal disc the size of the rough circle made by his palm out to the first knuckles of his fingers, as if to fit exactly there.

The rest of his fingers, and his thumb opposing them, bent more or less securely around its edges, which were flanged, so that he could turn it with an easy motion of his wrist. Against the sensitive skin of his palm he could feel the metal design writhing, squirming, poking out into his bones and sucking his flesh down into the little pocks it cut.

Then, realizing what the designs were, Eric recoiled and fell backward hard. What was now the door handle teemed with gargoyles, mouths gaping, hands reaching, ready to destroy him if he tried to use it to get inside where he might be safe.

But he had to get inside, because the pursuers were everywhere out here, swarming, crunching across rocks and swishing across needles and undergrowth to get to him, making trees sway and split, inhabiting trees, leering down at him from high branches and higher crags, spitting dirty water at him, grabbing at him, stuffing parts of him into their mouths. He made himself take hold of the disc again, actually had to steady his right wrist with his left hand and force his fingers apart.

The taste of metal was strong on his tongue and the roof of his mouth, as though he'd licked the handle trying to get in, and there was an odor both disgusting and alluring. Unable to straighten all the way, fingers clamped around the disc and palm pressed hard into it, Eric twisted sideways and threw up. But there'd been nothing solid in his stomach for many hours. Hot bile seared his throat and backed up his nose without getting rid of any poison.

He tugged on the handle while he was still retching, as if it were part of the same motion. The disc tipped toward him. The pursuers danced against the tender inside of his wrist so that he felt their clawed feet, their bulging eyes, their too many heads and swollen sex organs and tongues like long thick hair. "Don't let him go in there," some of them called to others. "Don't let him go!" He could hardly breathe. He thought about passing out but knew he wouldn't now.

Hands or feet or teeth came around him from behind in a nasty hug, digging into his waist. Thick liquid spouted into his hair. Using both hands, he turned the disc half a rotation clockwise, and the door opened as if he'd never meant to do anything else. All but falling across the seat, he managed to shut and lock the door.

When his breathing calmed and his heartbeat quieted, Eric just lay there. Everything hurt. His leg hurt so bad that he doubted he could have put weight on it. Jesse was in his mind. It was absolutely quiet in here. He was completely alone, and sober.

Turning his head on the seat and opening his eyes a little, he made out the dim, mottled shapes of pursuers outside the sanctuary of the car. The weight of them made the car rock on its wheels. They scratched and tapped on the windows. Some of them had climbed onto the hood and trunk to make faces at him through the windshield and rear window. Eric found himself almost wishing they'd get in, but he knew they wouldn't.

Jesse was in his mind.

He hadn't meant to kill Jesse, but he had.

Eric took a deep breath and began to cry. His pursuers milled for a while, grumbling. Eventually, they left him alone.

CHARLES DE LINT

May This Be Your Last Sorrow

FIFTY YEARS FROM NOW, Elfland came back.

It stuck a finger into a large city, creating a borderland between our world and that glittering realm with its elves and magic. As the years went by the two worlds remained separate, co-existing only in that place where magic and reality overlap. A place called Bordertown.

It was Joe Doh-dee-oh who told her about the gargoyle that perches on a cornice of the Mock Avenue Bell Tower, how if the clock in its belfry ever chimed the correct time, the gargoyle would be freed from his body of stone.

"I'm sure," she'd replied.

She waited for the teasing look to come into Joe's eyes, but all he did was shrug, as though to say, "Well, if you don't want to believe me . . ."

I'm nobody really; any glitter I've got's just fallout from people I know. Borrowed limelight. But that's okay. I never wanted to be anybody special in the first place. I like being part of the faceless audience—the people that attend the theatres and concerts, that sit in the dark and appreciate the skill of the performers. I read the books without any urge to write one myself. I'm the one who goes to the galleries, not by invitation on opening night, but later, when the anonymous people come to steal a glimpse of what made the artists' spirits sing so fiercely that they just had to find a way to give it physical dimension.

You'll find me in the back of a club, sitting by myself and enjoying the band, instead of trying to talk over the music to describe my own next project. I'm the one you see walking through a museum with the big goofy smile on my face because everything's just so amazing. I'm not full of ideas about what I'm going to do; I'm appreciating all the wonderful things that have already been done.

I think there's too much emphasis put on having to be Someone, on making something out of nothing. It's not a road that everybody can follow. It's not a road that anybody should have to want to follow.

I'm not making up excuses for having no talent—really I'm not. I don't know whether I've got any or not; all I know is I'm short on the inclination.

You know the old argument about whether talent comes from your genes or your environment? Well, I give lie to both. See, my mom's Deeva. You never heard of her? She was the "Elf Acid House *chanteuse*" as her recording company liked to put it. That was because, when the Change came, she was the first to take the visuals from across the Border and use them in her music and videos.

There was a time when all she had to do was just think about putting out a new recording and it'd go triple-platinum. She was the first of the post-Madonna dance artists who did everything—wrote, sang, produced, played all the instruments with nothing sampled, not even the drum track. She directed and choreographed her own videos, too. At the peak of her career she was a one-woman industry, all by herself. Amazing, really, when you think about it.

And my dad? He was Ned Bradley—uh-huh. *That* Ned Bradley, the one who played Luke on *Timestop for Chance*.

It's funny. I thought music'd make a way bigger impression in a place like this than a TV series would, but I guess I understand. I've gotta admit the show was pretty cool. I mean, he started shooting *Timestop* way before I was born, so it's like, really old stuff. The first show aired twenty years ago, right? But I could still relate to all those kids. It'd be so weird if reincarnation really worked and you could remember it the way they could. I think that's what made it so popular. It didn't matter what historical era they used for the background on any particular year, the continuity was so fascinating and the cast worked so well together that they just made each episode sing.

Anyway, so there's like more talent in my house when I'm growing up than anyone could know what to do with. Not just my parents, but all their friends, too. I guess the biggest disappointment to my parents was that I didn't show much of an aptitude for anything.

My mom must have tried to teach me to play a half-dozen instruments. She'd get real mad and tell me I wasn't applying myself; she wouldn't listen when I told her I loved music—just to listen to, not to make. That's something so alien to her that she must've just tuned it out. I mean, she still can't listen to a new recording—doesn't matter what style of music it is—without her fingers twitching and her wanting to head down to the studio to lay down a few tracks herself.

My dad's another story. I'm not unattractive, but I'm not as pretty as Deeva is, either—who really is? My mom sure isn't. She's just Anna Westway until she does that amazing makeup and puts on her Deeva wig, you know? I like her better as Anna Westway, but who's going to listen to me? Anyway, my dad tried to get me into commercials and bit parts in shows that his friends were producing—stuff like that—but it never took. I wasn't Deeva. I have no camera presence. Zip. Nada. Which my dad just *couldn't* believe.

You see when my dad's doing his thing—doesn't matter whether it's on the big screen or a dinky little TV set—he just commands your attention. I think the thing that really proves his talent is how he managed to never overshadow whoever was in a scene with him. With as riveting a screen presence as he had that wasn't exactly an easy thing to pull off.

Anyway, needless to say, I was a big disappointment to them both. They tried to get me interested in anything creative—writing, painting, sculpting—but none of it took. It was kind of embarrassing for them, I guess, but what could I do? I'm just me; I can't be anybody else. I wouldn't know how.

My parents kind of gave up on me by the time I turned thirteen. They didn't turn mean or anything, they just sort of forgot that I existed, I think. Mom was working on a comeback; my dad got a part in *Traffic*—yeah, he plays the holograph man. Great part, isn't it?

That was about the worst year of my life. It wasn't just the way things were at home. I was having the shittiest time in school, too. You know what I think is really weird? It's how everyone thinks that rich people can't have real problems. It's like, if you've got all that money, you can't possibly be hurting emotionally.

When I first started high school, people thought I was pretty cool, considering who my parents were, but that wore off real fast when I wouldn't, like, get them free tickets to some concert, or introduce them to that kid in dad's new show, Tommy Marot—you know, Mr. Heartthrob? I like to be quiet, but they just figured I was stuck up—with nothing to be stuck up about.

So that's why I ran away. There was nothing for me at home, nothing for me at school, nothing for me anywhere except here. I don't think my parents even know I'm gone. I used to check the papers, during the first few weeks, but there was never anything about Deeva and Ned Bradley's kid having turned up missing. No mention at all. I guess they were kind of relieved to be rid of me, that's what I think.

Why'd I pick this place? I dunno. Not because it's so cool. I mean, I still get a kick out of seeing elves and everything, but that's not really why I came. I think it was because I heard that this was a place where people left you alone.

And I love it here, I really do. It was tough at first, but

I'm staying with the Diggers now and they're really nice—especially Berlin. And Joe, even if he does tease me sometimes. So long as I pull my weight, I'll always have a place to crash and something to eat.

Nobody bugs me; nobody's trying to make me be something I'm not. If I don't want to talk, they don't get in my face about it. They just let me go my own way.

What I like the best is the clubs and galleries, though. It's like all the best talent from the outside world and across the Border's been distilled into this magic potion. You take a sip, and it just takes you away. Who needs drugs in a place like this? I get high on the music and the art; that's the real magic, I think. Something about being this close to the Border hones this edge on anything that's created in its shadow.

And I like the way nobody's pushy; they just leave you alone. That's the way it should be. People should just let you have your own space.

So I know I did the right thing. Really. I just wish I didn't feel so . . . lonely sometimes, you know?

I think you're the only one who really understands.

The stone gargoyle on top of the Mock Avenue Bell Tower watched the small figure climb down from the belfry. He enjoyed her visits, even if they always left a melancholy pang, deep in his stone chest.

When she got to the bottom rung of the ladder, she disappeared from sight. He shifted his gaze over the edge of the cornice, waiting until she stepped out the tower door far below. Her slim shoulders were bowed under her tattered jacket, her unruly tangles of hair hanging in her face to hide the tears that had been welling up in her eyes before she left the belfry.

He watched as she dried her eyes on the sleeve of her jacket, straightened her shoulders and then marched off down the street.

If he could speak, he would advise her to approach another human the way she did him. But he couldn't speak. And if he could, he doubted she would listen anyway. But he would still try.

She needed a friend. Anyone could see that, if they only took the time to look beyond her bravado.

The belfry clock chimed twelve although it was only the middle of the afternoon.

Was there ever such a bittersweet, forlorn sound? the gargoyle wondered, as he had far too often in the two hundred years he had kept watch over the city from the bell tower.

What might have been a sigh shivered his stone skin.

I think you're the only one who really understands, she'd said.

He did understand. He understood all too well.

Author's Note: Bordertown was created by Terri Windling and Marc Alan Arnold and is used here by their kind permission.

NANCY HOLDER

Little Dedo

BEFORE THEY HAD COME to Paris, Jeanne had not understood the idea behind gargoyles. Their purpose, Sam had patiently (and patronizingly) explained, was to frighten away evil spirits. They perched among the spires and balustrades of dozens of medieval European churches, but it was the gargoyles of Notre Dame that had attracted the imagination of the world. She wondered if they truly were the most stupendous and ugly of all the ugly little gargoyles that adorned the holy places of Western civilization.

Yet she still didn't quite understand how such squat, misfit creatures could keep evil at bay. How could you tell them apart from the things they were frightening away? She would have thought that magnificent golden angels or sweet, tiny fairies would be better at the job. The ugly would fear the beautiful, would they not?

Perhaps gargoyles were distractions. They fascinated the truly hideous because they were ugly enough to seem familiar. Something lovely would be too incomprehensible for things that had crawled up from the abyss. And while they were fascinated, St. George or whoever it was who slew evil things in medieval France (her namesake, Joan of Arc?) would charge in and destroy them.

Maybe that was why married couples fought about money, when what they were really struggling over was the survival of their individual identities. Or about their careers, when their actual objective was to stop themselves from killing each other.

Maybe that was why Sam seemed such a stranger now, so odd and different that he was beginning to frighten her. She touched her abdomen tentatively. With this new distraction, perhaps she was seeing her husband as he had been all along. They said that of women who married abusive men, that they just didn't see the evil inherent in them until they were beaten almost to death. Charming with the beauty of a handsome smile, a bouquet of flowers, and so-called "encouragement" to forge a life of one's own, they dealt the death blow while you hovered, staring at them, unable to look away as the mask melted and the putrescence glowed through the rotting layers.

She swallowed sick and sour bile and turned her attention to Sam's pointed finger. He must not know what she was thinking. There were no anchors here, nothing to save her from being cast adrift. She must not introduce the variable of marital disharmony into the thick Parisian fog of these weeks, this so-called celebration.

"Little Dedo," he said, and she followed his gaze. There he was, the ugly baby gargoyle, sucking his thumb of stone. Legend promised that he had been carved by a nun who had snuck into the cathedral in the dead of night and placed him among the grown-up gargoyles. The adults, poised and ready to take flight to loftier, more distant environs; the little monsters of protection, looming like attentive cats and dogs. At home, she and Sam had neither. They were too much work for yuppie couples such as they.

She wondered at a nun who would think of creating a baby gargoyle. A woman barren by choice, a woman who had denied herself what now lay inside Jeanne. The world's first career woman. Jeanne smiled unhappily, disliking the comparison but finding it apt. Despite all the talk of "balance" and the hipness of having children, it was still true that there was a mommy track and a success track in the world of law, which was now her field. This trip was to fete her graduation from law school. How could she tell Sam she was pregnant?

She thought of the horrible stories they had heard in England while touring various country estates: of tiny skeletons curled in fetal position tucked in the hollows of chimneys. The babies of servants not allowed to live, for their lusty shrieks would doom their mothers to being turned out as fallen women. Perhaps the nun had carved Little Dedo in memory of a child she had smothered in the nunnery, for herself or for a sister who had allowed the devil to tempt her into enjoying the fullness of life. . . .

"It's just like Disneyland," Sam grumbled, his voice making ghosts, as he put a coin in a box and picked up a candle. "You have to tip for everything."

Indeed. The two men who had escorted them to Quasimodo's bell had carried a yellow bucket to the tower. It was the job of Citizen #2 to sit on a stool and hold it out for your francs and centimes after Citizen #1 told you about the great bell and the poor old monster. You paid to buy candles to set before the statues of the saints dreaming of heaven behind wooden gates while the gargoyles stared down at them.

You paid to pray to them.

She sagged. He was unhappy with everything. They had been a week in England, a week in France, and he had gotten crankier and edgier with each day. If he knew she was pregnant, he would be more than unhappy.

"It's not even the real cathedral. Half of it's been rebuilt."

"No," she disagreed, then let it go. She had dreamed of going to Notre Dame ever since seeing *The Hunchback of Notre Dame*—the original black-and-white film, not the remakes. The cathedral was everything she had wished for, the chiaroscuro romance of the vaults and ceilings, the dim coolness that touched your cheek like a faint but understanding friend. The stones speaking stories, and changes, and eulogies.

She and Sam were from southern California, where

everything was new. It was astonishing to her that you could actually read a novel written in another century, then visit the places described there, and find them virtually unchanged. In Orange County, where they lived, the cathedral would have been a themed restaurant where "French" food was served—braised sirloin tips, omelettes, French bread and champagne. You could have purchased Quasimodo dolls. Disney might have arranged a tie-in deal, or sued the restaurant for appropriating what was, after all, a public domain property.

Jeanne had never found anything wrong with that. Her field was entertainment law. She had always loved the superficial amalgam of cultural "bits" with theme park structure. Why not build huge arenas and hire high school football players to joust one another in knightly garb? Why not charge kids a buck to pan for gold in an artificial river cleansed with chlorine? What did it hurt? Wasn't it the way the future would be, when everyone lived on space stations?

But suddenly, it was all wrong. Turned sideways; she flushed and shivered and remembered a time when she was so angry at Sam, incredibly furious, that she had driven herself to Disneyland. She had ridden the steamboat, and as it came along the island in the river, she stared at the fantastical shapes of New Orleans Square with a horrible vertigo and a sense that she had never been there before in her life.

"Finished?" Sam asked. There was an edge to his voice, as if he had come here only to placate her. As if somehow later, he would return with his learned colleagues and his discerning *amis,* who understood about gargoyles, and see the cathedral as it should be seen: quoting Hugo in the original, Rabelais and Moliere at his side.

"Yes," she said. "I'm done. Let's go to EuroDisneyland."

He checked his watch. In Europe he had often looked at his watch, although they weren't following a set schedule.

"You don't have to," she flared. "I can go by myself."

He looked shocked. "I didn't say I didn't want to go."

"But you act like it . . . oh, never mind."

He peered at her as if inspecting her under a lens. "You're

tired," he said. And the thing was, he was right. Being pregnant was a lot of work. She was tired and a little nauseated.

She wouldn't be able to go on all the rides at EuroDisney,
and she wouldn't be able to tell him why.

She raised her chin. She didn't care. She was tired of
doing things his way.

"I want to go now," she said firmly.

He inclined his head. *Noblesse oblige.* "Then of course
we'll go."

"Don't do me any favors," she muttered, but he didn't
hear her. He had processed ahead, holding court with imag-
inary judges and juries composed of people as clean-cut and
erudite as the extras on an old *Perry Mason* episode.

He had gone to law school first, specializing in divorce
cases. By the time it was her turn to go, life was comfortable
for them. They had a large stucco house with wall-to-wall
carpeting, *de rigueur* for an up-and-coming southern California career couple. It was not what Sam had grown up
with. He was from the East, and his patrician mother's house
was genteel and old, with plaster walls and bare wood floors
and plenty of bookcases loaded with first editions. Jeanne
was sure her mother-in-law thought her son had married beneath his station, but the woman was far too well-bred to
even hint at such a thing. Jeanne wondered what she would
think of the baby.

She had already figured out how to get to the Happiest
Place on Le Earth. It was the last stop on the line. It would
take forty minutes. She knew how much the tickets would
cost.

Yet Sam stopped in the underground station and double-
checked everything, assuring himself that she hadn't made
any mistakes.

"Little Dedo was cute, wasn't he?" she said, attempting
small talk to hold her temper in check, regain the sensation
of being in Paris, the wonder of it, the achievement. Sam
had been before, many times. "Sort of a cupid gargoyle."

"Oh, yes."   His supercilious smile set her teeth on edge.

"I know the story is probably bogus, but it's still fun to
imagine some little nun sneaking him up there."

He practically winced at the word "bogus." As if they were the kind of people who didn't use language like that. She remembered an old *New Yorker* cartoon that had tickled him: a chesty, pearl-drenched matron speaking to her husband, who looked like the younger brother of the little man in Monopoly. The woman said, "I wish we were the kind of people who ordered out for pizza."

"She's like my mother, isn't she?" he had said at the time, but even then, she suspected he admired people who didn't order out for pizza.

When he had gone to law school and she had slaved as an administrative assistant in the English Literature department, they had eaten untold amounts of delivered pizza. They got whatever was on special, whatever you got with coupons. Ordering an extra topping was an extravagance beyond them. The purchase of his interviewing suit had been a major event in their lives, although he had murmured something about buying his prep school clothes on Oxford Street in London while she had written the check. Taking the wind out of her sails even then, devaluing the moment as she had flushed with pride at paying for something so vital to their survival, his twentieth-century armor. He had not taken a dime from his mother, and nothing had ever been said about that one way or another. She had no idea if she had offered funds and been turned down, or sat back to see if her son and his Orange County wife possessed the mettle to make it on their own.

Now, in Paris, they got on the train and Jeanne watched the stops. In southern California, anyone who could manage it had a car. If you took public transportation, you were suspect. You were either an economic bottom-feeder or an innocent tourist who would soon be on your way to the emergency room. So now, riding buses and trains took on an allure of the forbidden. They seemed like theme park attractions, unreal, as if they would simply take you around in a circle and deposit you back where you came from. As opposed to getting you somewhere you really wanted to go.

"We're here," she announced breezily, grabbing up his hand. "Let's hurry. It's late."

"I'm sure we'll have plenty of time," he said. Always ready with a counterargument, always questioning whatever she initiated. He could win any debate. He could quiz her and trap her, and she knew soon she would stop going first, stop suggesting, and just wait to see what he thought or what he wanted.

She would be a terrible role model for the child.

She felt as if a bell were closing over her, the great bell of Quasimodo, and she would run around inside it for the rest of her life, a mouse.

For perhaps the last time, she ignored him and bolted ahead, tripping through the airy station toward the escalators.

EuroDisneyland! The entrance was enormous, with seemingly a hundred ticket booths waiting for their credit cards and wads of francs. She stood back and let Sam pay with the money that he had once assured her they had made together, although he had the high-powered job. She imagined herself taking her child to Paris not for Notre Dame but for Disneyland. A hotel stretched right over the entrance; at night you would be able to see directly into the park. What a treat!

Sam and his mother would find it incredibly common.

"Come on," she said desperately.

"You really are a kid," he said, but she could find no trace of affection in his voice.

But, Disneyland! Better than any kid could have imagined. It was different, it was bigger, and there was no one there. The French had not taken to Disneyland as the Americans and Japanese had in their respective countries. And the Germans, apparently, for whenever they saw another living soul, which was not all that frequent, Jeanne heard German. She spoke pretty good German, but her command of the language of class, of the upper class—French—was weak at best.

She heard a little German child tell his mother, "I hugged Bugs Bunny." She chuckled, doubting an American child would make the same error, steeped in American pop culture as he or she would be.

As her baby—as Little Dedo—would be.

Again, the vertigo, the unreality, of Orange County and the Disneyland that thrummed there with a life unconnected to her own. Off the steamboat there, the overlying blanket of unfamiliarity had traveled with her as she wandered into the shops, back out onto the streets. So mad at Sam, unbearably so, she had bought some perfume and daubed it onto her wrists, smelling it from time to time as if it were her own scent and she was looking for reassurance that she was still herself, like a dog that sniffs its own feces. *I'm still here. I'm still what I am.*

Now, as Sam put his hand on her shoulder and peered at her with exaggerated concern, her heart catapulted into her throat and she fought the urge to run, or to smell him, to find his scent and discover inside this stranger the young, eager boy who had loved her for the way she was.

"Sweetheart? Are you all right?"

He had said that before. And look what had happened to her. Her wrists—

—the scent not of perfume, but of blood—

They rode the rides, the pirates and the ghosts singing in French. She began to forget Sam was there. It was just she and Little Dedo on an exotic journey.

Then the park closed and the crowds made their way through the exit to an enormous boardwalk of restaurants and shops. It reminded her of the City Walk in front of Universal Studios in Los Angeles. Neon and clever architecture. She forgot Sam had been hurting her feelings all day and slid her hands around his arm.

"I'm hungry," she said, to have something to say.

"Just fifteen minutes ago, you said you weren't." Fifteen minutes ago there had been time for one more ride if they didn't stop to eat.

"Oh, Sam, I'm hungry," she said irritably, rudely.

"All right. All right. What would you like? More junk?"

"You're supposed to eat junk at theme parks."

He cocked his head, appraising her. "I'm only teasing."

No, he wasn't.

She chose a steak house only because it was expensive.

The emerging dynamic between them frightened her: she, demanding and vindictive, childish; he, paternal, grudging, the bestower of *largess*. Lucy and Ricky, when she was an attorney now too, for God's sake. It would not be a healthy environment for a child.

And she saw then that she was making Little Dedo into the real Little Dedo, transferring her distress to him or her, making him the reason she was so unhappy. The gargoyle that keeps away the evil spirits, the ones who say, *You are helpless. You are trapped. This is the way it will be from now on.*

He ordered a bottle of wine without asking her if she wanted any; she drank none because of her pregnancy. He looked at her curiously; she said, "I don't want any," and she sounded petulant. Angrily, she announced, "I want dessert." When they got home, she must see someone, tell someone what was going on. Get help.

Flee.

"Honey?"

One word, a common word, spoken from the lips of this stranger, one of Sam's words.

"Are we the kind of people who say things like that?" she asked shrilly. The people at the next table over glanced in her direction.

And then everything turned sideways again; the maze of bells and winged monsters clanging and flapping around her. She was disoriented beyond jet lag, beyond resignation, beyond anger.

"Honey?"

She blinked at this stranger, at this bell ringer, and her body heaved. She stood up unsteadily. Was she having a miscarriage?

Oh, God, Little Dedo.

"I'll be right back. I have to go to the bathroom," she said.

She ran from him, found the sign for the W.C., raced in and checked her underwear. There was no blood.

She retched into the toilet. Morning sickness, a reassurance. She was no calmer. If anything, she was dizzy, hot, cold.

She stayed in the sanctuary of the bathroom stall, her arms around herself, and began to rock back and forth. Perhaps if she pushed hard enough—

—Her eyes widened. What was she thinking?

Of gargoyles. Of hideous things pulsing inside her. Things gnawing through her, at her. Flying over the extent of her life and flapping away every good thing with their leathery wings because to others, those things were not good.

Not good enough.

"She just graduated from law school," she heard someone saying just outside the bathroom entrance. The voice frightened her because it was beautiful and because it should be familiar. "We're here to celebrate. This place is great isn't it? Someday we'll have to come back with our kids."

She dare not listen to Quasimodo ringing his bell. The ugly to frighten the uglier.

"Top in her class. She was under enormous pressure, but she did it."

Little Dedo, Little Dedo. That stranger's pride, so ugly. She pressed her stomach as the gargoyle baby moved inside. He shifted and rotated, descended, crawling toward her vaginal opening.

"She's trying to unwind. Jet lag and all, you know. Sometimes traveling is an awful lot of hassle."

Hassle? Do we say hassle?

The wings were stuck; she grunted at the pain and leaned back against the toilet tank. Her forehead was bathed with sweat.

Don't leave me, Little Dedo. Don't leave.

I'll die.

I'll kill myself.

Sweat poured down her face. The bathroom whirled.

I hate law school. I want to quit.

Oh, honey, just hang in there. It's been your dream for so long.

His dream. His. Praying to saints in another language, not

her language, her stucco tongue of theme parks and mangled French and her unbearable *bourgeois* upbringing.

White picket fence, Donna Reed, baking cookies.

High-rise office building, Ruth Bader Ginsburg, arguing in court.

The excruciating pain of birth exploded and radiated in all directions like talons, ripping everything to shreds, tattering, pressure, pressure, pressure . . .

. . . tattering her.

She bit through her lip.

How many bells had she rung? How many times had she climbed to the towers and sounded the alarm?

"Bit of Montezuma's revenge, I suppose." The stranger who was not Sam laughed gently. "That's what we call it in Tustin, where we live. Yes, very close to Disneyland. We go all the time. She's a real nut for Disneyland. I guess I am, too."

Not those kind of people. Not those kind.

Corporate suits. Impeccable manners. Prep schools.

She ground her top teeth against her bottom ones, incisors and molars. Blood streamed down her chin.

Then, in a rush of wind and freedom, Little Dedo flew from her body and flopped on his side. He was wet and slippery, an ashy gray. His limbs moved erratically. He began to mew like a kitten. The blood from her chin dropped on his face. He made suckling motions.

She reached out her hands and touched him. He was warm, not ice-cold as she had expected. She slid her fingers beneath him and picked him up.

He blinked at her, recognized her. The bond was made.

Her blood dripped. She ripped open her blouse and put him to her breast. Though he had sharp teeth, he didn't bite. He only sucked. The feeling of being drained coursed pleasantly through her body.

"She had a couple of really rough spots."

Leave of absence.

Dr. Epperling.

Medications.

Pressure, pressure, pressure.

Just give it one more shot, baby. You can do it.

A knock on the door. "Jeannie? Honey? You okay, honey?"

One hand cradling Little Dedo, she clung to the toilet paper holder and pulled herself to a standing position. She pushed open the door and staggered into the bathroom. No one else was there, but someone gasped.

There was a window. She opened it, crawled out awkwardly on shards she had not previously noticed. The glass must have reopened the scars on her wrists. Blood ran like rain down the side of the building.

Little Dedo stopped sucking and looked up at her adoringly.

"My darling, my life," she murmured, and opened her own great leathery wings. She flapped them once, twice, and flew into the air, over the boardwalk, and EuroDisney, and Sam, and high-rise office buildings and Ruth Bader Ginsburg and custom suits and secretaries, and picket fences and minivans and flew like

mad.

We're so proud of you; we're all so proud of you; you're going to make such a great lawyer.

mad

She should have gone to a prep school; she should have grown up in a plaster house lined with first editions. Her education was so limited. She was limited.

mad

Her mother: It's so different now. In my day, you'd have a baby by now. Maybe two. Don't you want children? Soon you'll be too old.

Flew like mad

angry, cheated, confused, terrified, wishing, wishing

to the land of the gargoyles.

At once the others flapped their wings and swooped down on her, lifting her and Little Dedo up, up into the rampart of Notre Dame, past the bell tower to the turrets, to the cornices and the darkness. A little nun sat there, smiling beatifically, as if to say, *Welcome, sister.*

The gargoyles gently lowered her; her joints stiffening,

her bones turning to stone; her blood congealing. In her arms she gathered Little Dedo, who was sucking his thumb.

She would never move again. She would never have to. It was finally, blessedly over.

"Little Dedo," she whispered, her mind clear and bright. The stigmata of her wrists, the crown of thorns of misplaced ambition.

Last words, last thoughts.

The theme park called Paradise, the holy infant called Little Dedo. The martyred mother—

—the sacrifice of external ambition!—

—exalted.

Grace à Dieu, God be praised, it is finished; she rose again among the other creatures of the air, of the magnificent golden, the beautiful, hearts of stone.

Shadows fell, but not on her.

Bells clanged, but she heard only the gathering of the fog, and the whispers of the saints.

Et voila, redemption eternal: Jeanne of the bells, of Paris, of the gargoyles.

ALAN RODGERS

The Gargoyle's Song

IN THE SMALL HOURS of the night, when the city wind blew hard and wintry from the north, Cathy's gargoyle sang to her. In the evenings, when she'd sit in her tiny room reading novels by the dim light that came from her bedside lamp, the gargoyle sang low steady tones, the sound of the wind whistling through stone, nothing more, nothing strange or *outré*: There was no haunting in her waking hours.

But late, late that night, in the moments when she lay abed alone in that brilliant city made of darkness, in the space between sleep and awake, Cathy's gargoyle sang the world to her.

She would have killed it if she could.

Cathy Gilman lived in New York three long years before she rented the gargoyle's room. That was the way she thought of it: It wasn't an apartment, or even a studio; it was a single room, bare and spare and almost functional when the heat worked.

It was the gargoyle's room. Oh, the gargoyle—a decorative-stone statuary cornice-waterspout, not especially or generically different from the gargoyles that thrust themselves from a dozen buildings in New York—the gargoyle didn't own the room, or live in it, nor had it ever to her knowledge passed through the room that Cathy rented early on a steamy July morning.

In the hottest part of summer.

When no one ever could have heard the song because the summer air in New York City is torpid, balmy, rank, and very, very still.

One night in late December the gargoyle sang a song about a place where life is always grand. *It doesn't have to be like this,* the gargoyle sang, staring out upon the world from its cornicine perch, watching every sight a woman's imagination can survey. *There is a world of possibility and wonder laid before you like a dream.*

Cathy Gilman almost woke when she heard that. How could it sing those words? The idea was so crazy and so wrong, like the stupid talk in art school that'd got her to move to the city in the first place.

New York is *the* place, everybody said. Careers happen in New York the way they happen nowhere else.

Everybody was about as wrong as wrong could be, Cathy thought. She hated New York City.

Hated it.

She rolled over, whispering obscenities. "Shut up," she muttered. "They only cut you out of stone. You never knew a thing about the world."

Later she lost track of whether she'd said those words or dreamed them. She was never certain of the gargoyle's song; when it sang to her, the music came as a strange melange of murmur and phantasm—a thing she always knew as it came to her but never could remember clearly.

She didn't have clear memories of the way that she responded to it, either.

The world is always bigger than you know, the gargoyle sang. *It loves you more than anyone could say.*

And Cathy Gilman cried, because that was the most hateful lie of all.

She fell asleep that way, still sobbing all alone with the wind and New York City wrapped in her imagination like a dream.

All the months she lived in New York City she never heard the magic that underlies the bitterness that is the city, and the misery of the place came on her so quietly and gently that she never realized and didn't even recognize it till the winter after she rented the gargoyle's room.

And heard the graven monster sing to her, devouring her dreams.

She slept soundly the first night of her haunting, and woke as rested as she'd ever been in all her days. Even then she knew what her haunting meant to her: She wasn't dullard hardheart Scrooge who'd need three ghosts on three successive nights to show him all the errors of his ways. The gargoyle had whispered its song to her, and she'd heard it, and she knew that it was true.

Time to move on, she thought as she rose from her bed, remembering the dream.

Remembering the song.

It wasn't as simple as that, of course; she had a life here, even if it was only half a life. She had commitments and responsibilities, and maybe moving on meant letting go of them, but even if it did she'd do it responsibly, giving notice, tying loose ends—if she was careful she could line up a job in—

In?

Line up a job before she moved wherever she was going to go.

Out of bed, now, and crossing the room to the shower stall. Turning on the water; putting coffee on to brew while she washed . . .

It was while she was in the shower that it came to her that she could still hear the song.

I'm losing my mind, she thought. And there was sense to that: Everyone she knew, all the folks at work and half her friends back home, they were all in therapy. Most of them because their insurance would cover it, and it wasn't like therapy was a cure or a salve, but it was somebody to talk to, anyway, and so long as the insurance covered it it was cheaper than talking to the bartender. *Maybe I should be in therapy, too,* she thought. And shook her head, thinking how people always seemed to get crazier and crazier in therapy, till finally the neuroses would absorb them and carry them away, like helium balloons set loose to climb the sky.

"I got it already," she said, climbing out of the shower. "You can stop now."

But the gargoyle sang on through the morning, till Cathy rinsed her coffee cup and headed for the door.

Later in the day, when she was as far from her gargoyle room as far could be inside Manhattan, she thought that she could still hear that song. But that was even sillier than the haunting, wasn't it? There was no way she could hear that thing from down on Madison in the thirties, was there?

Of course there wasn't. It was such a silly question!

But she did hear it. All day long at her dreary desk at the junk-mail agency; at lunch, as she watched the overdressed secretaries and sweaty salesmen and overconfident young executives scurry up and down the avenue; and on through afternoon, shimmering chords of it drifting through the glass in tune with the pastel brilliance of the setting sun.

"I hear you," she whispered, cutting repro by hand to force effects that the clumsy keyboard artists couldn't force from their computers.

Designers! Those people had the nerve to call themselves designers! And the truth was that they didn't know a solitary thing about design, none of them did, not a one—they had jobs because they had connections, or knew the software or even because they'd work for cheap, but they weren't designers, and their work wasn't worth the trouble it took to print it.

Not that Cathy cared. Of course she didn't care! She did her work well because she took pride in the effort, and she knew good work from bad work. But there was no joy in the paste-up or design of junk mail. Not for her. Oh, there'd been a time when it'd been something, what, a place to learn her craft? Because she had things she wanted to accomplish with her art, and she was going to accomplish them, by damn, even if she had to conquer all New York to do it . . .

She didn't feel that way anymore.

She wasn't sure what she felt, in fact. She kind of hated her work, but it fed her, and it was a thing that occupied the hours, the days—maybe she did know what she felt: bitter. Mad, almost. What had happened to her? Why wasn't she happy? Why wasn't she accomplishing anything?

She didn't know the answers to any of those questions. All she knew was the sound of the gargoyle, whispering a wordless song to her now on toward dusk, the skyline brilliant red the way New York skies can be some nights, beautiful, almost, if you can bear to savor beauty when it comes to you from endless clouds of car exhaust.

"Still here, Cathy?" It was her boss, Tom Fernandez, calling to her as he wandered by her door. "Time to go home! The Clark account isn't in that big a rush; no need to keep you here late this close to the holiday."

Cathy blinked, tried to smile. Close to the holiday? God, he was right, and she'd lost track of the days entirely: This was Thursday, and tomorrow was Friday, Christmas Eve.

She was supposed to take a train up home to Arkham tomorrow after work. She dreaded that trip, and she didn't know why.

Her boss was still standing in the door to her office, smiling. "You okay?" he asked.

Tom was a good guy, and he did well by Cathy—did well by all the folks who worked for him. Even so, she kind of hated him. She wasn't sure why that was, either.

Too damn cheerful, maybe. Too damn friendly when he had no right to be.

"Thanks, Tom," she said. "Lost track of time, I guess."

Tom said something chipper before he wandered away, but Cathy hardly heard him.

And not just because she was ignoring him, which she always tried to do when he was chipper.

She didn't hear a word that Tom Fernandez said because

that was exactly when the sun dipped below the horizon on the far side of the New Jersey Palisades, and when it did the song that had gnawed at her all day rose up to consume her, loud as a chorus thundering of angels.

If she'd had any sense she would have blacked out there in the office where some friendly soul might have found her and got her help before it was too late.

But how could she have sense? The sound was all-encompassing, so loud and so deep and so true that it absorbed everything around and about her. She couldn't think, and didn't try: She wandered out the door on autopilot because she'd meant to do that when the music took her. Wandered just that blankly uptown toward her apartment, and it was a damn good thing that nobody noticed her enough to mug her or she would have been in an awful awful state.

Up toward Broadway and 67th Street she found her sense and looked up to see where she was and what she was doing and she wondered how the devil she'd got that far uptown without getting herself run over by a cab.

The music was still with her, but it was softer now, eclipsed by the roar of the city. *I'm hungry,* she thought, and tried to think how long it'd been since she'd eaten.

Too long, was what. She'd had coffee in her room before she left for work, but nothing else. Daydreamed her way through lunch, ignored the coffee cart both times it'd come by—if she didn't put something into her stomach, she was going to be seriously ill, and damn soon.

There was a coffee shop on the corner; Cathy wandered in, dazed, and took a seat without waiting to be seated, and let the waiter find her—which he did in about the time it took her to get comfortable.

She ordered her burger, and smiled, and thanked him, and she tried to show him the kind of plain human courtesy that the ghosts taught Scrooge he ought to offer, even though that sort of courtesy is contrary to all custom and most mores in New York City. The waiter gave her a puzzled look, but that was just a look, and did it really matter? He still walked off disaffectedly when he went to fill her order, just as he'd've walked off if she'd hissed at him.

Cathy forced a smile.

It wasn't easy. She didn't feel like smiling—she felt like curling up in a ball and trying to hide from the world. Of course she did! Her head throbbed, and the music wasn't letting up, and if it didn't let up soon she was going to lose her mind forever.

What am I doing wrong? she wondered. *I heard the message! I'm still young. I can start over. And I'm not afraid to! If I can survive New York, I can survive anything.*

She'd made three phone calls from the office that day— two to people she knew back home in Massachusetts; another to a friend who'd moved out to California. Two of them offered her jobs while she was talking to them; the other sounded like he had something more ambitious in mind. He'd said, *Give me a day—I think I can put together a package you won't be able to turn down.*

Whatever *that* meant.

Now her waiter set the burger on the table in front of her, and smiled, and told her that she should ask if there was anything else she wanted (she thought that was what he'd asked—his accent was so thick it was hard to be sure). And . . .

The song inside her head suddenly and mercilessly reached a new and deafening crescendo, and Cathy nearly collapsed into her meal.

But didn't, just barely.

"Lady?" the waiter asked, looking concerned. "Are you all right? You don't look so good."

She looked up at him as directly as she could, but even so she moved slow as though the air were heavy, thick and sharp as sand. "I'm fine," she said, forcing down another bite of her hamburger. "Fine."

She didn't sound fine. At all. She could hear it in her own voice.

"You want me to call a doctor? It'll only take a minute if you want. I don't mind."

He sounded scared—or was that concerned? She wasn't sure.

"No," she said. "I'll be all right."

Her waiter frowned. "All right," he said. "You need help, you call me, okay?"

Cathy nodded, and finally the man was gone.

She sobbed when he was out of earshot. "Why?" she whispered. "Please, God, tell me why?"

God didn't answer.

The song didn't change.

She really was doing everything right, wasn't she? She had to be! She wasn't arguing with the song; she knew the song was right. She was going to leave. She didn't have any ties to this town, anyway; it didn't matter if she left it all behind.

She forced down a bite of the burger, and then another. It wasn't easy; her throat wasn't ready for food, and her appetite was more than gone—the whole notion of eating made her gullet ache. She forced herself to eat anyway, because the sound of the song was bad enough as it was, and she didn't think she could survive it if she starved herself.

One more bite, and she swallowed hard. It didn't go down well at all; she felt her throat cramp up in painful knots, and for a moment the pain was so intense that she was sure she would black out. But she didn't black out, and now it was time to go—gathering her purse and coat, looking at the bill, leaving money on the table.

"I'll take that," the waiter said. "You need change?"

She shook her head. "No, it's yours."

The waiter nodded, and he smiled, and he thanked her, but the smile didn't look like a smile and the thanks didn't sound like thanks because still worried or scared or both, he looked like a man in full-bore panic. In fact, she'd seen that expression on her brother's face the night his wife gave birth to their first child. It was an amusing expression, almost, but it was frightful, too, to see the man looking at her like she was about to die.

"Don't worry," she said. "I'll be fine."

A moment's hesitation, and now he looked as though he was about to say something, but held his tongue. "You're sure?" he said.

She nodded. "I'm a big girl," she said. "I can take care of myself."

A worried frown.

"Don't look at me that way, damn it," she said. "It doesn't help at all."

And there was just enough anger in her voice that the waiter backed away, and that was good, because she had to get out of there right then, *right then*.

And did, just barely: managed to get out into the sharp cool air before she passed out in that brummagem diner, and the air was like cool water on her face, forcing her back to her senses, forcing the music away.

The cold wind kept the song at bay all the way up Broadway to her gargoyle room. And it stayed at bay when she got to her building, as she climbed the stairs, as she opened the door to her room, stepped in, locked the door behind her, and collapsed oblivious onto the bed.

It was hours before it returned to haunt her.

It started in on her again at half past three in the morning. That was late enough that she'd got some sleep (thank God!) but it was still so early that it left her haunted four long hours through the night. At first she tried to sleep through it, but the song (wordless in her waking, but full of taunting possibility when it filtered through her dreams) was unrelenting, and finally she woke and put on coffee and set about tidying the room. What else could she do? They weren't nightmares, the dreams she had when she could hear the song, but they were close to that—they haunted her the way nightmares would haunt her, even though they were full of promises that were anything but untoward.

She cleaned the room and then started on the floor—sweeping, mopping, and now there was nothing to do but wax the thing. She never waxed the floor if she could avoid it but that night she knew she needed to keep busy, and the waxing couldn't go on long enough.

And didn't.

By four-thirty she'd finished with the floor, and it was dry, already, shining beautifully the way it did the time she'd

waxed it because her mom was coming down from Arkham
for a visit—

And the gargoyle was still singing.

Poured herself a cup of now-tepid coffee.

Sat at the kitchen table, trying not to hear. Trying to think
what was it she could do to hide from that sound, because
she couldn't take it any more; if it went on another moment
even one solitary fragment of a second she'd scream, she really would—

And then she did scream, and probably she woke up half
the people in the building. Someone pounded on the pipe,
she didn't care, she screamed again and launched herself at
the window with the clearest view of the gargoyle, and she
opened it to let a blast of winter wind force itself into the
room, and she shouted, "Shut up, damn you, I don't deserve
this! Can't you leave me with a moment's peace?"

The gargoyle's stone-grey skull swiveled on its fluted
neck.

And it turned to face her.

To look her in the eye.

It whispered words she saw but could not hear, and it
looked wounded, as though she'd said a thing so cruel and
so severe that its stone ears could not bear to hear. She'd
broken its heart, she thought, and she eased away from the
window. . . .

"Oh my God," she said. "Oh my God I'm sorry."

The gargoyle nodded.

I ought to run, she thought, backing away, turning away.

But she didn't. She stayed in the apartment, and she
didn't know why, or maybe she knew in a place she could
understand but never name. . . .

Went to her sink. Put more coffee and more water into the
machine, and watched it, listened to it gurgling. Trying not
to think all the while the room grew cold and colder still because she'd left the window open.

The coffee finished brewing, and she poured a cup, and
took a seat at the tiny kitchen table.

She stared at the south window, the closed window that
didn't have much of a view of the gargoyle even when it was

open. *I should be afraid,* she thought. But she wasn't frightened. Just the opposite, in fact—she was excited, almost.

Thrilled.

She didn't want to think why that might be.

I'm losing my mind, that's why, she thought, not for the first time. *And it's no wonder—it's past time to move on. Home to Massachusetts, out to San Diego—I'm not as young as I was, and if I don't get myself a life someplace I'll never have one.*

She thought about her brother and his wife and their beautiful little girl, and for the longest moment she thought her heart would break. She was lonely, wasn't she?

She *was* lonely. Of course she was! What else to expect in a city like this one?

As she sniffed, and looked for a tissue—

And saw the open window with its curtains blowing in the breeze—

—and there among the curtains was the gargoyle, perched on the windowsill like some grotesque and almost human bird of prey.

Staring at her.

She gasped, startled, and she thought that she would scream. But she didn't scream, and after a long moment it came to her that she wasn't even scared.

He's company, at least, she thought. *I don't want to be alone.*

"Don't just stand there," she said. "You might as well come in."

She turned away without waiting to see if he'd accept the invitation. Blew steam off the surface of her coffee; she stared vacantly at the lights outside the room's east window.

After a while she realized he was standing next to her, looking silently over her shoulder. "You might as well sit down," she said, looking up to face him. "There's coffee if you'd like some."

The gargoyle nodded. He didn't say a word.

Cathy shrugged, rose from her seat to fetch the coffee. Poured it, asked if her visitor wanted cream or sugar, but he didn't answer that aloud. Maybe she should have looked back to see if he nodded or shook his head, but she didn't have the heart for it, which was why she served the coffee black—

Served it.

That was the first moment when she got a real look at him, standing in the light in the room the way a man stands instead of perched on the wall or the sill like some great granite avial: There in her room as she turned around, coffee cup in hand, she saw him standing by the table, facing her, and he was beautiful, she thought, beautiful fantastic and so strange she never could imagine . . .

Staring for the longest time.

Till finally he smiled an embarrassed smile and said *"Coffee,"* as though that was the secret of the world, and took the seat beside hers at the tiny table.

"You spoke," she said, setting the coffee right before him. "I didn't know that you could talk."

He smiled again, and this time he didn't look embarrassed but amused. "You've heard me sing," he said. "Why would you think I could not speak?"

And she laughed, because he was right, it was funny, maybe it was the funniest thing she'd heard in all her days, and then they were laughing together, and that was beautiful and real.

"I don't know," she said, and she heard something wistful in her own voice, and she didn't understand that. "Your coffee's getting cold," she said. "I've got coffee cake in the bread-box if you'd like some."

The gargoyle took a sip from the cup, smiled. "The coffee's fine," he said.

His smile was stony and warm at the same time. It was a pretty smile, she thought, a smile she could watch for hours.

And thinking about that, about the smile and the warmth and the rocky solidness of him, it came to Cathy that there was no music in her head.

"That song," she said. "You aren't singing it anymore."

He looked at her with an expression that was almost quizzical, she thought.

"Don't look at me like that," she said. "You know the

song I mean. The one you made up to remind me what an awful place I'm in."

He laughed all deep and resonant and shook his head. "I sang that tune," the gargoyle said, "but I only heard it in your dreams."

She gave him a look of her own. "Don't tell me that. I know what I heard."

He shrugged. "You heard it," he said. "I can see that in your heart."

In my heart.

And she wanted to say a lot of things, then, like, *What the hell do you mean, looking in my heart that way?*, and *You think you're so smart, don't you?*, and *Can't you leave me any privacy?* but there was something in his manner that disarmed her, and she couldn't begin to wonder why.

"If you weren't singing all that time," she asked, "what exactly do you do?"

He shrugged, and looking at him she thought he'd moved the weight of the world to do it.

"Listening," he said. "That's most of what I do."

Later, when she thought back about it, it seemed to her that they'd talked forever that afternoon. About who she was, and everything she meant to do; about who he was, and how he didn't really know anything but what he'd seen.

Some of what he'd seen was terrible.

They shared things, too: a cup of coffee; the flavor of a cookie three days stale but still somehow rich beneath the staleness; the color that reflects from moonlight when it shimmers on the panes of a tall building made of glass.

It went like that until six-thirty, when she glanced up to see he'd drifted off to sleep while she was silent. He looked so beautiful that way, she thought, and she realized that the music in her head was silent, still and quiet for the first time in so many days, and Lord she was exhausted. . . .

She didn't stop to think how there was a strange man (or something like one) in the house—or maybe she did think of that, and didn't care. Either way, she pushed away from the table, stumbled the half dozen steps from the table to the futon, and collapsed onto it.

She slept three silent hours, her mind as quietly at rest as the minds of those who've worn their way through Purgatory and wait serenely for the Second Coming and their deliverance.

She woke at half past eight, which meant that she was late for work already, and there was no time for a shower or anything like that, and no way to take one with, with—*him* in her room with her—she hardly had a moment to get dressed, pulling clothes on without taking anything off unless there was something else on top, the way a girl has to change clothes at a beach sometimes, strange to do that in her own apartment but life is strange sometimes and that's the wonderful part about it—

—about it.

He was still at the table, but now he was a statue once again, still as stone where last night he was a thing of living breathing granite, and she thought, *What if he got stuck that way?*, and there was an awful moment of terror that she didn't understand and couldn't accept and couldn't deny, either, what was happening to her?

But there was no time; she had to be at work, and she was out the door, hurrying down the stairs to catch a subway packed with Christmas shoppers and other travelers on more workaday excursions, and it came to her, finally, what day it was.

It's Christmas Eve, she thought.

And it *was* the day before Christmas, and she had train tickets that would take her up to Massachusetts for the holiday that afternoon—she'd had the tickets for months, in fact.

She thought, *How can I leave the city when I love him?* And then she blushed, because it was crazy, the whole idea was crazy, a woman can't fall in love with a haunted slab of graven granite.

But all the way to work she daydreamed, thinking of him.

Daydreamed all morning at the office, and went to lunch at the Japanese fast food place two buildings east of her office still thinking of him.

This is what an obsession is, she thought as she picked at her larmen.

But she didn't care.

When she got back to the office there was a message waiting for her at the front desk.

It was from her friend in San Diego, and it meant that he'd put that job offer together, and she knew she had to call him even as she thought she never would.

The office manager came down the hall to send the receptionist home. Her own boss was just a few steps behind the office manager; he had his coat on and was heading toward the door.

"Cathy," he said. "You didn't get the memo? It's half a day today. Merry Christmas! Get your coat on! Go home to your family!" and he smiled wide and sincere the way you never do believe when you see it in an ad agency, even when it's Tom Fernandez smiling, no matter how Tom Fernandez was as real as real gets to be, in an ad agency or elsewhere.

"Thanks, Tom," she said. "Guess I ought to weed the inbox more often."

And Tom Fernandez laughed, patting her on the back, pushing toward the door.

"Merry Christmas, Cathy," he repeated. "Have a good holiday."

On her way home she remembered the train tickets again: she was supposed to leave for Arkham (via the train to Salem) at six P.M.

I need to buy Christmas presents, she thought. Her mom and dad; her brother Will and his wife.

Their baby.

Neat kid, that baby. Dimples that broke Cathy's heart every time she saw them.

She'd stop by that wonderful gourmet delicatessen, Zabar's, for the adult presents, then run up to the toy store on the corner by her building for the baby's gift. She'd get something that the kid could chew on, because the baby liked to chew on everything. Maybe in a few years when she'd chewed it half to death Cathy could remind the child how she'd eaten the first toy her aunt ever got her, and Cathy meant to laugh at that. It was supposed to be one of those neat and wonderful things that maiden aunts do for their nieces, but something in her heart went wrong, and she found herself standing on the IRT platform, sobbing as she watched the wall, waiting for the uptown train. . . .

And now she was thinking of the gargoyle, still as stone, asleep as granite in her room.

Waiting for her.

The train roared into the station, and Cathy climbed numbly into the car before her.

She was still numb five minutes later when it pulled to a stop in the station under Zabar's, but not too numb to recognize where she was, and plod zombielike out of the train; across the platform; up the stairs onto Broadway and into the Upper West Side.

What should I get them? She tried to think, but she couldn't think of anything anymore, and she wasn't sure why. So she went into the store and got a cart and wandered up and down the aisles mindlessly, waiting for inspiration to reach out from the shelves and sweep her off her feet.

Cathy loved that store. It was a cornucopia of strange treats from all the tucks and nip-ends of the world; she would have shopped there every day if she could have paid for it.

Shopping there for Christmas gifts should have been a great delight, a celebration in itself.

But it was anything but that.

As she wandered up and down the aisles, and up and down them once again with her big empty cart in hand, she found herself growing steadily sadder and sadder, till she could hardly move at all.

"Ma'am? . . ." someone asked as she stood motionless beside a great display of ripened olives. "Are you all right, ma'am?"

"Fine," she said. "I'm fine."

And she thought, *How can I leave him on Christmas?*

And if she'd thought about that she would have thought, *That's stupid, I'm not leaving him, he's just a statue, damn it,*

*a haunted statue gargoyle. You can't leave a statue that way
and even if I could I hardly know him.*

But she didn't think that, because she wasn't thinking,
and that was good because it was all wrong anyway. She
knew this: *I've got to stay home to make him Christmas dinner,* and she knew that was more important than anything
she'd ever done in all her days, and it was good that she
didn't apply a lick of reason to the things she knew because
the thing inside her heart defied all reason.

Now she was moving directly and so quickly through the
aisles, grabbing this and that and one of those to make the
most wonderful Christmas dinner any woman ever made in
a tiny room in hard Manhattan: roast beef and potatoes and
a dozen different condiments and salads, no one in New
York would eat a better Christmas dinner than they would
eat that night.

When she went to the checkout, she found an enormous
line waiting for her.

Enormous and slow, too.

It kept her waiting most of twenty minutes, and all that
time there was nothing to do but stand and stare and try to
stay calm and sane, which was hard, harder than it ever
ought to be because every moment that she thought, the
world around her left her feeling like an idiot.

It really did. She felt like a royal idiot, in fact. Imagine it,
her, Cathy Gilman, cooking Christmas dinner for a statue!
For a drainpipe, for God's sake!

On her way home from Zabar's, Cathy stopped at a shop
marked MEN'S CLOTHIERS to buy a gift.

She ended up wandering around that place for most of
half an hour. Not aimlessly or numbly, the way she'd wandered the aisles of Zabar's, but just about that fruitlessly.
She'd never bought a present for anyone like him! She'd
hardly even dated in the last three years, and now she had to
buy a gift for a . . . a . . . for her gargoyle, and what on God's
earth was right for anyone like that?

She couldn't begin to know.

Until she saw the hat. It didn't come to her how right it
was till the third time she walked past it: It wasn't all that

fancy or special or ostentatious. It was just a good leather fedora, warm looking, heavy, and wonderfully brown, the kind of hat men wear in the coldest windiest weather that New York ever sees.

"It looks like you've finally found what you were looking for," the salesman said. It was the third or fourth time he'd spoken to her, she wasn't sure which.

Cathy forced a smile. "I guess," she said. And paid the man, and left.

On her way up the stairs to her room, Cathy heard the couple in 2H arguing again, bellowing so loud and angrily that she thought she could feel their shouting in her bones.

We could be like that, she thought, and she laughed, because she was sure she never could.

And heard herself, and flushed with embarrassment. How could she think about a gargoyle that way? She was losing her mind. She needed help.

And still.

Still.

It doesn't matter what he is, she thought. *I love him and it doesn't matter. I can love him on his own terms, can't I?*

Can't I?

And she thought about settling down, and raising a family, and she'd never thought of children before in her life. The whole idea of having children scared her at the same time it warmed her heart.

And it wasn't like there were going to be children from a match like this anyway, was it?

It doesn't matter, does it, whether there are children? I don't want children anyway. And she felt as though she was going to cry again, and she didn't know why.

He wasn't there when she got to her room, and he wasn't on the cornice, either. That worried her some, but she told herself that there was nothing to worry about; he'd wandered off to run an errand, that was all. It was Christmas Eve and there were lots of errands to be run, weren't there?

So she put on dinner, and called home to Massachusetts to tell her folks she wasn't going to make it up for the holidays. "I'm coming down with something, Mom," she said. "I'll try to catch a train in a couple days when I feel better."

Her mom had worried at her for most of twenty minutes, which was sweet, in its way, but Cathy hated it, too, because she was afraid her gargoyle would appear at any moment on the windowsill or out there on the cornice or maybe even at the door. *Imagine him,* she thought as Mom went on and on about Dad's trouble at the office. *Imagine him arriving at the door with a good suit and flowers in his hand, maybe a present tucked under his arm,* and Cathy felt herself smiling so wide it hurt.

She didn't ask herself why. She didn't want to know.

Then finally he did show up, right at the darkest end of dusk, flying through the New York air quiet as a falcon come to roost upon her windowsill. She gasped at the sight of him in the air, stunned to see that her creature made of heavy stone could soar so easily through the sky, and Mom (still talking, now about the price of red meat at the markets up in Arkham), Mom was still on the phone, and she heard Cathy gasp.

"Cathy? Cathy, are you all right?" she asked.

Cathy didn't answer right away.

"Cathy!"

He was beautiful, she thought. So beautiful.

"I will be, Mom," she whispered, finally. "Just a little short of breath."

A pause. "You're sure?"

Cathy coughed. "Yeah. I'd better get off the phone, okay?"

"Okay dear. You call us right away if you have any more trouble, all right?"

Cathy promised that she would.

And hung up the phone. And crossed the room to open the window.

"I'm glad you're here," she said as he pushed himself beneath the transom. "It's good to see you."

The gargoyle smiled. "Did you think I would forget you on Christmas Eve?" and then he laughed, as though it was as silly a notion as he could imagine. He'd never do a thing like that; no one with a grain of sense would ever do anything like that, and he was right, of course. Cathy knew that.

Knew it despite the fact that she'd spent half the morning planning to do just exactly that to him.

"No," she said. "You wouldn't. What was I thinking?" A long, long sigh. "I've got dinner on," she said. "It should be ready soon."

"Christmas dinner," he said, and then he smiled.

She smiled back at him. Kissed her fingers, touched his cheek. "I ought to check on it now," she said, turning, crossing the room to glance into the oven and up at the timer. "Looks like half an hour. Can I get you something in the meanwhile?"

She glanced over her shoulder in time to see him shake his head. "I'm fine." And then, "It's good to see you."

She turned to face him. "It's good to see you, too." And looked him up and down, taking in the solidness of him, the granite musculature. Where had he come from? How could he be alive? She wanted to know, but she knew she didn't dare to ask. "Tell me about your day."

He shrugged. "I touched the world today," he said, and then he frowned. "I've never done that before—touching, I mean. I've always watched."

Cathy nodded. "You're changing, too, aren't you? Please don't ever change."

And then she laughed, because she knew that wasn't possible, because living things are always full of change; life is change, when you pare away all the details that confuse us: Life is about the world in motion, and everything else is a consequence of movement; an illusion or an afterthought.

After a moment he was laughing, too.

"I didn't mean to change," he said. "I never even meant to sing to you. But that song came from you so clear and true it woke me."

She crossed the room again, and now she put her arms around him. He was massively solid, heavy as a pillar of stone, and that only made sense, after all, because he was a carved pillar of good honest granite, old as time and marked by man, come alive by some device that neither of them could imagine.

She embraced him, and kissed his rough-cold stony lips.

"I love you," she said. "No matter how you change."

Her stone-gray lover blinked, and blinked again. "I love you too," he said.

Cathy Gilman sighed. "I know," she said. "I can feel it in your heart."

The timer went off to tell her that the potatoes were ready to come out of the oven, and Cathy stepped away to see after dinner.

"What did you touch?" she asked. "What did you see?"

He frowned. "I don't have the words for it," he said. "I never . . ."

And something snapped way down in Cathy's gut, and she heard herself saying a thing she never knew she had inside her.

"What's her name?" she asked, her voice all full of sarcasm and pique.

He looked confused, or maybe that was surprised, and the thing that Cathy didn't recognize came up all big and ugly, devouring her.

"Her? . . ." he said. "I don't—"

"Tell me her name!" she shrieked, and then she let out a bellow of blind rage.

"I don't understand. I never—"

"I bet you never did," she said, even though it wasn't what she meant at all. She had her hands on his shoulders, now, and she was shaking him back and forth, no, not shaking him, she couldn't shake him any more than she could shake a pillar made of stone. *"Get out of here!"*

"I—"

"Get! Get! Go!"

And she gave him one great final shove, toward the window, and he tumbled toward it like a statue toppling from grace. He crashed into the floor with such force and angular momentum that Cathy felt the building trembling beneath her toes.

"Get out of here!" she screamed again, and now he stum-

bled toward the windowsill, climbed onto it, and turned to look her in the eye.

"I never did you any wrong," he said. It wasn't a denial, or an excuse; he said it like an accusation, reproaching her for treating him so harshly. "I never did."

"GO!" she screamed.

And he took wing and flew away.

When he was gone, she took their half-finished dinner out of the oven and left it cooling on the counter.

She staggered to her futon on the far side of the room, kicked it open with her foot, and collapsed onto it.

And slept deep and hard and quiet, the way she always did when hopelessness consumed her.

As Cathy slept she had a terrible, terrible dream. The worst dream that she'd ever had, and worse than that: She dreamed she saw her cold-stone lover with another woman, walking on a moonlit seashore. They were beautiful together, heartbreakingly beautiful, walking hand in hand in the waves up to their ankles, and now he stopped and took the woman in his arms to kiss her passionately as a wave came thundering down upon them—

And Cathy woke screaming. She rushed to the window and flung it open, not minding how a tempest of a snowstorm had come up as she slept, and when the window went up cold gusts of snowy air blasted over her. . . .

He was back on the cornice, statue-still and lifeless—looking as though he'd never touched her. Moments ago he'd been so full of life, fluid as a stallion, and now— he was wearing the fedora that she'd bought him, even though she'd never got around to giving it to him. How had he gotten that? She wanted to know, but that wasn't the question that she asked.

"I want to know her name, damn you," she shouted. "I swear to God, I'm going to kill her, you hear me?"

Somewhere in the distance a church-clock tolled twelve.

Midnight.

And it was Christmas.

"I'm going to kill you, too," she screamed. "Stop ignoring me, damn you! Look at me!"

As her gargoyle lover turned to face her, and the vicious wind caught hold of the fedora, blowing it away into the night.

And snow-lightning flashed four times across the sky, turning the city into a castle made of bright light.

"God *damn* you," she screamed. "God damn you straight to hell."

As she heard the words she'd said, and thought how terrible they sounded—how terrible they were.

And lightning flashed again, right *here,* right *now,* and it struck him, struck her gargoyle lover from the precipice, hurling him to earth.

Cathy screamed when she saw lighting strike her gargoyle. She screamed four long beats, and then the scream was out of her, and she was watching him fall to the ground wheeling head over heels over head over heels and around, his wings burned and broken by thunder.

His back split wide in midair, exposing his heart to the wind and the snow and the cold as he tumbled five stories to explode on the pavement like a bag of dirt.

Cathy screamed again when she saw him hit the ground and shatter. And took off out of her room and down the stairs not thinking how it was Christmas in New York, the middle of a blizzard and she'd catch her death without a coat; she didn't even notice the cold when she got to the ground floor and bolted through the lobby, into the cold.

Gasping and sobbing in the wind as she came to her knees on the sidewalk, digging through the snow and the dust and the shattered granite with her gloveless hands, there in the middle of it was a man in a brown coat and a red scarf; her lover crushed a man as he smashed to earth. *Dear God,* she thought, *I need to call an ambulance.* She tried to lift the man out of the snow and the cold and the dirt, she was sobbing and wailing, her teeth were chattering as she did—

As the man moaned, and she saw his hat.

His hat was a good leather fedora, and Cathy Gilman knew that hat.

The man moaned again, and asked, "What happened to me?"

The cold rushed down into her belly as she realized that she knew that voice, and that she'd know it anywhere.

"You've been hit," she said. "I'm going to get you to a doctor."

"Just help me up," he said, turning to face her, and yes, yes, it *was* his voice—

His face.

"You're sure?"

"I'm fine," he said.

And it was undeniably true.

"It's cold out here, and you've had a fall," she said. "Let me take you in."

BRIAN LUMLEY

The Luststone
(excerpt)

———✦———

THE ICE WAS ONLY a memory now, a racial memory whose legends had come down the years, whose evidence was graven in the land in hollow glacial tracts. Of the latter: Time would weather the valley eventually, soften its contours however slowly. But the memories would stay, and each winter the snows would replenish them.

That was why the men of the tribes would paint themselves yellow in imitation of the sun god, and stretch themselves in a line across the land east to west and facing north, and beat back the snow and ice with their clubs. And *frighten* it back with their screams and their leapings. With their magic they defeated winter and conjured spring, summer, and autumn, and thus were the seasons perpetuated.

The tribes, too, were perpetuated; each spring the tribal wizards—the witch doctors—would perform those fertility rites deemed necessary to life, by means of which the grass was made to grow, the beasts to mate, and man the weapon-maker to increase and prosper upon the face of the earth. It was the time of the saber-tooth and the mammoth, and it was the springtime of Man, the thinking animal whose destiny is the stars. And even in those far, dim, primal times there were visionaries.

Chylos of the mighty Southern Tribe was one such: Chylos the Chief, the great wizard and seer whose word was law in the mid-South. And in that spring some ten thousand years ago, Chylos lay on his bed in the grandest cave of all the caves of the Southern Tribe, and dreamed his dream.

He dreamed of invaders!

Of men not greatly unlike the men of the tribes, but fiercer and with huge appetites for ale, war, and women. Aye, and there were gross-bearded ones, too, whose dragon-prowed ships were as snakes of the sea, whose horned helmets and savage cries gave them the appearance of demons! But Chylos knew that he dreamed only of the far future and so was not made greatly fearful.

And he dreamed that in the distant future there were others who came from the east with fire and thunder, and in his dreams Chylos heard the agonized screams of the descendants of his tribe, men, women, and children; and saw visions of black war, red rape, and rivers of crimson blood. A complex dream it was, and alien these invaders: with long knives and axes which were not of stone, and again wearing horned helmets upon their heads to make them more fearsome yet. From the sea they came, building mounds and forts where they garrisoned their soldiers behind great earthworks.

And some of them carried strange banners covered with unknown runes and wore kilts of leather and rode in horse-drawn chairs with flashing spokes in their wheels; and their armies were disciplined thousands, moving and fighting with one mind. . . .

Such were Chylos's dreams, which brought him starting awake; and so often had he dreamed them that he knew they must be more than mere nightmares. Until one morning, rising from his bed of hides, he saw that it was spring again and knew what must be done. Such visions as he had dreamed must come to pass, he felt it in his old bones, but not for many years. Not for years beyond his numbering.

Very well: The gods themselves had sent Chylos their warning, and now he must act. For he was old and the earth would claim him long before the first invaders came, and so he must unite the tribes now and bring them together. And they must grow strong and their men become great warriors.

And there must be that which would remain long after Chylos himself was gone: a reminder, a monument, a *Power* to fuel the loins of the men and make the tribes strong. A driving force to make his people lusty, to ensure their survival. There must be children—many children! And their children in their turn must number thousands, and theirs must number . . . such a number as Chylos could not envisage. Then when the invaders came the tribes would be ready, unconquerable, indestructible.

So Chylos took up his staff and went out into the central plain of the valley, where he found a great stone worn round by the coming and going of the ice; a stone half as tall again as a man above the earth, and as much or more of its mass still buried in the ground. And upon this mighty stone he carved the runes of fertility, powerful symbols that spelled L U S T. And he carved designs which were the parts of men and women: the rampant pods and rods of seed, and the ripe breasts and bellies of dawning life. There was nothing of love in what he drew, only of lust and the need to procreate; for man was much more the animal in those dim forgotten days and love as such one of his weaknesses. But when Chylos's work was done, still he saw that it was not enough.

For what was the stone but a stone? Only a stone carved with cryptic runes and symbols of sexuality, and nothing more. It had no power. Who would remember it in a hundred seasons, let alone years? Who would know what it meant?

He called all the leaders of the tribes together, and because there was a recent peace in the land they came. And Chylos spoke to those headmen and wizards, telling them of his dreams and visions, which were seen as great omens. Together the leaders of the tribes decided what must be done; twenty days later they sent all of their young men and women to Chylos the Seer, and their own wizards went with them.

Meanwhile a pit had been dug away from the foot of the great stone, and wedged timbers held back that boulder from tumbling into the pit. And of all the young men and women of the tribes, Chylos and the Elders chose the lustiest lad and a broad-hipped lass with the breasts of a goddess; and they were proud to be chosen, though for what they knew not.

But when they saw each other, these two, they drew back snarling; for their markings were those of tribes previously opposed in war! And such had been their enmity that even now when all the people were joined, still they kept themselves apart each tribe from the other. Now that the pair had been chosen to be together—and because of their markings, origins, and tribal taboos, the greatest of which forbade intercourse between them—they spoke thus:

"What is the meaning of this?" cried the young man, his voice harsh, affronted. "Why am I put with this woman? She is not of my tribe. She is of a tribe whose very name offends me! I am not at war with her, but neither may I know her."

And she said: "Do my own Elders make mock of me? Why am I insulted so? What have I done to deserve this? Take this thing which calls itself a man away from me!"

But Chylos and the Elders held up their hands, saying: "Be at peace, be at ease with one another. All will be made plain in due time. We bestow upon you a great honour. Do not dishonour your tribes." And the chosen ones were subdued, however grudgingly.

And the Elders whispered among each other and said: "We chose them and the gods were our witnesses and unopposed. They are more than fit for the task. Joining them like this may also more nearly fuse their tribes, and bring about a lasting peace. It must be right." And they were all agreed.

Then came the feasting, of meats dipped in certain spices and herbs known only to the wizards and flavored with the crushed horn of mammoth; and the drinking of potent ales, all liberally sprinkled with the potions of the wizards. And when the celebrant horde was feasted and properly drunk, then came the oiled and perfumed and grotesquely-clad dancers, whose dance was the slow-twining dance of the grossly endowed gods of fertility. And as the dance progressed so drummers took up the beat, until the pulses of the milling thousand pounded and their bodies jerked with the jerking of the male and female dancers.

Finally the dance ended, but still the drummers kept to their madly throbbing beat; while in the crowd lesser dances had commenced, not so practiced but no less intense and even more lusty. And as the celebrants paired off and fell upon each other, thick pelts were tossed into the pit where the great stone balanced, and petals of spring flowers gathered with the dew upon them, making a bower in the shadow of the boulder; and this was where the chosen couple was made to lie down, while all about the young people of the tribes spent themselves in the ritual spring orgy.

But the pair in the pit—though they had been stripped naked, and while they were as drunk as the rest—nevertheless held back and drew apart, and scowled at each other through slitted eyes. Chylos stood at the rim and screamed at them: "Make love! Let the Earth soak up your juices!" He prodded the young man with a spear and commanded him: "Take her! The gods demand it! What? And would you have the trees die, and all the animals, and the ice come down again to destroy us all? *Do you defy the gods?"*

At that the young man would obey, for he feared the gods, but she would not have him. "Let him in!" Chylos screamed at her. "Would you be barren and have your breasts wither, and grow old before your time?" And so she wrapped her legs about the young man. But he was uncertain, and she had not accepted him; still, it seemed to Chylos that they were joined. And as the orgy climbed to its climax he cried out his triumph and signaled to a pair of well-muscled youths where they stood back behind the boulder. And coming forward they took up hammers and with mighty blows knocked away the chocks holding back the great stone from the pit.

The boulder tilted—three hundred tons of rock keeling over—and in the same moment Chylos clutched his heart, cried out and stumbled forward, and toppled into the pit!—and the rune-inscribed boulder with all its designs and great weight slammed down into the hole with a shock that shook the earth. But such was the power of the orgy that held them all in sway, that only those who coupled in the immediate vicinity of the stone knew it had moved at all!

Now, with the drumming at a standstill, the couples parted, fell back, lay mainly exhausted. A vast field, as of battle, with steam rising as a morning mist. And the two whose task it had been to topple the boulder going amongst them, seeking still-willing, however aching flesh in which to relieve their own pent passions.

Thus was the deed done, the rite performed, the magic worked, the luststone come into being. Or thus it was intended. And old Chylos never knowing that, alas, his work was for nothing, for his propitiates had failed to couple. . . .

Three winters after that the snows were heavy, meat was scarce, and the tribes warred. Then for a decade the gods and their seasonal rites were put aside, following which that great ritual orgy soon became legend and eventually a myth. Fifty years later the luststone and its carvings were moss-covered, forgotten; another fifty saw the stone a shrine. One hundred more years passed and the domed, mossy top of the boulder was hidden in a grove of oaks: a place of the gods, taboo.

The plain grew to be a forest, and the stone was buried beneath a growing mound of fertile soil; the trees were felled to build mammoth-pens, and the grass grew deep, thick, and luxurious. More years saw the trees grown up again into a mighty oak forest; and these were the years of the hunter, the declining years of the mammoth. Now the people were farmers, of a sort, who protected limited crops and beasts against Nature's perils. There were years of the long-toothed cats and years of the wolf. And now and then there were wars between the tribes.

And time was the moon that waxed and waned, and the hills growing old and rounded, and forests spanning the entire land; and the tribes flourished and fought and did little else under the green canopy of these mighty forests. . . .

Through all of this the stone slept, buried shallow in the earth, keeping its secret; but lovers in the forest knew where to lie when the moon was up. And men robbed by the years or by their own excesses could find a wonder there, when forgotten strength returned, however fleetingly, to fill them once more with fire. As for old Chylos's dream: It came to pass, but his remedy was worthless. Buried beneath the sod for three thousand years the luststone lay, and felt the tramping feet of the nomad-warrior Celts on the march. Five thousand more years saw the Romans come to Britain, then the Anglo-Saxons, the Vikings, and still the luststone lay there.

There were greater wars than ever Chylos had dreamed, more of rape and murder than he ever could have imagined. War in the sea, on the land and in the air.

And at last there was peace again, of a sort.

And so in a way old Chylos was right, for in the end nothing had come of all his works. But in several other ways he was quite wrong. . . .

CHRISTA FAUST AND CAITLÕN R. KIERNAN

Found Angels

———◦⟡◦———

HERE'S THE SCENE: HOLLYWOOD Boulevard, frying pan hot on another August afternoon filled with fat, sunburned tourists and their teeming children. And the stone lions standing silent guard before the faux Oriental deco glamour of the Chinese Theater, watchful pair, too stylized, too serene, to ever be real. Unforgiving sun like napalm on the skin and as always, radiohead man, black old man and his bizarre, constantly-expanding headset of foam and circuitboard, plastic flowers and television parts. A tattered clown in sweat-smeared greasepaint assaulting anyone who comes too close with his desperately cheerful antics and unwanted balloon animals. Neatsuited studio robots with their smiles and suckerpasses to sitcoms and game shows no one's ever heard of and never will. Giggling Japanese schoolgirls snapping each other's photos while college freshmen from some place far away where everyone is white suspiciously eye a pair of baby gangstas in line to have their fat girlfriends' faces superimposed over the faces of bikini-clad models. The Metrorail construction, pointless

burrowing through unstable terra-cotta earth, so traffic
snarled as usual, headache pound of jackhammers and
trucks forever backing up to blend with the stench of hot asphalt and exhaust. And above it all, Angelyne reclines on her
slick pink billboard, do-it-yourself fame, airbrushed goddess
of empty sparkle watching over her gaudy flock.

Kev used to think of Angelyne as his guardian angel,
back when he first drifted in from the desert, an unloved
middle child 15 years old and still street soft, still prone to
silly daydreams. Whenever it seemed like trouble might gel
out of the hot night air, if a trick turned mean or the Friday
night Lowriders thought maybe he was looking at their
women the wrong way, he would picture himself up there in
her static pink world high above the heat and dirt and angry
hands where everything was perfect and cartoon pure and
nothing ever changed or went bad in the middle. He would
imagine himself up there with her, above it all, and the trouble would skate over him like a summer storm.

Older now, twenty-one and still sparechanging in front of
the Chinese Theater, too old for angels or escape, and he's
just another street punk; deep, piratedark complexion part
tan and part dirt, scraggly mohawk tired and drooping to one
side and nearly four inches of dark root below the faded an-
tifreeze green. No shirt and scrawny chest covered with
shitty tattoos. Pierced nipples and scars, lots of scars, mostly
self-inflicted, some neat, symmetrical, and the rest wild and
ugly. Dirty fatigue pants slung so low on his birdwing hip-
bones that the dark fluff of his pubic hair peeks over the
waistband. Ancient jump-boots held together with duct tape
and his face like some small and cautious scavenger.

"Spare a quarter," muttered, planting his big foot next to
the fossil prints of Myrna Loy's tiny high heels. A very wrinkled woman in some kind of uniform gives him a dollar and
a religious tract, two stingy drops of salvation; he stuffs both
into his pocket, sick of this crap, decides he'll head over to
the Needle Exchange to see who's hanging out.

Following the stars to Cahuenga under the whiteblue sky
and the sun burning down through his scalp as he passes the
dead theaters: The Vogue, The Egyptian, The Ritz, The Fox,

The Pacific, Hollywood ghosts unable to cross over, trapped inside their own rotting corpses while tourists snap photos of the marquees and pretend everything's just like it used to be, like it's 1935 and the world is bright and shiny, innocent black and white, Technicolor perfect. Still walking, past Frederick's and Playmates and around the corner, lingering at the newsstand, browsing porn until they kick him out. When he finally gets to the Exchange, it's just Teddy and two other guys out front with Sharpie and Blanca and this shitugly puppy with a piece of rope around its neck and it keeps straining toward him until its eyes bulge out of its head. Kev crouches down to pet it, so maybe it won't kill itself trying to get to him.

"Cute dog," he says, still hoping Sharpie might fuck him and knowing he doesn't stand a chance. Once, he was able to get her to put her cigarette out on his chest and that gave him jack-off material for a week.

"His name's Elvis," Sharpie says, brushes stiff pink hair out of her smackdull eyes, quick disdainful smirk. He can see the underside of her big, braless tits peeking out at him from under her cutoff Black Flag T-shirt. Then Blanca startles Kev by squatting down beside him, all skinny insect legs and nervous twitches; the ugly dog leaps at her and she swats it away.

"There's an art show 'cross the street," she says, like he should give a shit. "Photos, not paintings. Me and Sharpie and some of the guys. We all posed," and she leans in, knifeslash lips brushing his ear. "We were naked."

"Huh?" Stupid, but what was he supposed to say? He looks up at the underside of Sharpie's tits again, subtle stare and thinks about the exquisite fire of her half-smoked cigarette punching into him like a poison arrow. He swallows hard, and looks away.

"It's not like that though," Sharpie says. "She's an artist."

"Yeah," and "That's right," as Blanca stands, tottering in cheap heels. "A *real* artist."

The gallery really just an empty storefront and he guesses that's probably part of the art, people who can afford rent and food and clean drugs, and they think showing off their stuff in this kind of place is more artistic. But the pictures *are* good, not just good, fantastic, and they make a hot tangle inside Kev's hungry stomach as he moves slow down the line of goateed hipsters and club girls in clunky black shoes and unflattering glasses. And it's not just the exposed bodies of his friends, Carlos making gang signs over his big flaccid dick, bony Blanca flipping off the camera, or even Sharpie, crouched and her fingers hooked in the air like claws; it's the other things, mostly, the statues, that make the spit dry up in Kev's mouth. The stone things lurking behind the familiar faces and vulnerable, naked bodies. Maybe they're supposed to be people, but people that have been twisted, broken and then put back together wrong; some have sharp spines like porcupines or strange fish, and others have bent and stubby wings sticking out of their narrow backs, careless, unfeathered jut and spread: wire for bone, cement for skin.

"Do you like them?" Sandsoft voice and he turns around too fast so he knows he looks stupid again; the woman is standing very close, head shaved smooth and goldbrown eyes, hawkeyes that miss nothing. Her face all cheekbones and sharp chin, sharp but pretty. She's wearing some kind of military coveralls, army surplus shabby, and a necklace made of delicate bones, the bones of birds, or snakes, or rats. They are exactly the same height.

"Yeah, um . . . they're . . ." And he feels those eyes on him like the burning tips of cigarettes. "They're wonderful." He watches the toes of his boots while he talks. "When I was little, I used to have this dream over and over about being turned into stone. But it wasn't a nightmare, you know? It felt . . . safe." And he wishes immediately that he hadn't said that, something he hasn't thought about in *years,* and why the hell is he telling her, strange wetdream images and he knows he's fucking blushing now, and the knowing just makes his face feel that much hotter, that much redder.

"I'm the artist, you know," she says, finally, and "Oh," he says back, pointless little sound lost in the drift of other people's pretentious conversation. A crumpled pack of cigarettes from one of her coveralls' dozen or so pockets, filter quick between her thin lips, and she lights it with a shiny Zippo.

"I want you to pose for me," she says, inhales deep and holds the smoke a moment, then lets it spill out slow as she speaks. "Will you do that? Pose for me?"

"Uh . . ." and *Jesus,* he wishes he'd just shut the hell up, keep his fucking mouth shut since there's nothing coming out of it anyway and he knows she's probably making fun of him, teasing, some big kick she's getting messing with his head, some kick making them all think runaways and street trash and those creepy statues are deep.

"Well, will you?" She's getting impatient and he's afraid she might just walk away, disgusted, and maybe that would be for the best. Except he doesn't want her to.

"Right now?" he says, already knowing that he'll go, telling himself it's only because there might be money, might be dope or food or maybe even sex with a hot shower after and a real bed to sleep in and what the hell else has he got to do?

"Why not?" and she looks around them, then, taking in the restless crowd preening for one another, sweating for art, and something he can't read moves fast across her face like a shadow.

"What about your show?" he says, follows her eyes across the art fags and posers, shoulder-to-shoulder as they point and lean close to stare, ooh-and-ah, practiced interest for her black and white and gray portraits of the street kids and hookers and the scowling stone shapes behind them.

So she smiles, expression as sudden and sharp at the corners as the hollowcheek corners of her face, and "Fuck it," she says. "I hate these people."

Her loft, cavernous space downtown somewhere off Alameda, just past the Disneyland shine and consumer-friendly sterility of Little Tokyo, more warehouses gone to galleries and cheap apartments, studios and maybe floating raves and fetish clubs, or just sitting empty. Out of the air-conditioned bubble of her little black car and they walk together over crumbling asphalt and gravel, side by side and she's silent, barely even acknowledging his presence. Tag-scarred fire door and then up a steep flight of iron stairs that clang and echo under their boots. Another gray fire door and four locks before she opens it on more air-conditioning, meat-locker chill after the stairwell oven, heavyair gush into the hall; she goes first and he follows her, steps into the dirty light leaking in through big windows washed over with a thin, uneven coat of paint the color of melted chocolate.

And the statues are everywhere, like he's walked into a trap, ambush, except they don't move to jump him, knock him to the concrete floor and kick his skinny ass with their hard feet. But maybe they're just waiting. Lined up neat and patient like gargoyle soldiers along both sides of the long room, clustered at both ends, and places where they've been plastered right into the fucking walls. Some dangling overhead from rusted chains and tackle. Kev gasps loud, scared girlsound, and he knows she's heard because she stops, that smile that might not be a smile again, and says, "You're not scared of *them* are you?"

"No," he says, *no,* like the things aren't giving him the fucking heebie-jeebies. "They're cool. I just didn't know . . ."

"There'd be so many?" she says, finishing for him, and that isn't at all what he was going to say, isn't what he's thinking, but he nods anyway. "I guess I should let people buy some of them." She looks around, lingering gaze over their bizarre anatomy and her fingers reach out to brush a spine, a rusted wingtip. "People always ask, but I don't think I could bear to part with any of them."

He imagines her working on these twisted figures, careful hands shaping them with needles and wires and sculpting knives and he feels obscurely jealous, as if they are her myriad watchful husbands, grown familiar with her touch while he, the new and awkward lover, is left waiting, wondering.

Maybe the statues can hear him thinking these things because they seem to lean closer, prick rough, suspicious ears, and he shrugs his shoulders for her, for them, as if it doesn't matter. The cold apartment air smells like dust and chemicals, and the faint hint of something bad underneath, dead cat smell, but he pretends not to notice.

There's a circle of ratty old furniture that might be antique, scratched wood and cotton puffing out through torn upholstery, two chairs and an old-fashioned sofa surrounding a crooked coffee table weighted down with ashtrays and sketchbooks. He sits down when she points at one of the chairs.

"You got a name?" and he nods again, "Kevin," he says, "but Kev's okay. That what everybody calls me instead."

"Okay. You want a beer, Kev?" Ironic twist to his name in her mouth and of course he wants a fucking beer, something icy and wet, and the buzz so he won't mind all the damned stone faces watching him. She nods and disappears into the clutter and gloom; he stares nervous at the stained and tattered covers of her sketchbooks, wondering what might be inside until she comes back with a sweating amber bottle in each hand, PBR, though he'd expected something fancy, green glass and German labels, but this is good enough, better really. Long swallow and he feels better at once, even though the stink has gotten into his sinuses and makes his beer taste a little funny.

She sits across from him on the sofa, sets her own beer, untouched, on the table, not a sip and the bottle making another ring on the scarred wood. He tries to imagine Sharpie in this place, surrounded by the statues, drinking this odd, intense woman's beer and trying to look tough no matter how she really felt.

"I don't really want to take your photo," she says.

The mouth of the bottle clinks against his teeth and he swallows, nervous gulp, wipes his lips on the back of his hand. Kev wonders if she's coming on to him; she still hasn't touched her beer, just watches him and he tries to imagine what it would be like to fuck her, let her do things to him.

She stands, slow walk around the table, her long and callused hands out to him and because he can't think of anything else to do, he takes them and they are terribly cold. She pulls him to his feet, leads him to a cluttered ring of odd tools and camera parts, brushes and open pots of dark liquid, faintest oilsheen iridescence. A spash of raw white light from a naked bulb hanging overhead and she stands him at the center, *puts* him there, but no instruction, so he waits to see what's coming next.

She leans close and at first he thinks, hopes, she might kiss him, but instead she sniffs him, *sniffs* like an animal, gentle ebb and flow of air from her nostrils as she moves inches above the delicate skin of his throat, down across his shoulders, chest.

"Unh . . ." So fucking *smooth,* Kev. "I guess I oughta shower. It's been a while, you know." But it's not like the smell of his pits could ever compete with the chilly stench of this place.

Her eyebrows bunch together and he notices for the first time how the hairs have been plucked completely away and drawn in again, careful shitbrown bow, and she shakes her head sharply, dismissive. Studying him now, serious face that's almost funny, detached mask; he notices the X-acto knives there among her tools and his heart beats a little faster.

"Undress," she says. Commanding, in control now, probably in control since she first spoke to him back in the gallery and that crowded, noisy place seems years away. He wrestles off his boots, peels off his filthy pants, and she takes them away so Kev stands naked, starting to shiver, feeling excited and vulnerable and waiting to wake up. Because this has to be a dream, a dream and maybe he's really curled up with Carlos or someone else huddled next to him against the night.

"What you gonna do to me?" B'rer Rabbit whine, *Please don't hurt me,* please *don't use those sharp knives on me. Please don't throw me in that briar patch.*

"Make you immortal, Kev," says B'rer Fox, foxfaced woman, and that's such an artist thing to say, *I want to make you immortal,* so goddamn Hollywood and he wants to laugh but doesn't. She might be crazy, might be a total fucking Froot-Loop. Might be gonna kill him, cut his throat with her neat and shining row of blades.

"I have to warn you," she says. "It hurts."

Her eyes send a rush of heat over his skin, goosebump

tide, and he feels lightheaded. He's seen the urban primitives around, their elaborate scars, lace on skin traced from a hundred or a thousand wounds, or one single, perfect cut. There's no more being cool, no more pretending it doesn't matter and he doesn't have to tell her that he wants it, needs it more than anything. His body speaks for him, the eagerness between his legs, plain enough for her to see.

She reaches for one of the pots, stained white porcelain, rim chipped and something inside the sticky color of caramel that she stirs around with a fat brush; he isn't really surprised when she begins painting the stuff onto his bare skin, but it burns, cold heat and the brush back and forth until he's coated head to toe and the burning is almost unbearable. He tries to speak, to move, but the liquid has done something to him, every muscle frozen, paralyzed but not numb. He feels *everything,* the burning gone now, faded and his skin suddenly so sensitive: faint warmth of her breath and the icy air-conditioned breeze that flows like mercury over him, thinks maybe he can feel even the specks of dust floating down through the light as they settle on his body.

And he is scared now, real fear because this *is* real, no dream and so scared he would probably tell her to stop, if he could, if his frozen jaw and tongue could shape the simple words. If it shows in his eyes she doesn't see, chooses a knife and makes the first cut. Sure and certain stroke, the blade moving at the center of his chest.

The pain is overwhelming. And the pain is divine.

The shallow, faltering cuts performed in secret with eyes squeezed shut, pleasure in one hand and pain in the other, nothing next to this, the clumsy plucks and twangs of an orchestra warming up compared to the bottomless music of her scalpel. And as she works, the fine line between his fear and his desire, any distinction, dissolves, as she pushes the thinnest silver wire through his skin, weaves it into complex patterns, drives needles through his cheeks and eyelids, through the velvet skin of his dick and the inside of his thighs. Oddly-shaped metal components, gears and struts and jagged fragments of smashed clocks or music boxes. Dead bees, beetle husks, pressed into gaping cuts and held in place with crossed pins. Something huge and barbed worked up inside his ass, protruding brush of copper wire like a tail between his legs. She works patiently, moves oblivious or indifferent to his ecstasy or fear.

From the floor, twisted frame of metal rods, rust and spindly joints like skeletal umbrella batwings, and she drives the pointed ends between his shoulder blades. Heavy skewers through the tough skin of his back in careful, measured rows, and then she's in front of him again, razorthin fish bones through his lips and nostrils; always checking, always stepping back to squint thoughtfully at him. And he thinks he loves her, then, this moment of absolute pain roaring through him, over him, and his love seems so true and obvious, something left in plain sight he's been missing for years.

Another container and plaster or cement smeared and dribbled on with her bare hands, hands moving faster now, making her way up from his feet, fast but thorough. Thick coat to sting and burn in the thousand cuts she's made and the stuff starts to harden almost immediately.

Around him, the others seem closer, now, hungry faces turning to watch this initiation and he wonders for a brief moment who they used to be, before her. Before she brought them here and changed them, bent them to her tastes, made them something important. There's a bright, brief flash of panic when she begins covering his face, gut-deep flinch that soon passes as cool, blanketing peace settles over him. And Kev, if he *is* still Kev, realizes that everything before doesn't matter, the long days sweating on the streets, cold desert nights in alleys and dumpsters, and all the other shit before he came to L.A. That it never mattered, never *could* have mattered; there is only now and her and the others, unchanging family like old dreams. He can hear them, soft wordless welcomes that seep up from inside him, subtle chorus flowing like his blood used to and he struggles to join in, eager baby steps that grow gradually stronger.

Pressure beneath his arms, sudden weightless shift and it

feels like maybe he's being hoisted into the air. But sensations from outside are dull and muffled things, far away while the voiceless chorus grows stronger, her at its mute center. This blazing goddess who loves *him,* loves them *all* and he is not afraid, knows that he'll never be afraid again, knows that for the first time in his life he belongs.

JO CLAYTON

The Hour of the Sisters

1

Shimmering under the impact of the heat which had seared the land since the drought had begun more than three years ago, the night sky was a bowl of white porcelain with the full moon sitting on the blunt peaks of the mountains of the East like a pie plate of scalded milk. A twisted, triangular shape pierced the lower arc of this curdled white—the Master of Waters, the Gargoyle named Cottonwood, patron demigod of the county called Cottonwood.

Timoas dropped to his stomach, wriggled through the coney-run in the manzanita until he reached the first of his snares.

The cord was gnawed through, a tuft of brindle fur glued by a drop of blood up near the knot. Sucking air through the gap between his front teeth, he dug a battered ball of cord from his pocket, peeled a length free and cut it off with the broken blade of an old pocketknife. When he had the new snare in place, he wriggled on to check the rest of the line, harvesting a plump kangaroo mouse and a skinny young coney more bone than meat, resetting the tripped snares with grubby, deft fingers.

He whispered the ancient draw-charm over the snare nooses and whispered it again as he moved between them, a simple charm whose power lay not in the words but in the rhythm of the song. "Soo oon soo soo, coney run this round. Soo oh soo ooh, four foot run this round. Soo oon soo soo, come little, come big, come and be found."

The first at the meeting tree, a lightning-split cedar oozing crystallized sap from its heart, Timoas bent down the weak side, straddled it and sat there, once again whistling breathily through the gap in his teeth and bouncing as if the split wood were a hobby horse. After a while, he touched the small lumps in his game bag, lifted a scowl to Cottonwood rising like a tower from his Nest. "Hey, ol' garggal, you gotta do better'n this or my mam 'n my pa they gonna say hellwitya, burn the talk drums and go be good churchers like the priest want."

"Who you talkin' to, Timo?" Lionin rose from his section of the manzanita coney-run, limped round a thicket of broom and fetched up next to the tree.

"That up there." Timoas jerked a thumb at the stone figure looming over them, then pointed it at the ragged canvas sack his cousin carried. "Get anythin?"

"Not a sausage. Even lost the cord. Coyote."

Their cousin Machoan strolled from behind a patch of deerbrush. "Me, I had fat ones in five of my nooses." He kissed bunched fingers and waved them at the figure on the cliff. "Thanks be, ol' garggal."

Lionin stretched his shoulders and scratched at the small of his back. "I reset my snares with coyote avert over them. Maybe second round be bringin' better luck."

"Let's go get us some shrooms, huh? And there's ol' carp sleeping in the splash pool. You and me can tickle him out, don't you think, Lio?" Machoan kicked a clod of dirt that broke over the toes of his bare foot. "M' belly growls ev'

mornin' these days and I'm sick of it." He shook the dust off
his foot and turned. "Hey, Timo, what bit you?"

"Somethin' funny up there. Am I seein things or did ol'
Waterbug lift a leg and give hisself a push up?"

"Huh?" Lionin stepped away from the tree, tilted his
head back and shaded his eyes out of habit. "Hey! Macha,
come see. He stop spoutin' and he walkin' cross the top of
the fall like he weren't made outta rock. Hoo! lookit that."

Machoan shivered. "Let's us get outta here."

Timoas swung his leg over the broken tree and stood up.
"Me, I'm not goin' home without meat and a mess of
shrooms." He slapped his game bag, then went stalking into
the trees.

Lio and Macha looked at each other for several breaths,
then, reluctantly, they followed their bolder cousin deeper
into the forest.

2

Vesta lifted her head as she heard the clatter of broken stone,
a cascade of sharp, often overly sweet chimes produced by
fractures of the Gargoyle's Nest-rock, a sound she'd been attuned to since the day more than five Cycles ago when she
emerged from the egg. Her thorny white hair stirred and
sharpened. "Cottonwood has left the Nest." She spoke over
her shoulder at the shadowy figure standing in the doorway
of the house called Mud. "He's coming for you, this time.
Game's End was decreed the instant our Gargoyle put foot
to ground. That's the Rule, Sister. This time I will have my
prize." Grim satisfaction deepened her voice to a growl. She
dropped her head again and frowned at the painting that
rested on her knee.

Though she habitually wore pale gray lace and silver tissue, painted her lips and nails with ashes of rose so that she
walked through daylight pale as a patch of fog, the blobs of
plastic paint squeezed onto her palette were harsh and
bright, splotches of saturated color.

It is Ash, she told herself with fierce determination.

That's what she is. Screaming red on a storm wind. Green so glaring it reeks of poison. It is her.

Yet the harder she tried to convince herself, the greater her certainty grew that somehow she'd lost it. Once again her eye had failed her for she'd let herself be blinded by the twists of her own mind rather than looking simply and directly at what stood before her.

Ash had lost the Game. As soon as the Gargoyle claimed her, Ash would sleep in the mud at his feet until the repair of the layered Worlds was complete, until the burn-damage of the drought was healed. And for the rest of the new Cycle she would serve as his voice and as the link between him and the outlying aspects of the multiple entity Cottonwood.

Vesta smiled at that image, covering her mouth with her hand as if she meant to protect her triumph from the abrasion of reality. *Ash will be tamed,* she thought and nearly burst with excitement. She'll be pliant and docile, her wildness scrubbed off. She'll learn the Rules and keep them. Obedient Ash. And Father will see . . . She broke off because that speculation led into dangerous places in her head. Ash lost. I won. That's beyond dispute.

Vesta glanced at the failed painting for a last time, then flung it out across the river. Dropping brush and palette onto the step beside her, she hugged her slim knees and watched avidly as the canvas sailed through awkward curves, skimmed through the heat-withered leaves of the cotton-wood saplings that grew on the largest of the tailing isles left behind by long-gone mining barges.

Down and around the small square went, in and out of shadow, never quite touching the whippy limbs of the saplings, down and around until it splatted onto the shallow, muddy water and sank gradually out of sight among the weeds. "And so might it be," she whispered. "One day. So might it be, image and body made one, sharing the same fate."

Ash came from the shadows of the doorway and kicked through the curling scum on the floor of the porch. "Your prize," she said, her laughter filled with mockery as she tilted her head to the side and turned a bright black eye on

Vesta. "I just might start to worry if you ever forgot must, ought and supposed to be. But that time hasn't come, has it?"

Ash had long black hair, smooth and shiny as a waterfall of tar. Her skin was soft olive and silvery brown with touches of blue and green in the shadows that gave shape to her face. She wore a white silk shirtwaist tucked into a black gabardine skirt, dark nylon stockings with seams, black shoes with heels of mid-height and silver court buckles.

Vesta pinched her lips together. "I won the Game," she said after a short pause. "I doubled your score and drove you from the board. You can't deny that and you can't change it."

She heard the beginnings of hysteria in her voice—born of anxieties developed over the long centuries of rout and frustration in her dealings with Ash, but there was enough certainty in her this time that she banished the quaver without appreciable effort. "You can't change that," she repeated. And smiled.

3

Shoulders hunched, hands in the pockets of his loose trousers, Timoas stared nervously at his bare toes and waited for the next batch of questions; his hair was sodden from the mix of heat and nervousness, his shirt and trousers were blotched with body sweat and he could smell himself. As he waited, he cursed his cousin's weakness. If anyone else had seen anything, they'd had the sense to swallow the sight and keep their heads down, but Lio had to start chattering with the first person he met.

Pel the Bruhman leaned forward, eyes fixed so hard on Timoas that they felt like augers drilling holes in his head. "The Elders are finished, the rest is mine," the Bruhman said. "Sit." He pointed at the three-legged stool placed in a shaft of light burning down through a hole in the roof of the sweat tent. "Tell me about the last thing you saw."

Reluctantly Timoas shuffled to one side and lowered himself onto the hard wooden seat, his knees folded down, his lower legs wrapped around the stool. "Well, my cousins and me, that's Lio and Macha, we were poachin' in brush and forest, don't care what you say bout that, ain't something that shames us. We was second-running our snarelines, cause ol' coyote got mosta the first run. Me, I din't look at waterfall because if anythin' weird was happening, I din't want to know about it. I 'spect Lio and Macha was doin' same or tryin', but Lio sometimes he get bit by somethin' and nothin' to do but he hasta scratch itch, because I hear him yell. So I think maybe somethin' has got him so I turn and I see him pointin'. I don't wanna look, but I do and I see this . . . this somethin' which I do *not* wanna know about, crawlin' headfirst down cliff from top of waterfall. It has six legs all thorny and weird looking so I know even if I don't wanna know. It's Garggal.

"He's putting his weird feet down on a special kind of rock. The way I know it's special rock is cause whenever ol' Waterbug touches it, it crack and grumble and start shinin' and the shinin' don't go away for the longest time even when him, he has gone past the place. And I think I hear a sound like bells 'cept Macha say he don't hear nothin'. Ol' Lio he gobblin' goose talk and wavin' his hands like someone shovin' a tickler up his arse. So we grab him and get outta there."

In the darkness behind the Bruhman there were rustles and restless movements, a slide of light along the side of a face, his family squatting in crooked rows, elders to the fore, with the rest packed into the space remaining, his brothers, sisters and cousins pushed into the curve of the sweat tent's back wall, all of them listening to the Bruhman's questions, all of them judging Timo's answers in a way that made his skin itch.

Pel the Bruhman rocked forward on his toes, his eyes turned inward as his hands darted like the nose sting of a flitterby, touching Timoas on hands, shoulders, knees, elsewhere across his body, quick, faint prickles that piled up and piled up, growing into a shivery hurt that Timoas was determined his family wouldn't see.

With an odd sound that was part grunt and part moan, the

Bruhman rocked onto his heels and let his hands drop onto his thighs. He turned his head so he was speaking over his shoulder, but his eyes were shut so he was looking at no one. "Go home," he said. "The boy stays."

4

When Ash laughed again, a careless easy sound, Vesta flung palette and brushes over the stair rail and closed her fingers until she could feel her nails cutting into her palms. "I won," she said fiercely. "Our Father said I won. You heard him. You heard every word he said."

The crack-clash-clatter of the Nest stone grew louder, closer. Vesta's breath came more quickly as she tried to hold on to what only moments before had been certainty and satisfaction.

"That was then." Ash's head turned with a soft swish of her long black hair. "If you expected Our Father to stand meekly aside and allow himself to be given to the Burning without fighting it . . ." She waved a hand at the figure sitting in the back seat of the battered flivver drawn up beside Vesta's roadster, both of them parked in a turnout near the point at which the stairs from Mud House touched the River Road. "Is that a man prepared for sacrifice?"

Vesta twisted her hands, refusing to look down. "The Rules, Ash. The Rules of the Game. The Cycle's Endtime has been declared and the Day of Sacrifice is confirmed. The Gargoyle has left the Nest."

"Ah. Rules. Has Father ever paid attention to those?"

Vesta stared at her sister. "He bribed you. How? What has he got left . . . No!"

"You have always underestimated his grip on life. I don't say fear of death, because that's not it."

"His Powers . . ." Vesta's cry was filled with incredulity. "You can't use those. You'll ruin everything."

"Rules and Turns. You're so damn rigid, Ves." Ash walked to the far end of the porch, vanished around the corner of the house. Only the humming memory of her voice was left—then the clatter of her feet on the stairs.

"She did it to me again. And I let her."

Pain struck to Vesta's heart as she watched their Father welcome Ash with an affectionate hug. The Dark Sister had always been his favorite. She closed her pale fingers around the crumbling wood of the rail. "He despises me," she moaned, the words drowned in the whine of the wind. "He has from the day I emerged from egg. How can you possibly hate someone a few moments old?" She dropped her head on her arms again, shuddering with a loathing that made her despise herself and a nausea that threatened to leach away the last of her strength.

The sudden roar of an over-powered motor drowned the clatter of the shattering Nest stone and the patter of insect feet. Hastily Vesta straightened and scowled at the driver.

He was a superlatively handsome young man—an entertainer if the guitar case on the front seat was any indication—with perhaps a little talent and, from the flash of his eyes, a lot of impudence. Handsome and young. Very young. His face was flushed and glowing with happiness, as if he'd won the prize of his life.

"The Orlando." Vesta unclenched her fingers from the rail, wincing at the sharp small pains from the splinters driven into her flesh. "She found an Orlando to sing his own death. No wonder Our Father bought her deal." Her voice faltered. Everywhere she looked, Ash had won.

Ash lifted a hand in a mocking wave.

As if that was the signal he was waiting for, the Orlando started the car rolling forward; a few breaths later it had turned a bend and vanished into the night.

5

In the Corn Tassel clan farmland there was a small patch of ground set aside from the Common for the use of the Bruhman, a place where he grew food and herbs and whatever else he needed to sustain his role in the Web of the Bruh. Pel the Corn Tassel Bruhman took Timoas there and squatted beside one of the hills with its multiple plantings of corn, beans and melon. He motioned the boy down beside him, scooped up a handful of earth so dry and dead that Timo flinched when Pel poured it into his hand. Pel tapped the boy's wrist. "What's wrong with that dirt?"

"Same what's wrong with everythin'. Dry."

The Bruhman got to his feet. "Come." Without waiting for a response from Timoas, he walked away, moving swiftly along the raised paths between the family plots of the Corn Tassels, heading for the river intermittently visible between the yellowed leaves of drought-killed cottonwood saplings.

They picked their way across the mud and gravel flats and knelt beside the weed-choked flow of murky water. Pel dipped his empty hand into the river and poured a trickle of the water he scooped up into the hand that held the dirt.

The dirt floated. Its dead gray color didn't change.

"Take a pinch and spread it out."

Timoas did what he was told. "Dry. Like water din't touch it at all." He dropped the rest of the handful to the ground by his feet and rubbed his palm clean against the side of his shirt. "How come?"

"Gargoyle's gone." Pel brushed his hands together, bent and brushed off his knees. When he straightened, his face was paler than usual and there was a glitter in his yellow brown eyes. "The sun burns and the moon makes lunatics; fire rules and even the deep Forest starts to die. The Gargoyle leaves his Nest and the water is unclean."

He started back across the riverbank, climbing toward the worn blacktop of the River Road. Silent and confused, Timoas trudged after him.

6

The clatter and crash of broken stone was so loud this time that Vesta wheeled around, hands raised to ward off what she expected to see breaking through to this reality, coming for her.

An oval shimmer roughened the air for an instant, then was gone.

Abruptly she was too frightened to stay on the porch any

longer, too frightened to stay in a house that had proved more of a trap than shelter.

Heels clumping heavily on the stairs, soft leather instep flaps slapping on the concealed shoelaces, she ran down the rickety stairs to the River Road where her own car waited, a smoky gray roadster, the color softened yet further by a layer of dust. Running served no purpose, she knew that, but her flight gave her a sense that she was at least doing something.

I didn't win. I lost. Yes. I lost the Game because I stopped playing too soon. Lost it! I listened to Our Father. I trusted Him. Traitor! Thief! He stole the Game from me and gave it to Ash. Because He likes her. Because He hates me.

Vesta slid into the roadster, settled herself beneath the steering wheel, her skirt smoothed into neat folds. She leaned over, took her driving gloves from the abdit's hollow and tugged them on, the soft buttery leather gleaming in the light from the full moon.

No! Not not not lost. I won't allow it to be lost. Why do you let Ash get to you, Ves? Take her at her word. Bend the one Rule and the Game's not over. Keep playing until there is no time at all. Go for the blood. The blood. The blood. Go for the blood of the Sacrifice and you've got her. And Him. The End of Cycle Rule is still there. Make Him bow to it. He Burns this time. I swear it. Our Father's life force will power the Change of Cycles and everything will be right again. She squeezed her eyes shut, set the tips of her fingernails against the pale skin of her face, the nails that held the cold poison-paste. *He Burns.*

The Gargoyle stone broke no closer to Vesta, but neither did the sound retreat.

Night after night she drove the back roads of Cottonwood County searching for Ash—or wove her ghostly car through the ice trucks that carried fruit and produce from Cottonwood County to the markets in the great cities of the Southlands.

The increasing desperation of the growers and the pickers, the scorched desolation of the farms, the smell of starvation and poverty spread like a blight across the County—none of that reached her. All she felt, knew, thought about, was the Game and how to reactivate the lethal clash between herself and her sister. How to force the conflict to the edge of death, drawing into herself the Power that came from walking such shattered extremities, the bloody bones of their Father, of the Orlando and Ash.

But first she had to find Ash, so by scry and eye she sought her sister across the fields and the forest of Cottonwood.

7

The Gargoyle's Nest was a truncated cone of tight-grained marble as blue as watered ink, veined in white, black and indigo, the slanted top a ragged platform of twigs and branches carved from that marble, with a deep hollow in the middle. Tucked among the branches there were detailed images of mushrooms of various sorts, young conifers mostly less than a foot high, sprays of lilies and lupin, paintbrush and poppies and other flowers.

Timoas reached out tentatively and touched a poppy; he shivered at the silky feel of the carved petal, then brushed his fingers along one of the pine branches. The texture was right, the slightly fuzzy feel of the bark, the smooth warmness of stripped inner wood. He moved his hand again, stroking his palm along what felt too real to be real.

The tumbled pile of boulders they'd come around when they finished the climb up the cliff was the same pale, ink-colored marble as the Nest, fragments large and small as if this were at once the quarry that provided stone for the carving and the dump for the bits that were discarded after the carving was finished. Timoas leaned on one of the larger boulders and frowned at the trickle of murky water oozing down the face of the stone cliff. "Where ol' garggal crawl off to?"

"Said too much already." Pel reached for one of the carved branches and fitted his toes into a niche between two others, pulled himself onto the Nest wall and started climbing. When he reached the top he swung around and sat with his legs dangling.

"Apprentice with me," he said abruptly.

Timoas tilted his head back and stared up at the Bruhman. "Huh?"

Pel looked older than time and twice as shabby, with his stubble and his untidy hair, the white shirt and twill trousers that were castoffs from the mayor's laundry basket. Castoffs, that's all he had. Apprentice with him? Why would anyone bother?

The Bruhman waved a hand in a rueful acknowledgment of the thoughts he read flowing across the boy's face. "Listen," he said. "I need an apprentice. You need a job. Even if I can't promise much, it's not so bad a deal. No wife, no family—you'll have sons but they won't know you're their father and you can't claim them. On the other hand, you aren't responsible for raising them. You'll have to learn to read and write; I'll teach you so that's no problem. You'll have to deal with demons and soul eaters; no sweat there either. You won't starve, you'll always have a roof to keep you dry and you'll never lack women to warm your bed."

"But . . ."

Pel shrugged his shoulders impatiently. "We haven't got time for going round and round. Yes or no."

Timoas leaned on the boulder and stared down at the skim of water that barely covered the bottom of the catch pool at the base of the falls. His youngest uncle, Nemmat, lived in town and had a hauling business with a couple of stake-bodied trucks; even with the drought he was successful enough to be negotiating for an icer. Nemmat wanted Timoas to come work for him. No pay, just a piece of the business. Pa was pushing for it, but Nemmat was the tightest man with a coin Timoas knew and the boy had a strong suspicion that his uncle's promises were like summer mirages, pretty enough but always out of reach.

His mind abruptly made up, he pushed away from the boulder, marched to the Nest and began climbing.

8

Ash danced, her bare feet kicking through dust and bark, thudding on the thick mat of pine needles, her voice rising and falling in a lyrical, lilting, wordless song.

Her face Changed, chin sharpening to a point, nose like a knife blade, eyes huge and multiple, dark skin hardening to chitin the color of bleached amber.

Her body Changed; her hands hardened to claws, her fingernails to micro-pointed stings; four cellophane wings as long as she was tall uncurled from slits along her spine. As soon as they dried, they began a powerful vibration, burring and humming, playing continuously behind the wordless song and the soft rhythmic thuds of her feet, weaving a web of compulsion across the Sacred Danceground of the clearing in the forest pines.

Vesta drove deeper and deeper into the forest, her white-thorn hair curling tighter and closer to her head, the ends sharpening till they were as hard and deadly as the thorns of the white deathrose.

Her Change began.

Her face reshaped itself, the cheeks spreading outward, the skin hardening into chitin until she seemed to wear a porcelain mask. Her hair dropped into a sharply defined widow's peak and her chin pulled into a point until the wasp's heartshaped head bloomed out of the more human one she ordinarily wore.

Four paired wings transparent as cellophane unfolded from her shoulders and back; her chest broadened and angled sharply into a keel to provide power to those wings. The rest of her bones hollowed for lightness so she could fly when the time came.

Her hands hardened, fingertips turning to claws, fingernails to stings, deadly stings with a powerful poison in the paste they carried.

The sun heated her body and turned her hair to silver, touched the opaque white of her chitin and glinted from her newly facetted eyes—eyes black as jet, cut and polished to reflecting planes.

9

The Bruh Web was a haze of misty light floating after Timoas, billowing sky-to-ground, rolling along at a constant distance behind the Gargoyle, soul-emblems caught in the mist, the visible elements of the symbolic power bodies of Bruhmen from all the Clans of Cottonwood County. Silver threads like lively wireworms looped swiftly from that Web, waving blind foreparts, feeling/smelling the air, searching for him—falling short until Pel caught his arm, slowed him, and the gap between him and the Bruh Potency grew smaller and smaller.

The wireworms touched him, wrapped themselves around him—each touch shocking him, burning him, at the same time sealing him deeper into the Web. Whispers came to him, words that passed through Pel and took shape from his voice, words that passed by Pel and were as shapeless and antique as the Web itself.

He was part of it now, the whispers told him, a very small new part, but important; as youngest, he was both Heir and Focus for the power of the Web. Listen, the whispers said, hear us . . . .

"In the Realm of Cottonwood, Cottonwood stands Watch and Ward.
Purified and plentiful is the water he provides.
In the Realm of Cottonwood, Bruh Web stands Watch and Ward.
Shield of the Gargoyle, Focus of the force.
Wide is the Web Wielded by the Heir
Full is the Flow . . . .

Focus . . . Bruh flows through you, Timoas son of Mattan . . . Youngest of the Bruh . . . the Heir . . . the Lens . . . the Stander between stings . . . Capture the Sister . . . drain her . . . her poison powers the Change

. . . Protect the Gargoyle . . . tap and sap . . . wasps in mein and mind . . . don't let them touch him! Feed the Gargoyle . . . build his strength. . . ."

The air quivered around Timoas son of Mattan and turned silver.

The Nest vanished.

The cliff vanished along with everything else but the depleted, dried-up river and the path that ran beside it, a ribbon of gray dust wandering in long lazy curves between low hills carpeted with black grass. The sky was silver, the stars were black and the fat half moon that sailed through barren clouds seemed beaten from a lump of tarnished pewter. Mushrooms, black fern and shadow flowers were everywhere around him, and great white webs spun by mottled white/gray spiders weaving in and out of leaves like pointed black shapes cut from carbon paper, rustling in the wind that plucked at Timoas's hair and stung tears from his eyes.

Some distance away the Gargoyle waited, head swiveled so he was looking back at the boy. His forelimbs were raised high as if he were lifting spears toward the moon and his lower four legs were bracing his long flat body so it stood like a slab-sided tower atop one of the barren hills.

When Timoas started toward him, the Gargoyle turned and went trundling off, those six thorny legs see-sawing through leisurely arcs.

"Run, Timo!" Pel's eyes burned and he shoved his hands repeatedly toward the boy. "Run!"

The shout waking a sudden exhilaration in him, Timoas flew along the track, gray dust billowing about his feet, the Web behind him, thrusting him forward, Cottonwood dark and mysterious ahead of him, the distance between them shrinking with every step he took until he was running at the Gargoyle's side.

"Got you," he cried and slapped his hand against the reddish brown chitin that armored the foremost of Cottonwood's shoulders; the sound his palm made was a reverberating crack that broke across the tarnished bowl of the sky and melted into his own outcry.

"Ahhhhh," he shrieked. "Garrrr galll!" Power surged through him, starting waves of shudders and twitches as the touch initiated a link that was sudden, frightening and terribly powerful—so powerful that for a moment he lost all sense of himself as a separate being.

The link shook him, whirled him up, slammed him hard onto Cottonwood's broad back, the wind knocked out of him, broken blotches of darkness jigging and jagging around him. At the same time Cottonwood's wing cases tilted and rocked under him, easing him into the crevice between them.

He folded his legs and arms, straightened his back to initiate the easy sway he used when he was riding his father's mule and he settled down to let the Gargoyle carry him wherever it was they were going.

10

Vesta sent her roadster swooping off the road, brought it to a stop beside the battered old flivver. Through the dark verticals of the pine trunks she could see the long low block of the cabin and beyond that the flicker of the fire. The music from the guitar rose and died with the soughing of the wind, the song of Sacrifice played by the Orlando who didn't know his true role, mingling with the call of owls and loud roar of the wind in the needles.

She swung her legs from under the steering wheel, bounced to her feet on the roadster's leather seatcover. Her wings buzzed loudly, lifting her into the air where she powered herself into a steep arc that took her high above the ragged crests of the pines. She hovered a moment to watch the Rite of Sacrifice Exchange unfold beneath her, then howling and hissing with fury, she darted toward her sister.

When she was close enough to cry Challenge, she changed the dart to an aerial dance of brief, swift flights above the point where Ash was dancing. "*Game*, I cry Game and Game again," she shouted hoarsely, "until the Gargoyle himself chooses the winner and carries off the loser."

The sun was low in the west, near the rounded tops of the coast mountains, the shadows long and inky black on the bark-littered ground, but the fire that burned in the clearing was still daylight pale, popping loudly from the resin in the wood, the embers from the herbs flaring to a last burn.

Ash's wings whirred. She rose smoothly upward to face Vesta, her hands darting in threat gestures explicitly deadly. "Challenge accepted and altered. To the Death. Though the Cycles end forever and the World Herself cease to be, let the Challenge between us be to the Death."

"Alteration accepted. To the Death."

11

The Game Board was a shimmering, translucent collection of cubes, jewel-colored cubes drifting in slow, elegant orbits about each other, bursting momentarily into liquid sprays as—feral, furious and beautiful—the Wasp Sisters erupted through them, coalescing once more into their simple eight-sided forms as the Wasps flung themselves elsewhere.

Angular, lanceolate, rushing and deadly, the wasp dance went on and on. Counting colors, building cube strings, advantage points garnered by Rule—enhancing the odds that the Sister with the most points would win the ultimate Game. By the same Rule-Set, Death was the ultimate Counter that cancelled all other points.

Feints initiated, broken off.

Clawed, sting-pointed fingers, stabbing at faces, arms.

Bodies zigging and zagging through the cubes—six directions, up and down, north south east west, each way a different color, the spin uncertain, the change continual and unpredictable.

12

Timoas gagged at the stench that the wind blew into his face from the Danceground—a blend of rage, loathing, and fear that burned down his throat and set his stomach churning. He crooked his arm across his nose to block out the wind, but that didn't help much and he was reduced to breathing as shallowly as he could since the Gargoyle had picked up his pace until he was racing across unmarked grass like black fur and seemed to be using the stink as his route guide.

The whisper from the Bruh Web rustled in Timoas's ears, sometimes clear, sometimes so hazily obscure that he didn't bother with the struggle to understand what the Web was trying to tell him.

the Game . . . insert self into . . .
watch for Ash . . . Sister with black hair . . .
follow Cottonwood's moves . . . knows in nose, in
grabble and fumble all erratica and oddities
paired and unpaired . . .
must have one of the Sisters . . . MUST have Sister . . .
MUST HAVE SISTER . . . .
must kill Father . . . or see the man dead . . . time is
termination . . . at end . . . cessation . . . life is finale
. . . swan song . . . Cycle and Male Being merged as
one and both are condemned to completion. . . .

TICK TOCK. Like the clunk-clang of the village clock in Cottonwood's central Plaza, the Gargoyle Realm marked the draining of the last impulses of the old Cycle. TOCK TICK TOCK. Counting sounds filling the space below the silver sky. TICK TOCK TICK.

Then the Gargoyle's run was finished. The air dissolved before him and they were back in Timoas's Realm, racing under the oaks and pines, fir trees and cedars of the forest Timo had played and poached in since he was old enough to run about alone.

Racing toward a clearing that pulsed with Power, the clearing where the Sisters fought their Game toward the death of one of them.

13

On the Danceground the Father moved in a wingless version of the Wasp Dance—his fiery breath heating the air about him, his boot heels thudding on the needle mat, his arms bent into the stiff, stylized gesture-forms that hoarded power for killing strokes. Physically, he was a small man, his head no higher than Ash's shoulder, yet there was a solidity to his presence that seemed to render the space he occupied much larger than his size would warrant.

He danced that Power.

Vesta, glancing at him, knew he had not yet paid over the price of his survival.

She knew suddenly and with absolute certainty that he was planning a second betrayal.

Her anger bloomed again. Traitor! Thief! As much as she hated her sister, the idea that their Father would extend his treachery against Ash sparked almost as much fury in her as his earlier betrayal of herself.

In that moment of distraction, Ash struck at her.

Vesta hissed and twisted rapidly to one side, arched her body and swung her clawed fingers at Ash, trying to use her greater strength and swifter reaction time to turn back the blow, missing her sister's amber chitin by less than the width of a hair.

On the ground the Orlando backed away from the Father, his lip curling with distaste.

Their Father used that aversion as if it were reins on a bridle, nudging, backing, turning the Orlando toward the Killing Site, the virtual altar visible only to him and his daughters.

As unaware as he had ever been of his true role, the Orlando continued to play the Dance, the music plucked from the strings drawing into its song the power and magic that shivered in the cooling air of the Danceground. He could feel that power—that magic—vibrating into his fingers and assumed it was the gift that Ash had promised him.

Cottonwood burst into the clearing and careened about its edges. Timoas clung to his rocking, plunging perch, terrified and excited, struggling to serve his assigned role as Focus to the Bruh Power. Feeding the Gargoyle. Watching the Sisters flinging themselves at each other.

Wingcases flicked wide. Cottonwood increased his speed till the wind of his going tore tears from Timoas's eyes, then he leapt toward the soaring Sisters, his lacy flightwings whirring louder and louder as they bit into the erratic currents of magic that coursed through the air of the Game area.

As the great soaring bulk of the Gargoyle crashed into the orbiting cubes, his thorny forelimbs reaching for Ash, the Father leapt for the Orlando, a knife like a silvergilt thorn jutting from his fist. Once again he was betrayer and thief—this time stealing from his favorite Dark Daughter what he'd sold her for his rescue. If he took the Blood of the Sacrifice himself, it was his by right no matter how much work Ash had put into finding the Orlando and bringing him here. He didn't have to pay her anything.

Fury burst through Ash as she spun away from Vesta and in the middle of that swerve saw what was happening. Her wasp chitin was scratched in several places, the scratches yellowing as the poison worked on her; her heart fluttered with the rage that flooded her, her breathing went shallow and whistled as if she were wheezing.

Vesta started after her Sister, but whirled away before she got close enough to threaten Ash as she fled the sudden swipe of the Gargoyle's foreleg.

The Bruh Web went silent as Cottonwood's drive redirected itself from Ash to Vesta, the powerflow hovered, neutral until Timoas tightened Focus and once again became the lens through which that potent force would pour, feeding Cottonwood, grounding him doubly, first in Cottonwood Realm, then in his true abode, Gargoyle Realm.

Ash twisted her body. Wings beating furiously, she dived through the board, bursting cubes without calculation, color spraying randomly about her plunging body, her arms outstretched as if she desired to embrace what her wrath was driving her to kill.

Her fingerstings dug into the Father.

Her finger claws tore at their Father's flesh—flesh that

melted off his bones until he was no longer a man but an animated skeleton gamboling through a macabre jig.

With a high warbling scream Ash pulled free the knife rattling in the fleshless fingers and drove it up under the Orlando's ribs until the long shining blade pierced his heart.

A silvery ribbon shimmered briefly between the Father and the Orlando, then flared to white fire as it touched Ash; an instant later it was gone, the promised power transferred to the Bright Sister.

The bones of the skeleton fell apart, tumbling into a scatter that looked much like a dead bear after vultures then maggots had finished with it.

Cottonwood's forelegs clamped on Vesta.

As soon as the black-tipped thorns on those legs touched her, her body changed once again. The Wasp Aspect of the Game melted away and Vesta wore her humanity on the outside once more, her long white lashes resting sweetly on the delicate curve of her cheek.

Ash hovered briefly above the pile of bones, then fled the clearing.

The Game cubes lingered a few moments longer—as long as both Sisters were present and Game-in-Potential still existed—but the moment the Gargoyle vanished with his prize, their precise and delicate orbits decayed and their colors faded; in seconds they were erased from the air.

With the power fed into him from the Web, Cottonwood leapt into the Gargoyle Realm again, carrying Vesta in his forelegs, Timoas on his back. He raced to the Nest, wingcases still extended so he was half flying as he ran along the gray ash of the cinder path, gray dust boiling in clouds like thunderheads around and over him. Timoas clung to the rough and lumpy back as he continued to feed the Gargoyle and—all fear wiped away—reveled in the play of power around them.

Tenderly, affectionately, Cottonwood laid Vesta in the hollow of his Nest. With Timoas helping him—though Timo didn't know what he was doing or why—he curled the Sister's unconscious form into a curve that would leave room for him to stand his Guardian's Watch over the Cottonwood Realm. Then he left the Nest and moved into the gelatinous mud of the dried-up river that fed all the other rivers in the Realm.

Timoas stood on the bank and stared as Cottonwood arranged himself into the pose the boy had seen a few hours ago—hours that seemed like centuries now. He lifted his thorny forelimbs to a heat-whitened sky, braced his great abdomen on his four hindlimbs and threw back his head, his mandibles opening to a great and somehow terrible gape.

Water gushed forth from that gape, a pure, air-filled arc that caught the glow of the moonlight and amplified it until the night pulsed with whiteness.

Water gathered behind the Gargoyle, filling the river from bank to bank, flowing slowly at first, then more and more swiftly until it was curling round Cottonwood with a deep, booming roar, leaping out from the lip of the cliff into a second arc that filled the catch basin below, then began swelling the dead rivers of the plain, the creeks and streams of the forest. . . .

Cottonwood woke from his trance. He lowered his arms and waded from the river, ignoring the tug of the powerful current.

When he reached the bank he knelt and began splashing water onto the soil there, wetting it further with his saliva, kneading it, turning it into malleable earth-spheres.

"Grab an armful of those."

Timoas looked up. Pel stood beside the Nest. "Huh?"

"That's our part. The Sister has to be packed away until she's needed. Ever seen a mud-dauber's nest?" Pel yawned. "The sooner we start, the faster we'll finish. Me, I want my supper and a good long sleep. Like I said, you fetch the workings from ol' Cottonwood there, I'll pat her down. Then we'll go rest up so we can enjoy the fruits this night's work is going to bring us."

•   •   •

Thus the Rule of the Cycle's End was fulfilled by the Transformation and Sacrifice of the Father.

The Rule of the Beginning of a New Cycle took its place.

The Gargoyle Cottonwood stood Watch and Ward over Cottonwood County and it, in its turn, stood watch and Ward over him.

WENDY WEBB

Smiling Beasties

———⚬———

THE HOUSE WAS ASYMMETRIC.

Tendrils from a creeping rose swayed in the windless afternoon. It escaped imprisonment from the low wrought-iron fence that contained this asymmetric house, and pricked the skin below her knee with a sharp thorn. Rebecca Stern jumped at the sting, stepped back instinctively, and wondered at how something so fragile, so vulnerable, could at the same time be so hurtful. She looked up at this house and its marvel of architecture that was at once auspicious and aloof, and rubbed the soreness from the sting.

The house seemed to hold its breath at Rebecca's discomfort. To the left of the Tudor-arch double door, a single equally arched window pointed heavenward like a pious eye below an imperious brow. Then, by a trick of light, or the sun dipping behind a cloud, the eye seemed to wink.

She raised a hand to her forehead to block the glare of the sun that had reappeared in magnificent force and watched the house fall into deep shadow. Its modest width on the tight, overgrown lot was offset by the towering height of an-

other two stories punctuated by a torso-shaped finial atop
the cupola. The finial figure seemed to stand vigil over all
those who dared approach.

Reaching deep into her briefcase, Rebecca checked the
file against her memory that this was indeed the right address. Few clients could afford such elaborate dwellings and
therefore didn't command her services, however involuntary
in either situation. But this house, in the noted first subdivi-
sion of Atlanta, was out of the ordinary by the architecture
and the inherent wealth of the community. By all reports, the
client situation was disturbingly familiar.

Even if the house was asymmetric.

A dusting of rust fell across her shoes as she turned the
latch to the gate and entered the front yard. Here, the once
carefully managed garden was overgrown so that the stone
walkway leading to the large verandah had been reduced to
a narrow and treacherous path past sticky plants, an undisci-
plined variety of colorful flowers, and the skittering of small
creatures underbrush. Taking the wide steps one at a time,
she moved into the shadow of the porch and felt the temperature drop to an almost uncomfortable cool.

"May I help you?"

The voice from deep shadow, or perhaps it was the question, took Rebecca by surprise. "Yes. I suppose you can. Are
you Lillian Wicker?"

"I am."

"I'm Rebecca Stern from Social Services, Ms. Lillian."
She stared deep into the shadow for a closer look that was
not forthcoming. "May I call you Ms. Lillian?"

"I find that address condescending, don't you? Mrs.
Wicker will do just fine. But you seem a nice girl, so you
may call me Lillian if the rules allow it."

"The rules?" Rebecca blinked in the dark and leaned forward to see her newest client. "I don't follow you."

"Don't you?" A quiet laugh punctured the air, then was
cut off abruptly. "I know why you're here."

"Then you got my letter."

"I did. As cryptic as it was, I've received letters like that before. And the consequent visits." The quiet turned ominous.

Rebecca shifted uncomfortably in the cool air, the dark, and with this woman who refused to make herself visible. "I would have called—"

"You would have failed. I have no need for a telephone. My needs are amply taken care of." A pause. "Whatever happened to that nice young man, what was his name?"

"Paul?"

"Ah, yes. Paul."

"He's no longer with us." Rebecca shifted her briefcase from one hand to the other. "Really Mrs. Wicker, I've so looked forward to meeting you, but it is a little dark here. Could we go inside?"

A small chuckle. "I like the dark, and the quiet. That is, when I'm not tending to my garden. But where are my manners?" She emerged from the comfort of shadow, a slight woman scarcely five feet tall. Stark white hair, brushed on one side, but a mass of tangles on the other, was pulled back in a braid and pinned up. Her dark blue skirt and jacket, once fashionable, were wrinkled, caked in gray-white dust, and worn thin and frayed about the cuffs and various points at her waist. She was dressed as if to attend an afternoon event some decades ago. Or to receive expected visitors. "Better?"

"Yes. Thank you."

"Do you like my attire? Paul always did. He said it set off the blue in my eyes. I could always tell when he was sincere. His dimples appeared on either side of his smile. Dimples on both sides. One doesn't see that very often, does one? You say he's no longer with you?"

"He's no longer with the office."

"Why?"

"I don't know, Mrs. Wicker."

"But you have your suspicions. Everyone has suspicions."

"I'm here to find out about you."

"Indeed." She smiled then, and waved her hand toward the massive front door lined on both sides by diamond-shaped glass panes. "Do come in."

Rebecca nodded, released a tense breath she didn't know she held, and scanned the entrance outside the door. Encircling the pointed arch of the entrance were a congregation of faces with their grotesque features forever captured in stone. An animal of some sort jutted out from the eaves with its permanent snarl bearing sharp teeth. A humanlike face was caught in a battle of emotions somewhere between sadistic humor and excruciating pain. Myriad impressions touched each hardened and fixed face, but collectively it was their eyes—dark, shallow, knowing—that met hers with bare truth and without chance of ever backing down by blinking. She gasped.

Mrs. Wicker clapped her hands with open glee. "Oh. I see you've met some of my friends. Family, really. I like to think of them that way as they protect me from those who would do me harm. You don't know anyone who would do me harm, do you? Of course not. Come in. Come in."

Rebecca Stern pulled her gaze from the disturbed faces and followed Mrs. Wicker into a front room. "Are there more?"

"Naturally. One can't be too careful in this day and age. All I have to do is look up from any window to see them watching out for me. Ah, here we are."

The sitting room was small and circumscribed with built-in bookcases from floor to ceiling filled with dusty leather-bound volumes. Across from the aged marble fireplace was a settee covered in threadbare gold brocade that hinted at a more opulent time. Two scuffed wing chairs flanked the fireplace, and it was in one of these that Mrs. Wicker took her place. Near her was a life-sized bust of a dour-looking man.

Rebecca sat in the settee and proceeded to open her briefcase. "You have a beautiful home, Mrs. Wicker."

"I like it. Always have. I was born here eighty years ago and have lived here ever since."

The flurry of movement in the briefcase stopped. "Nowhere else?"

"No need. My grandfather was a successful industrialist and sought this area for its proximity to the city and its wide open green space. This used to be wilderness at one time.

Now you can see the Atlanta skyline from my backyard. Things have changed quite a bit over the last century, have they not?"

"They really have." Rebecca pointed to the bust that sat on a pedestal level with Lillian Wicker's left shoulder. "Is that your grandfather?"

Peals of laughter echoed through the room. The woman stopped suddenly, but the sound reverberated around corners and down halls until it, too, fell silent. "Heavens, no." She turned to the bust and addressed him: "Did you hear that, Walter? Our Rebecca thinks you are my grandfather. Now don't get yourself in a state. She didn't mean it." Mrs. Wicker turned to Rebecca. "Did you, dear? Just say you didn't mean it and he will be fine."

"Who is Walter?"

"My husband, dear. Who else? Quickly now. Say you're mistaken and all will be forgiven.—"

"Mrs. Wicker, I don't think—"

"Say it *now*." The old woman's face turned red with instant fury.

Rebecca paused, considered this turn of events and knew that the extraordinary reports from the neighbors were probably more accurate than she had expected. "I was mistaken."

"There now," Mrs. Wicker said, stroking her husband's head, "don't you feel better? That's right." She leaned over to kiss him on the forehead and turned conspiratorially to Rebecca. "He always did have a mean temper. But it passes quickly." Then back to the plaster bust with a little girl voice offered in soothing tones, "Doesn't it, Father. You like it when I stroke your head, don't you? Yes, you do."

Rebecca shifted uncomfortably in her seat. This was the worst part. Evaluating a client for their ability to take care of themselves was always hard. The right report from her, peppered with the accepted terminology of the office and state guidelines, meant the end of independence for people like Mrs. Wicker. Rebecca didn't take this responsibility lightly, but she couldn't stand by and let the elderly fend for themselves when they weren't capable, mentally or otherwise.

She wished now more than ever that her colleague, Paul,

had continued with this case rather than simply abandoned it, and everything else, without so much as a two-week notice. His work load had fallen to her and the few left in the office, all of whom were already months behind with their own cases. Lillian Wicker had waited an unjust period of time for a continuance of her evaluation. And dimples or not, should Rebecca ever run into him again, she would give Paul a piece of her mind and then some.

Clearing her throat, she opened the file and looked up at the elderly woman still stroking her husband's head. "Mrs. Wicker, I have a few questions to ask you."

The old lady smoothed her wrinkled skirt, brushed away gray-white dust, and looked at the caseworker with open contempt. "I told you, I know why you're here. So let me save both of us some time. I know who the president is, and I know what year it is. I know my name and yours. So now we've both played the game and you can be on your way."

"It's not that simple, Mrs. Wicker. I have reports from your neighbors clearly indicating unusual noises in the middle of the night, and strange behavior—"

"Busybodies. Every one of them." Her voice rose an octave. "I've lived here for eighty years and they've been here for only three or four. Their despicable children pick my dear, dear buttercups and leave their plastic toys on the streets. They are the ones who should be removed. Not me."

"I never said anything about removing you."

A tiny smile touched the corners of Mrs. Wicker's mouth. She stroked her husband's head and nodded as if something had been spoken. "Of course, Father. You're right. You're always right." She returned to the conversation with Rebecca in a lighter tone. "I'm not some crazy old woman with twenty-three cats. Oh, I had one. Once. It was missing an eye from an ugly fight, but I took it in anyway. Then it scratched me and I did something about it."

"Mrs. Wicker. My files indicate you have a daughter."

The old woman's face brightened then. "Oh, yes." She launched to her feet, rifled through a drawer, then dropped a photograph into Rebecca's hands. "Here she is. Lovely, isn't she? At least she was."

Rebecca Stern glanced at the picture, then looked quickly away. A knot lodged in her throat at the sight and she tried to massage it away.

"After the accident, Daughter was never the same. She underwent plenty of reconstructive surgery, but the scars never completely went away. She was left a bitter and vindictive woman."

"Do you ever see her?"

"All the time." She stroked the bust. "Isn't that right, Walter?"

A shadow crossed the hallway between the sitting room and the kitchen.

Rebecca caught the motion out of the corner of her eye. "Is someone else here?"

"My servant." Mrs. Wicker's hand went to her mouth as she stifled a giggle. "Pardon me. We are not to call help 'servants' anymore, are we? And Henry's really only a part-time handy man. I've known him since I was a young woman." She whispered, "Truth be known, the meager fee I pay him—when he shows up—keeps him in inexpensive wine." Her voice rose to a normal pitch. "I suppose the tea is ready. I'll just get it. You do like tea, don't you? Of course you do. Who doesn't?" And with that, she was gone.

Rebecca placed the file next to her on the settee, stretched, then walked to the entrance hall for a closer look at the dining room. The diamond panes from the arched window dropped dappled light across the breadth of the large table that would easily seat ten. She wondered how long ago that many people had dined in this room, and in this asymmetric house.

The flutter of bird wings pulled her attention to the large window. She followed the movement and found herself looking out on the front garden from a different perspective than when she had first arrived. There, tucked in among tangled boxwoods and the threatened buttercups, were broken slabs of stone. She looked closer. The surface part of a disfigured face, one eye staring sightlessly at the heavens. The upturned mouth was void of teeth in its wide death grin, and its eyebrow was thick and arched as if the face had been caught mid-expression.

A chill ran through her and she crossed her arms to bring back warmth. Following the line of the acutely angled roof, she could see the place where the grotesque face had at one time been anchored. It was smooth, almost polished, as if the wound had healed itself. But it was empty, too. Naked in its stark relief.

An unexplained sadness caught up with her then. This stone face, this protection from harm that poor Mrs. Wicker so desperately claimed, had fallen from grace and lay placidly among the ruins of the garden, this house, and her mind. Her industrialist grandfather had built this house in imitation of another era, and here it stood with what appeared to be little change for over a hundred years.

Rebecca turned to the dining table touched here and there with the dust of moth wings and hollowed insect bodies, and glanced at the floors now cracked and peeling with age. Small fissures traced fingerlike projections across the ceiling, and moisture leaks left permanent stains of circles within circles.

There was no one to care for this house anymore, nor, perhaps, for the mistress of the house. The wound from an anguished stone face may have healed itself, but no hope remained that the same could be done for Lillian Wicker. Time had taken its toll on this place and its inhabitant.

There was nothing else for Rebecca to do but her job. As painful as that was, she knew there was no choice. The pitiable old woman had stayed relatively alone far too long, and in her own way had become as desiccated and hollow as the insect bodies. The asymmetric house had produced in its last gasp a kind of quiet symmetry after all. One had inadvertently forced the care of the other. The only salvation left was if Mrs. Wicker's daughter could watch over her mother and lend the protection she needed.

"Sugar?"

Rebecca whirled at the voice. "I hope it's okay to look around."

"Come drink your tea before it gets cold. I've taken the

liberty of pouring you a cup. A slice of my grandmother's recipe for English Dundee cake goes quite well with tea. I think you'll agree."

"Thank you. It sounds lovely," Rebecca said, as she followed the woman back to the sitting room and resumed her place on the settee.

Mrs. Wicker went to the rolling cart that had appeared in the sitting room before the singular gaze of her husband, Walter. On it sat an ornate silver tea set, a small round cake cut into modest portions, and a thin crystal vase of symmetric blue and purple cowl-shaped flowers. "Sugar?"

"No. But I'll take cream if you have it."

"Just like you, Father," Mrs. Wicker said to the bust. "One so sweet doesn't need anymore sugar, does one?" She clucked lovingly, stroked his head, then passed the tea with a small slice of cake to Rebecca. The shiny, lean knife sliced through the cake easily, and she settled comfortably in the wing chair next to Walter to sip her tea and nibble cake like the consummate gracious hostess.

Rebecca cleared her throat and said, "The cake is wonderful. And the tea. Thank you very much for your hospitality."

"But you've made up your mind anyway."

"I'm sorry. I don't follow you."

Mrs. Wicker nibbled the cake, and pressed a crumb to her husband's lips. "You always liked Mother's cake, didn't you dear? Yes you did. And you liked games, too. I never cared one whit for games. Always thought them a waste of time. So you quit playing them." She leaned close to the bust and whispered in his ear. "Just like that." Her lips brushed against the ear and she stroked his head rhythmically. "And now things are all better."

"Please, Mrs. Wicker," Rebecca said, rising to place the empty plate and saucer on the rolling cart. "This is difficult enough as it is."

The shadow passed in the hallway again, then was gone.

Startled by the motion, Rebecca stared, shook her head, then returned to her ward. "I'm trying to do what's best for you."

"Are you?" Mrs. Wicker asked in anger. "Who better than I would know what's most suited to me? I am happy here among my friends and family. They watch over me. They protect me." She paused in consideration, then spoke quietly. "It is at this moment a courteous guest would recognize she is most unwelcome and leave."

"I can't do that."

"No. I suppose not."

Rebecca sighed in exasperation, and rubbed her hand across her face. The photo of Mrs. Wicker's daughter floated on unseen air currents from the settee to the floor to lay at her feet. Breathing deep, she offered the only thing left to her and this odd woman. "You say you see your daughter all the time. Is there any way I could meet her? Maybe talk with her?"

The old woman leaned back in the shabby wing chair with revelation and relief etched across her wrinkled face. "Is that all you want? Well, of course. All you had to do was ask." She added a quick aside to Walter. "See, Father? The games are coming to an end. Shame on you for thinking otherwise." Smoothing her wrinkled skirt, Mrs. Wicker eased herself out of her chair, and approached the window with a beckon to the case worker. "There's someone I want you to meet, Daughter."

Rebecca followed the woman to the window and looked out. "I don't see anyone."

"Look up, dear. Always look up."

Slowly, ever so slowly, Rebecca's gaze traversed the arch of the window, focused through the distortion of diamond pane glass, and came to a stop at one corner of the eaves. She stared.

It stared back.

Numbness rose in her tongue and throat. Then in her face. Her mouth opened in shocked silence.

The contorted mouth of the stone facade mocked her. Its scarred, and picture-perfect disfigured face waited as if in anticipation of—

—what?

Her vision blurred, then dimmed as if the lights had suddenly been lowered. She leaned heavily against the windowsill.

"Oh," Mrs. Wicker said with a hint of sadness, "you don't like her. And I did hope you two would get along. Didn't you, Walter? Of course you did."

A chill grabbed Rebecca. She shivered uncontrollably, and clung to the wall to remain standing but felt herself slide with new weakness in her knees. "Something's happening. I don't feel too well."

"Don't you, dear? Was it something you ate?"

Rebecca shook her head. Confused, she shifted her eyes to another corner of the eave. She blinked, then forced a liquid gasp.

This stone face was new. The effect of pain belied his otherwise youthful smooth skin and handsome features. And there, on both sides of the gaping mouth stopped short as if from a scream, was the unmistakable indentations of dimples.

"No." Her lips formed the words, but there was no sound forthcoming. Nausea welled in her stomach. She turned weakly to see Mrs. Wicker blow softly on the petal of a cowl-shaped flower in the thin crystal vase.

"My darling family of buttercups," she cooed to the flowers, "you and Grandmother's English Dundee cake always take care of me as well, do you not?"

Rebecca launched herself at the old woman, but fell short in a stagger. Grabbing the back of the wing chair, she fought for balance.

The shadow appeared in the hall between the sitting room and the kitchen. This time it stayed.

"Not yet, Henry. You know we must wait." She brushed away gray-white dust from her skirt and jacket, then leaned close to the bust of Walter. "Right, Father? You of all people know I'm right."

A spasm of pain gripped Rebecca across the middle. The muscles of her face froze in a distorted grin for a split second, then passed. She whimpered.

"Soon now. And all will be well again."

Panting for breath, Rebecca stepped toward the bust. "Please. I was only trying to protect you."

"You did, dear. And you will." Mrs. Wicker's hands rested briefly at the nape of Walter's neck, and then the stroking across his head began anew. "Be kind to our guest, Walter. Tell her."

But he didn't need to.

Rebecca looked into the dark, shallow, knowing eyes of Walter's bust, then followed the line of his high forehead to the shiny, thin veneer of his scalp. And there, where the plaster was worn down by years of loving strokes, was a wisp of gaunt gray hair.

Mrs. Wicker smiled warmly, and gently touched Rebecca's damp, cold face. "You'll protect me from harm, won't you? Of course you will."

MARC LEVINTHAL AND JOHN MASON SKIPP

Now Entering Monkeyface

1

It's always tough to meet a legend. Tough for the legend, and tough for you.

Frank knows this, knows it all too well. He remains, however, vastly unconsoled by the understanding. He is soaring through the infinite in a low-budget space-shuttle—the interstellar equivalent of a Greyhound bus—in the company of sixty-seven painfully ripe-smelling strangers. (He has counted them. More than twice.)

Moments before, the captain had advised them all to direct their attention out the window to their left. Suddenly, they're all crowded on his side, looking out the greasy windows at the surface of Mars, and one of its most famous landmarks.

Said landmark is also his destination.

He squints at it till his stomach hurts.

"It doesn't look anything like a goddam monkey face," Frank mumbles at last, as the shuttle burns the last few thousand miles to the spaceport.

"Sure it does!" yells Bradley, a cute little freckle-faced kid whom Frank will despise till the day he dies. "Can'cha see his sungoggles?"

"No."

"I still can't see it, honey," Bradley's oversized mother complains, clutching her rumpled *Weekly World News*. Monkeyface is on the cover, next to the headline LOVE SE-CRETS OF MARTIAN HEAD!; so, Frank notes, is one whole hell of a lot of airbrush work.

But this woman is that special kind of stupid: the kind that believes that spinach causes cancer, or that Bat Boy and Lisa Marie Presley's daughter gave birth to Corey Feldman in a time machine. She has also been a monumental pain in the ass, from the moment they cut loose of Earth's ravaged atmosphere: foghorn snore, sulphurous bowels, voice that sounds the way it feels when you bite down hard on tinfoil.

The woman leans closer, unspeakably pungent, acci-dently elbowing Frank in the head. "Ow!" says Frank, but no excuse me's are forthcoming. The kid yells something—he always yells—about why can't you use your mamagina-tion. Frank, in turn, blissfully mamagines cramming the little bastard right back into his mother's womb. Then he leans forward—far as he can away from her armpit—and re-news his attempts to see.

Could be any number of things, he thinks, turning his head sideways and back. Could be, like, a lady's shoe, or a boomerang stuck in a pile of dogshit. Fucking idiots. It's like seeing Jesus on a tortilla. You can see anything on any-thing, for crissake!

Then again, it's still hard to make out something even a mile across from this high up. And judging from some of the oohs and ahhhs, *somebody* besides Bradley must be seeing this thing.

Frank gives up, disgusted, unstraps himself, and cau-tiously stands before the throngs. "Stay outta my goddam seat," he warns the adorable moppet; then he elbows his way down the corridor to the head, grabbing seats when he can, pulling himself along.

He's thankful for small favors: He only has to piss. And

he's starting to feel a little less green than he has for the past two weeks. Mercifully, the perpetual dry-heaves stopped about a week out; but the nausea has lingered, like the stale puke smell that hangs around the shuttle.

He closes the door, makes a grab for one of the paper dick-cups and attaches it to the vacuum hose. As he fastens it over his spout, the unnerving grabbing sensation gives way to relief as the pee drains out of his bladder. It almost makes him happy.

The last time he remembers "happy" was the day Snid e-mailed and told him about the opening at his gas depot: Somebody waiting in line for a lichen-dusting gig finally got called.

"MARS NEEDS WOMEN . . . AND MEN!" So the lame MarsCorp slogan proclaimed. MarsCorp needed bodies: That was the truth of the matter. Therefore, MarsCorp checked your pulse, ran you through the Disease-O-Meter, and didn't ask you too many more questions. Bingo.

Frank could have gotten into the Terraform program any number of ways, but he waited to do it Snid's way. Snid had a dream (translation: scam), which he refused to discuss with Frank until he got there; but Snid guaranteed that it would turn them both into rich men, and fast.

True, Snid's record didn't bode well for the future. There was the chinchilla farm, the AMWAY thing, and of course the big Baldness Cure fiasco: the one that had sent Snid on his merry-all-the-way to Fuel Depot 807, Cydonia, Mars, in the first place.

Still, Frank had a feeling about this one. Snid liked to shoot his mouth about everything, to everyone; and the fact that he didn't this time made Frank wonder if his pal hadn't finally struck gold after all.

He remembers thinking, as he closed the door for the last time on his little rat hole apartment—beating impending eviction by mere hours—what some asshole had once said: even a busted clock tells the right time once a day. Or something like that.

That moment, that feeling, was sort of like happy. This,

on the other hand, is not. He spends a moment in the spider-cracked mirror, remembering precisely that fact.

"Yuck," he says, surveying his thin, greasy salt-and-pepper hair, his haggard complexion in the ugly hallogen light. Frank is fifty-five years old, and all he's got to show for it is paunch and wrinkles, creaks and complaints (plus a crappy little suitcase, the clothes on his back, and a handful of pocket change, diminishing fast).

Truth is, life has not been kind to Frank. Every dream he ever had fell apart, drifted off, was brutally dismembered, or—worst of all—never even came close. He is so far past mere "disappointment" that the concept invokes bland nostalgia in him.

He thinks to himself, Hey, I mean, here it is! The glorious Future of Humanity! Soaring to distant galaxies; reclaiming hope for the children of a dying planet. It's a golden age, alrightee.

And where the fuck am I?

I'm in the reeking commode of a ValuJet shuttle, trying to make sure I don't piss all over myself.

He waits a moment for the last drops to get sucked off before he removes the cup and shoves it in the waste receptacle. Even so, when he takes it off, a tiny golden globule escapes from his penis, does a merry slow caper around the toilet cubicle. The one serious design flaw in the human body, he thinks. Besides nostrils and sinuses.

And everything else.

2

The drive from the spaceport takes about seven and a half hours. It doesn't look much different to Frank than parts of Nevada he's driven through. The one big difference is that, if you got out to stretch your legs or take a whiz, your lungs would be in for a big, bad surprise. Not to mention that it's a bit chilly out there without your woolies—gets to be 95 below sometimes.

Of course, Bemy the driver tells him in clipped Bombay English, parts of the year are nice and warm; you could go out with a mask on and almost think you were back home. Almost.

The pressurized bus rolls through spectacular vistas of mountain ranges that rival the Himalayas, seem to poke out through the atmosphere (as Bemy tells him, some actually do). These are punctuated, on a regular basis, by mind-numbing stretches of desolation. Bemy doesn't have much to say about that.

Frank doesn't mind; he's just relieved to be free of all those people. (He's also slightly alarmed by just how much of the smell was him.) He spends a lot of time with his feet up on the seat, looking around, thinking too much about too little, slipping sporadically into alpha state. A long stretch of that goes by, and he almost dreams.

"Getting close now," Bemy says at last, rousing Frank out of a half-doze.

"How the hell can you tell?" Frank says, blinking his eyes.

Out of nowhere, a sign jumps up over the horizon:

> FUEL DEPOT 807—3 KILOMETERS.

And then, looming up right behind it, a gigantic, leering hand-painted chimpanzee dressed like an Egyptian, bearing the legend:

> NOW ENTERING MONKEYFACE
>
> POP. 12
>
> MYSTERIOUS CYDONIAN ARTIFACTS
>
> GIFT SHOP AHEAD
>
> VISIT ANGRY RED'S SALOON

"Sonofabitch." Frank gets that sinking feeling. He knows Snid's handiwork when he sees it.

Bemy's grinning ear to ear. "Think I'll get a drink or three while I'm here."

"Sonofabitch."

"Might buy one of those little monkey heads for my kid."

Frank's got his head in his hands. "Fuck!"

"Maybe one of those Monkey T-shirts."

3

His name is Sidney, but for some arcane reason, lost in the mists of time, he has always been known as Snid. No matter where he goes, no matter what new community he finds himself in, people who started out calling him Sidney eventually find themselves calling him "Snid."

Snid has not aged well. Ten years younger than Frank, but you wouldn't know it now. He has half as many teeth as he had at age one. He claims it's something in the water. Frank's ecstatic about that.

Snid takes a swig off his seventh straight Pabst. His adam's apple bobs in his scrawny throat like a Pez dispenser locked on semiautomatic. He's nearly bald on top, but hanging on to his mohawk, which means that there's a thin strip of baby-fine wisp streaking dead center down the length of his dome, and then a scraggy little strag-tail in the back.

It's the most retarded fashion statement Frank has ever seen, but the horror doesn't quite end there. Snid's tattoos, done as a teen back in the year 2040, are no longer even legible. They just look like bad ink smears. He's got them all over his body, but he still wears his vest wide open—tattered tie-die, with fringe—and his beer gut poking out through the breach like a mange-ridden medicine ball.

"Anyhow," Snid continues, "why am I not surprised that you think it doesn't look like a monkey face?" He shows all his teeth in an enormous grin. "Because it doesn't." He wags his finger in front of his face like a conductor's baton. "Because it DOES INT."

Snid takes a quick toke, and without exhaling, leans forward with a crazed conspiratorial leer. "Because when the U.N. Forces came up here and saw that face, that sphinx, that fucking mother-of-all-gargoyles—you know what I'm saying?—carved right into the Martian rock . . ."

He exhales, eyes gleaming, immediately takes another toke. "You know what they did, right? I mean, I think it's pretty obvious."

Frank slowly shakes his head.

"They came up here in their little Black Shuttles and—

pffft!—*chemically altered* the outside of the Monkeyface."
Exhaling dramatically, once again. "They didn't fuck with
the insides. No no no. Because that's where the shit is, man.
That's where all the shit is."

Frank stares at him, and Snid stares back.

"Y'see 'em coming out of there sometimes, man." Snid
tries to pass him the joint.

Frank looks at the joint, looks back at Snid. "You're a
fucking idiot, dude. Has anyone ever told you that?"

Snid breaks into that half-panicky, all-defensive, too-famil-
iar snivelface. His pale arms flap in protestation, smudgy wattles slapping the air. "There's nothing . . ." He falters. "I'm not
saying anything that's not . . ." Again. He sucks in breath, eyeballs balooning in moist entreaty. "There's *proof* . . . !"

"How much did those T-shirts cost you, anyway? What
made you think you would sell more than one of those
things a week, anyway?"

Snid attempts a weak response. Frank is not in the mood
to hear it.

"Hey," he says. "Fuck this, fuck you, fuck the fucking
monkey face, alright?"

He storms out of the room, Snid stunned into silence.

And then it's just Frank, in the parking lot, surveying the
grandeur that is Depot 807. He lights a cigarette, just to
commemorate the event.

There's a whole lot of Martian dirt. A few crummy hov-
els. A hot dog stand. All of it's enclosed in a terraformed
bubble, maybe thirty acres square, color of an Army blanket.
There's also a road that runs straight down the middle of
town. It ends in duel airlocks. They might as well be Hell's
gates.

Although, actually, he feels more like a tenant in a roach
hotel.

He thinks about Earth, about how depressing it had become. Wearing breathmasks on the streets. Mutant rats. The
whole ordeal. Suddenly, in retrospect, Earth doesn't seem
all that bad. There was a vibrancy to it. Mostly terror, but
still . . .

Frank finds himself suddenly longing for White Castle

wormburgers, teenage violence, the occasional toddler in flames. He pines for the constant sirens, the religious mania that took off around Millennium, the endless holovision bullshit, the bottomless corruption of home.

A tear wells in his eyes. It's almost embarrassing. If he had any pride left, he'd kick his own ass. But that commodity seems as far away as the ruins of Mann's Chinese, on that island of rubble once known as L.A.

Something opens up inside of Frank: a canyon at his core that is screaming to be filled; a now-accessible receptivity, yawning and yearning for meaning. He feels sobs well up as well, chokes them back, then says fuggit and lets them come.

They do. He's too numb to bawl—too completely in shock—so the sobs are like seizures from an engine utterly drained of oil or lube. He takes it as long as he can.

And then he can't take it no more.

Calling upon faith that he has never once possessed, he finds himself ridiculously praying to God. Face uplifted. Hands in the air. Desperately praying that there's an upside to destiny; praying for a solitary sign that this is not, oh please please please, the single worst move he has ever made in his whole dumb goddam stupid fucking life.

As if in answer, a mutant rat scurries across the street.

"Oh, good," he says.

And then Snid is there, still holding out the joint, like some kind of sacrificial offering. He pats Frank on the back with his free hand and says, "Swear to God, dude. This place is gonna be a gold mine."

An ugly toothpick woman appears in the street. Snid waves at her. She snubs him cold. "That's Sara," he says. "She's one red-hot woman. Won't be long before you can afford her love."

Frank doesn't have the strength to shake his head.

"Did I mention," Snid inquires, "that I'm running for mayor?"

4

Nothing changes, except that he's here. One truck rolls by about once every two hours, at least this time of year. Frank sits in the gift shop, tapping his toes, waiting for a trucker to come up, stick his retinas in front of his scanner, and ask for a pack of chewing gum or a slurpie or maybe where can a guy get laid around here?

Well, there are in fact four female humans here that run a kind of whorehouse/Laundromat, but personally, I'd go right across the hall to this hemisphere's largest collection of holo-porn for your wanking enjoyment, if in fact you actually want to enjoy yourself, pal. But as long as you're here, can I interest you in a fine plastic replica of a reconstruction of the original Monkeyface? Or one of these cute little stuffed monkeys in an Egyptian getup? Or how bout one of these "I've been to the Monkeyface" T-shirts?

Not me, he thinks, not in a million fucking years. I'll sit in this goddam place, I will take the money, I will live down the humiliation of ending up working in a gas station on Mars, but I'll be damned if I'll pimp or hawk these stupid Made-in-Taiwan pieces of shit for any reason.

He glances over at a row of Monkey toys against the far wall.

Frank wonders what would possess a man to take his hard-earned cash—money that he could have saved against his old age—and plow it back into this crap. The little simian heads look as though they are almost nodding their agreement.

Am I right, monkeyheads, am I right?

You are right, they seem to agree. Their faces beam in total blissful acceptance.

Frank is suddenly sceptical. Are you agreeing, my little friends, or are you in fact mocking me? Are you mocking me? For I am not a man to be trifled with. I can stand so much, and then . . .

A trucker is standing in front of the register, face mask pulled up over his wooly cap. He gives Frank a funny look before gazing up into the retina scanner. "Fill it on fifteen."

The register dings, and the monitor on Frank's side scrolls the driver's ID and credit info.

"All set," Frank says. "And have a really nice day, okay?"

The trucker dons his mask again, though he doesn't really need to; and in a moment Frank hears the northern airlock whoosh as it cycles. Another customer, Frank thinks, but nobody comes. Evidently, it was somebody leaving.

A few minutes later he hears the faint whine of the truck's hydrogen turbines as it rolls away. Once again, he is immersed in the ancient Mar-tian silence.

"Fuck this. Computer! Music. 'Highway to Hell'."

The computer complies. The antique strains of AC/DC, headbanging across from nearly a century ago, rise and kick away the oppressive quiet.

Frank always did enjoy the old stuff, never could go for the Ninja Gothic Kareoke Disco or whatever the hell they were shoving down people's throats this week. That's what he'd been trying to do back at the Dung Club, but nobody was buying it. Nobody liked the live acts he was booking. (Of course nobody really knew how to play rock and roll anymore—sure they could copy, but the *feel*—it was a lost art. Fucked him out of that job.)

But hey, look at these guys, he thinks. They seem to be enjoying it. The bobbing, spring-headed variety of monkeys rock sympathetically to the thudding kick drum. The stationary variety on the far wall seem to like it as well.

However, the Monkeyface plastic replicas appear to be on the fence, not sure whether or not it would be proper to admit to a pleasurable sensation. Kind of a fart-holding face.

"What is with you fuckers?" he asks them out loud, annoyed by their gassy stoicism. "Don't know how to have a good time?"

The Monkeyfaces eye him—in fact, it seems like they're all just staring at him—and the effect is entirely unnerving. Little monkeyfaced gargoyles, hording some kind of secret. Withholding the facts.

Just like Snid's Black Shuttles . . .

"I gotta get outta here," Frank hears himself say. Truer

words were never spoken. He thinks this, looking into those blank monkey eyes, and a chill wiggles through him, yanks him up on his feet.

There's a sign on the door. It says CLOSED, from where he's sitting. He walks over to it and flips it around. It's early afternoon on Mars. Snid will be pissed, but it's impossible to care.

"I gotta get outta here," he says again.

And then locks the door behind him.

5

It looks a lot like Ayer's Rock in Australia from this side. Bigger, though. It's a mile wide, and maybe a third as high. Frank's gotten used to the scale of things, like everyone on Mars does after a while, but this is still a majestic and lonely sight.

What he hasn't gotten used to is the solitude.

This, he guesses, is part of his therapy. Shortly after the feeble sun had cleared the horizon, he'd nabbed the settlement's Helsina 50, a kind of pressurized shopping cart on bubble-wheels, and rolled out over the plain down to the Face.

The Helsina is a cheap, dependable ATV; it's the Volkswagen Bug of Mars, and has made a few wiley Icelanders into rich men.

This particular ride is murder on Frank's hemmoroids, and the torpid drone of the engine does not inspire confidence. The fear of being stranded twenty kilometers from Monkeyface-proper (with only his Mars-wear between himself and certain death) lurks in the back of his mind.

It looks less like a Monkeyface from close up than it had from space. Or a face of any kind, for that matter. It looks like a big rock. Twenty kilometers away to the southwest are more big, portentious rocks—"The City"—that probably look even less like what people believed they really were.

Snid said that "The City" was where Martians lived before they died out, and we showed up.

"What the hell am I doing out here?" Frank mutters to

himself as he approaches the rough wall of the Face. He puts his gloved hand out to touch it, almost expecting some cosmic, magnetically encoded knowledge to take possession of him and impart the mystic wisdom of the universe. But it behaves pretty much like a rock the whole time. He takes his hand away and looks up the side, into the pale red sky.

"Well," he says to no one in particular, "that was great. What a fucking waste of time."

He smacks his hands against one another and starts walking back to the Helsina.

He thinks he hears something.

Of course, he knows right away that it's stupid. There is no one around for twenty kilometers in any direction. But still, every time he starts to walk again, he (imagines) he hears it, out of the corner of his ear: a rumbling, a hum, a ringing. It buggers description, partly because it isn't there (he knows), and partly because it is an alien thing, almost a non-sound. A carrier wave for some kind of zeitgeist to be decoded somewhere in his hindbrain.

"Oh, and what exactly are you being told, Mr. Radiobrain?" he asks himself.

Things long hidden, the non-sound tells him.

And something happens.

He sees the plain transformed; an overlay appears, and all around him are people—well, not exactly people, but close enough—and they're doing people things. Well, not exactly people things—the mannerisms and movements are a little different—but basically, they are people. They're wearing clothing that looks vaguely Aztec, vaguely Egyptian. Like something out of an old Heavy Metal comic, he thinks; and some of them are rolling through in some kind of wheeled contraptions bellowing steam. Some walk right through him.

And some of them are wearing a kind of helmet, black priestly robes a-flutter in their wake, and Frank can see one of their faces for a moment. It looks him in the eyes, kind of looks through him . . .

. . . and it is, of course, at that precise moment that Frank feels himself leave his body: floating above it, airlift-

ing like a skydiver film in reverse, up and up, while below him the whole of Martian civilization spreads out: "The City" a city indeed, with suburbs that extend for miles in every direction . . .

. . . and at the center of the sprawl and bustle—looking more and more like some infinite, incredibly complex hi-tech ant farm, the higher he goes . . .

He sees THE FACE.

He sees the Face, in all its glory; and he's amazed that he ever could have missed it before. It is not like the cover of the Weekly World News. *It is not like a monkey at all. Or maybe it is, but it's eons beyond. Like the difference between a paremecium and the Pope.*

The Face that looks up at him—mile wide, a third as high—is a carving of exquisite refinement and brain-devouring scale. An obviously superior civilization, calling out to some deity far beyond any half-baked, tepid vision cooked up by the mind of Man.

The Face is wise. The Face is calm. The Face knows all, and bides its time. The Face looks like it could just lay there forever. Completely content. Completely at peace.

And then it opens its eyes.

And that is when Frank begins to scream, mind wrenching as free from his soul as his soul has wrenched free of his body. Screaming as the mile-wide Face of Mars tears free of the soil and BEGINS TO RISE: *enormous throat blowing up through the dirt, making way for miles of seismic displacement as shoulders almost too huge to imagine plow up from below. Pierce the surface. Rise up. Shrug off mountains that vanish in great plumes of dust, like a smoke machine roughly the size of Rhode Island kicking up a cloud cover for the resurgence of the King . . .*

And then it's done. It's gone. It's all gone. He is back in his shoes, and the Martian world is silent. Frank staggers for a moment, then catches himself.

And all he can say is, "What the fuck was *that*?", the resonant edges of his words impossibly echoing off the sides of the Face.

Just a rock, now. Nothing more.

Then he's dabbing at his helmet as if he could catch the sweat now sluicing down his forehead, and he is thinking, what was that? WHAT WAS WHAT? WHAT WAS WHAT? Well, let's see. Okay. I'm just out in the middle of nowhere, stressed out because I am working at a gift shop in the middle of Asswater, Mars, and I . . . had a little episode. That's all. Just . . . saw a tableau of the Lost Civilization of Mars, complete with Monkeyheads. That's all.

And he thinks about how Snid planted this shit in his head. And he thinks about how it means nothing at all. Maybe it's just something leaking in from the Martian atmosphere. Maybe he just needs to take a deep fucking breath. Maybe he's been drinking too much. Or not enough.

He looks at the rock. It's just a rock. That's all.

He climbs back into the Helsina.

And stomps the pedal.

Hard.

6

That night, he dreams.

And in the dream, he is sitting at the gift shop/gas station counter. He hears the rumble of the trucks, the tick and tocking of the clock. There are monkeyheads, yes. They are watching him closely.

He sees a shadow whisper past the front door.

Cold dread wells up inside him; but in the dream, he is terribly calm. He feels himself rise, move toward the door, and there's no fear in the gesture.

But there's fear in his heart.

He steps through the door, and the shadow is there: not a shadow at all, but a black cloaked figure. It is running toward the gas pumps, arms flowing up and out like wings; and now Frank hears somebody screaming. But only for a moment.

Frank comes closer. The shadow stands before a burly, squirting man: first the throat, then the belly, opened up and flowing heavy. Frank comes closer, watching the shadow reach one arm up inside the trucker's torso; watching the shadow root around, more than elbow-deep, in the chest cavity.

Watching the meat-plop of wet red innards, corruscating onto the trucker's boots and into the dirt.

As the shadow comes out with a still-beating heart.

And pops it into a bag.

There is more screaming now, from a bus that's parked at the second bank of pumps. Frank sees a pair of familiar faces, pressed against window glass. The trucker collapses, and the shadow takes off; closer now, Frank sees the Aztec/Egyptian motif of the garb. Weird golden cuniforms around the cowl that conceals the head; more ornate golden squiggles as piping for the cloak.

Frank feels himself running, trying to catch up with the shadow. The shadow rounds the front of the bus, races between the bus and the pumps. The bus driver ardently scratches his ass, clueless till seconds before the end. When it comes, Frank can't see it.

But then the shadow whips and turns.

And Frank sees the blade in its black-gloved hand. Sees the blood and the steel and the black matted sleeve. Then he looks in the eyes of the Martian before him. Black, inpenetrable eyes. White, inpenetrable features.

The Martian shadow comes toward him, as the bus driver dies. Frank watches it all; but in the dream, he does not move. The Martian shadow walks right into his face.

Then passes through him.

As if he were not even there.

Frank turns. The Martian walks toward the front of the bus, where the door still hangs open. It steps inside. Frank follows, up the steps, past the vacant driver's seat, and walks the narrow course toward the back of the bus.

Beyond the shadow, he hears the howling of a woman and child.

It is at this point that Frank realizes he's walking through a dream. Up until that point, it had been too real. But somehow, recognizing the voices, he goes, "Hey! That's Bradley!" And it all starts to turn.

Suddenly, it all begins to make dream-sense. He knows a

wish-fulfillment fantasy when he sees one. And here's one now. Like that scene at the Face. Suddenly, he feels weirdly complicit. And not at all guilty.

While the shadow grabs Bradley and hacks off his head, Frank finds himself drawn to the cowering mother. She's as awful as he remembered her, and he loves her expression. It's completely terrified, and just as clueless as they come.

She flaps her arms as the shadow descends, but there's no self-defense in the gesture at all. She's just a fun bullseye target for some unconscious virtual role-playing game.

When she dies, it's not nearly bad enough.

Then the Martian shadow-icon moves back through Frank again, and he follows, away from the carnage. He almost feels like the game is running him, but dreams are strange, and he is consciously along for the ride.

The inside of Angry Red's is dank and hopeless as ever. Seven people are inside. That's half the population of 807, including Frank, who doesn't see himself seated at the bar.

The Martian-shadow hacks its way straight down the line of worthies: not pausing for hearts, but simply destroying. Severed neck. Torn-out lung. Gonads sliced up to jawline. A pair of eyeball piercings, and a slit throat for ballast. By the time Angry Red—a scrawny Irish/German mix—gets it up to find his handgun, his tongue is skewered to his pate: blade raking against the man's two front teeth as the point ventilates his hindbrain.

In dreamtime, the whole ordeal seems to take maybe a minute or less.

Now Frank is actively having some fun. Angry Red is a prick, and the rest are all drones. Not a soul worth preserving in the whole damn batch, including Sondra, who's the hottest of the laundry whores on hand.

Frank finds himself wanting to make whoopie with her corpse, absolved of the need to address her personal quirks with his social graces. But the shadow Martian stand-in is on the move, and he is moved to carry on in his voyeur's position.

So he finds himself racing down the street in pursuit, and the next stop is Sara's laundry love-in emporium. The washers and dryers are silent, but there's sound from above, and it's the base noise of heinous amour. Without a moment's hesitation, he races up the steps toward the second-floor brothel that houses, as it turns out, another half-dozen of Cydonia's finest.

They all die and die and die.

In his dream-head, he does the calculations. This leaves two, counting the absence of the one who just left. Lichendusting: a good call for whoever the fuck it was.

With a little time to spare, the Martian shadow goes over the victims.

Removing hearts, and bagging them.

Leaving very little left to be done.

But the fear returns to Frank as he follows the shadow back out onto the street, through the pluming Martian dust and toward the gas pump/gift shop fulcrum. There, he knows, the real Frank is just stupidly sitting around: waiting for the bus and truck to pay up and get out of here.

He finds himself thinking *oh no, oh no*; and he picks up his pace, but the shadow does, too. And he finds himself running, as the shadow takes off, and there's no way to make himself run fast enough.

He blows through the door, and all at once, he's in his chair.

And the shadow is standing directly before him. Seeing him now.

Seeing him clear.

Monkey boy, the shadow says. *And Frank has nothing to say. Monkey boy, we thank you for the hearts.*

Please deliver them unto me.

And Frank is rooted in his chair, watching a million years of perished wisdom patiently advance. He watches the face get closer, closer, from a yard to a foot to an inch.

In the dream, Frank intuits a subtle and ugly thing. Is amazed by its power. Is amazed by how far beyond all that he's known this dream seems to penetrate.

Frank feels himself lifting the bag. Feels the thump and the roll of the wet human hearts. They are rolling, from solid squirting here to spurting there.

All encased in the bag that he holds in his hand.

And then he sees the face of Snid, staring dumbstruck, and the dream starts to de-rezz. Sluicing light into the tangible darkness.

Reclaiming life, as it blows through the dream…

7

… and suddenly, he's sitting in the chair behind the cash register, just as he had last seen himself; and there's Snid, precisely where the shadow had stood in the dream.

"Frank, Jesus, don't hurt me . . ." Snid is saying; and Frank thinks, why would I want to hurt *you*?

Frank stands, and Snid backs away, cowering. "What's the deal?" Frank says.

And then Snid turns into the Shadow.

Frank blinks, looks at Snid, only Snid isn't there; and the walls start to shift from coal black to dull gray. It's like the dream is a colorless transparency, draping itself over the waking world.

Then Snid is back; and on the walls, the monkey faces are approving.

Frank continues to watch, fascinated, as different parts of Snid shift back and forth into Shadow. Shadow, then Snid, there long enough to repeat, "Don't hurt me . . . don't . . ."

Then that singsong, too, melts into the resonant carrier wave-song from the Cydonian plain.

Frank comes around the counter, puts his arms out to cowering Snid. "Of course I won't hurt you, you shithead . . ." he says.

And then he sees the bag he's clutching in one of his own outstretched hands: paper and plastic, with dark brownish blood seeping through the soaked paper, pooling in the bottom against the white plastic.

The Shadow stops cowering and approaches Frank. Putting out its arms. Mirroring Frank.

Take it, the Shadow thinks at him. *Take your face, Monkeyman. Come take it, Monkeyking.*

And now the Shadow wears a face—sad, lovely flat beyond-simian face—and the coal black eyes pin him even as he approaches it to merge, to receive (he knows) his own true face.

As they press together—front to front, arms out-stretched—they merge; and the resonant note ramps up to a crescendo that strangely twists back into Snid's tortured screams as Frank lets him drop, strides to the front door, popping yet another into the fresh bag of hearts.

His offering to the People.

He can hear them already, as he walks toward the southern exit of ghostly Depot 807. Can hear the cheers, in the ancient tongue, soon to be revived again.

They are cheering for him, for the next great champion.

The One Long-Awaited, finally back where he belongs.

"ALL HAIL MONKEYFACE!" they call out as one as he pauses, humbly, at the door.

"ALL HAIL MONKEYFACE!!!" they call out again, and he is nearly overwhelmed by the glory.

"ALL HAIL MONKEYFACE!!!" comes their delirious cry.

Then he opens the airlock, and lets in the sky.

LUCY TAYLOR

Tempters

———

THE DOCTORS HERE AT St. Benedict's Hospital say I nearly died. That I lay bleeding on the deserted street for perhaps two hours before a pair of blokes on their way home from a nearby pub came upon me.

As for what caused my awful wound, I said I took a tumble on the wet sidewalk and landed on a broken bottle. I can tell the doctors doubt my tale, but they're pretending otherwise.

In the meantime, I have to piss off out of here and finish what I started, then rescue the kids and return to London. For the *sheela-na-gig* and her mate torment me even now. My mind's become their Garden of Impure Delights. Their vile fantasies run rampant like a garden of gorgeous but unholy blossoms.

It all began when my wife Sybil stole my kids away.

The first time I saw Vic and Heather after she took them, it was playtime at Wee Ones Daycare Center, and they were in line behind other kids to go down the sliding board. Six-year-old Heather, a strapping girl in red shorts and a *Lion*

King T-shirt, went first. Vic, a tubby boy with his mother's
cinnamony hair and valentine-shaped mouth, hesitated, ignoring the other children's cries to get on with it, then
wooshed down with a look on his face suggesting a skydiver
with a deflated chute. He broke into a wide grin at the bottom and scurried 'round to join the queue again.

How beautiful they were that day, small, clothed cupids
with dimpled flesh flushed pink beneath the morning sun.

Watching them, the decision I had agonized over for
weeks was made: At first chance I would snatch the kids and
get them away from here.

By God, I've never broken the law before. I wasn't raised
that way. But these were my kids—a part of *me,* my flesh,
my being—how could I let them go?

Funny how life alters people, brings out things in them
they'd sworn were never there, makes them into something
completely different from what they were. Me, for instance,
turning into the devoted father after my babies came along.
Who'd of dreamt it!

I never wanted kids, you see, but the wife insisted on it.
You know how women are. Don't feel complete 'til they've
pushed out one or two more squalling mouths on an already
overpopulated planet. Sybil had Heather first and then, less
than two years later, Vic. Wonderful kids. So perfect in their
purity and innocence it was tempting to believe they be-
longed to another species entirely, the species of children,
who were of a different ilk completely than the world of de-
spoiled, deluded adults that had produced them.

Adults like my wife, for instance.

When we'd first met, I thought her feces smelled like
fresh bread and her tears were holy water. Eyes the color of
Delft china, long shiny auburn hair. A big-hearted woman, I
thought she was, like my Mum. But later, after the kids came
along, I began to see a streak of meanness that at first I'd
taken for charming cheekiness. A slutty-sweet way of rolling
her hips and lowering her eyes that, more and more, she reserved for other men.

Still and all I loved Sybil. Would never have walked out
on her, not hardly. Yet she done it to me. No note, no call. All

she took was the kids' toys and her jewelry, everything that is, except her wedding ring, which she left atop a pile of fag ends in an ashtray. Perhaps she figured there was nothing left to say. Who knows? Like wicked children, women are. You can't know what goes on in their minds. Secretive lot, always whispering behind their hands. Plotting, planning strategies a man can only guess at.

I had my suspicions, too, about how Sybil treated the kids. Nothing overt, you understand, but small things, subtle signs that I felt hinted at an unhealthy physical intimacy. For one thing, Sybil nursed the kids an excessively long time, almost as if it were she who needed the experience more than they. I remember growing queasy at the sight of Vic, a husky toddler, pawing at her swollen breast, wrapping his fat pink mouth 'round the nipple. And sometimes she allowed both in the bed, touching up in ways that made me wonder where one draws the line between normal parental love and a pervert's vile inclinations.

When Sybil left me, it only confirmed my fears that her relationship with the children was something other than a natural mother's love and that her desire to end our marriage was more the need to have the children to herself than the desire to escape from me. An idea which kept me up many a night, pacing the floors of our flat in the West End, imagining all sorts of unsavory activities she and the kids might be engaged in.

But I was fortunate in one respect—Sybil had not only left me, but her young man as well. The lad had a problem with alcohol. One night he rang up, pissed as a newt and blurted out the name of the town my misses had moved to. I'm not certain it was an accident—I suppose lovers feel the bitterness of rejection as much as jilted spouses.

The next day I quit my job as a chippie for Thames Construction, motored north to Kilpeck-on-Tees, a sleepy village a stone's toss from the Scottish border, and rented a modest room at the Copgrove Arms. I had a bit of money saved and planned to take my time.

With a bit of detective work, it didn't take me long to locate the flat Sibyl had rented and to learn she'd taken a job at Wee Ones Daycare Center, run out of the church hall next to St. Cuthbert's Cathedral on Mulligan Street. Heather and Vic were enrolled there, and often, watching from my vantage point in the cathedral grounds, I would see the three of them going in together, Sybil in the middle holding onto the kids' hands.

St. Cuthbert's Cathedral, I discovered, boasts a large and immaculately-tended garden that extends from the west side of the building to a low hill leading to the day care center and its adjoining playground. Lily of the valley, iris, and white and yellow roses line the winding paths. A hedgerow aids in blunting the playground clamor.

At mid-morning, during playtime, I could sit on a stone bench, pretending to read, and spy upon the children. Sometimes I'd see Sybil, too, if it was her day to be playground supervisor. I noticed she'd cropped her hair off to a bob and she was growing tubby.

Once in a while, I got there early and strolled the garden, admiring the flowers and the statues of the saints. It was while doing this, meandering along one of the quiet paths, that I got an appalling shock.

I couldn't believe what stood before me. What I saw was like one of those vile Soho strip joints—oh, not that I attend, you know, but I'm aware of what goes on—but not here! Two old statues, human, more or less, dwarfish in size and lewd beyond description. The male, an ape-like thing with bald head and bugged-out eyes, wanked his enormous rod with both hands, looking as if he meant to climb himself. A feverish look of manic sexuality lit his moronic face. Next to him, a grinning female reached between her buttocks to spread herself wide open as the Cheddar Gorge.

In disbelief I ran my fingers into the female's granite trough. You could have thrust a boxing glove inside with room to spare. How could anyone, I thought, ever desire intercourse after seeing sexuality depicted in such a disgusting manner?

But that, I guessed, was the point. The clerics of another age intended to portray sex as bestial and nasty, the vagina in particular being the pathway straight to Hades. The purpose of these exhibitionists must be to cool rather than inflame, revolt rather than arouse. Totally opposite to anything desirable. Any act of copulation between them would have to be grotesque, repulsive, even comic.

I found myself resenting the sculptures and the clerics who had commissioned them. Well and good, perhaps, for the Middle Ages. But in the modern world? I wondered why the gargoyles had not been relegated to a cobwebbed cubbyhole in some obscure museum, fit to be studied by that special type of scholar who uses academic research to rationalize a fascination with filth.

Pondering such things, I saw an old vicar approaching, his gait wobbly. I watched him release from his robes a flask of the type one brings to a rugby match.

I greeted him with an amiability meant to assure him I in no way cared what he might be imbibing at 8:30 in the morning, and asked why statuary such as this should be on display in the Cathedral garden.

"Ah, the *sheela-na-gig* and her brother," the old man chuckled. His whiskey-breath popped me in the nose like a rolled up newspaper.

"The what?"

"The female's of a type known as a *sheela-na-gig*," he said. "Celtic in origin. These two are among the finest in the British Isles. Better even than those in the cathedrals at Tugford and Whittleford."

He said this with pride, as though cathedrals competed with one another as to which possessed the most revolting statuary.

"Originally," he went on, "the *sheela* and her mate were part of St. Cuthbert's east facade, but by the eighteenth century it was decided their presence violated Christian sensibilities, so they were buried out front of the cathedral. A couple of years ago, when they widened Mulligan Road, the statues were rediscovered. Our local archeologist claims they're twelfth century, probably modeled after the Frankish gargoyles. Wonderful, aren't they?"

Thinking drink must have taken a toll on the old geezer's wits, I remonstrated, "But they're indecent."

He eyed at me as though I'd questioned Mary's chastity. "If these offend you, consider that some cathedrals in Southern France have far more shocking statuary—anus lickers, snakes entering a woman's vagina, men with phalluses that—"

"So we're to count our blessings that the statues aren't even more disgusting?"

The vicar's veneer of tipsy cheer was wearing thin. "By depicting lust in such a manner, the gargoyles warn us of its evils. A quaint notion in these times, to be certain, but insightful as to the nature of the Medieval mind."

So saying, he continued on his stroll, pausing only to give the privates of the flagpole climber a passing pat.

All right, I thought, *they're but statues. Let it be.* But I could not. For it seemed to me they embodied the very core of human ugliness, depravity, the dirtying up of all things good and innocent and clean. Putting ideas in people's minds. Ideas that wouldn't have been there had such images not stirred them.

My point was proved days later when I came upon a young girl in perverse dalliance with the male gargoyle. Torn jeans, a nearly see-through blouse, the torso of an undernourished teenaged boy. In need of a good scrub, that one. She fondled the male, running her hand up and down the enormous shaft, cupping a palm 'round the grapefruit sized testicles as if to weigh them.

I cleared my throat. "Disgusting sight," I said, referring as much to her as to the statues.

She whirled, looked flummoxed for a moment, then let forth a peal of laughter.

"The wanking artists? I think they're cool. Me Mum's a jewelrymaker and she's done pins and pendants of 'em. The little wanker, he's real popular. The fairies give 'em to their lovers. A dick big as a man's waist. Don't I wish . . ."

Black bars seesawed across my vision. All I could think was that this bird probably posed exactly like the *sheela* when she took a man to bed. Legs splayed, prying herself apart as if for a self-administered gynecological examination. *Come look at me. See everything. I have no shame. Come join me.*

"It's revolting," I said. "They reduce love to a dirty joke, an obscene music hall routine. What in hell are you laughing at?"

That silenced her. Her orangey-pink mouth twisted as if to spit out something sour. "What're you, from the Mary Whitehouse League or somethin'?" She continued sliding her hand up and down the granite shaft. A female Pan playing an oversized lute. I felt the pressure of each fingertip inside my pants.

"Stop that!" I seized her wrist and bent it back. Her face went stark white, causing her lipsticked mouth to appear brighter and more clownish. "Go! Get the hell out of here! Don't think you're fooling me. I know what you're about."

I let her go. She bolted, rewarding me with a stream of vulgarity that didn't stop 'til she was nearly out of sight.

In my head, I heard again my Mum's voice as she stood above me, belt in hand. *Don't think you're fooling me, you evil boy. I see through you, Harry. I know what you really want. Don't think you've deceived me.*

This is an evil place, I thought. *An evil town, evil people. No matter what, I must rescue my kids from here.*

Weekends were the worst, as I had no easy means of spying on the kids. On Friday I motored down to London, not quite certain what I meant to do, but restless, needing something. Under the jaundiced light of a lamppost, I spied a pack of youngsters. They wore drab, ill-fitting clothes that looked to have been scavenged from a rubbish bin. But if their attire was plain, their bodies were anything but. Spiked hair in colors most often found inside a Chinese restaurant, labyrinthine tattoos scrawling up bare biceps, exposed cleavage. Beneath the sludgy glow of the lamppost, their ornate piercings shone.

Tarts and rent boys, the lot of them. Why else to display their bodies in the dead of night on a London street corner? And so young—the ages my Vic and Heather'd be in half a dozen years—these slut-eyed youngsters arranged across the curb like a lewd display of manikins in a porno-shop window.

The eyes, the stance, the wanton vigor all echoed the appalling figures in the churchyard. A lad with a crotch so achingly defined it brought a blush to my face just to look at him. A tiny girl with nipples peeking through the top of a halter so black and shiny it looked to have been dipped in motor oil.

I felt them gawking at me, sizing me up. Their stares like indecent touches. *What does he want? A boy? A girl? Both perhaps?*

I hit the accelerator, rounded the corner, then found myself making another left-hand turn, steering 'round for a further peer at the ragged mob of them, in particular the girl in the black halter.

Bugger the perverts who'd cast an eye in her direction! She ought to be at home in bed, or studying her lessons. Where were her parents? What sort of people might they be? Or perhaps they were like my wife. So self-absorbed they wouldn't notice as their child grew from an adorable innocent to a slinking tart. Might even secretly jag off on it—I may be only a humble chippie, but I've read my Freud—offspring acting out the ugly fantasies of the repressed parents.

I know what you are, Harry. Don't think I don't. You've not fooled me for a minute.

And suddenly, as though my fury had been stored in a box that had got suddenly violently overturned, I felt rage inundate me. Like drowning in an acid bath. The fury blinded me, brought spasms to my hands. The car careened across the island in the middle of the road, tires making scorched-cat sounds. The street kids flung themselves out of the way of my vehicle, which leapt the curb and plowed into a rubbish bin before swerving back into the street.

Later on, I examined the tires and bumper. No one got hit, I don't believe. No blood I could find.

The following week, I finally got my chance at Vic and Heather. With the playground supervisor distracted by a lad

with a scraped knee, my kids decided to investigate a hedge-
hog near the hedgerow where I'd hid myself.

"Heather! Vic!" I stage-whispered. Heather's eyes
widened. Vic looked simply stupefied. For a moment I'd the
idea he didn't recognize me.

I called them to come over to me.

"Does Mum know you're here?" Heather said.

"No, it's a surprise, I've come to take you two for ice
cream."

"We're not supposed to go with—" she almost said
"strangers," then stopped herself.

But Vic broke in, exclaiming, "I want mint with sprin-
kles!"

"I'll have you back in no time," I said. "Your Mum won't
even know you were gone." Gripping each by the hand, I led
them toward the gate and the carpark beyond it, not the more
direct route, where we'd have a greater chance of encoun-
tering the drunken vicar, but along the narrower, winding
path passing the cathedral.

Where *they* were, but I wasn't thinking of them then.
Only of spiriting my children out of there while I had the
chance.

Heather saw the gargoyles first. She scrunched her face
and made the kind of *bleh* sound she used to make when
Sybil served sprouts.

But Vic, in his enthusiasm, ran into them, and stopped in
his tracks, eyes huge with horror and amazement.

He seemed to rise several inches off the ground, as
though someone had yanked him up with a noose, then he
burst into hysterical sobs. I tried to calm him, but his
screams were drawing attention. A teacher ran up the em-
bankment toward the garden, searching out the source of the
screams.

"I've got to go," I said. "Don't tell your Mum I was here.
Promise?" They nodded, and I loped rapidly away.

After that day, foul dreams commenced to plague me.

That night, I watched the gargoyles creak loose from the
stone and lumber toward the playground, mouths working

like the jaws of obscene nutcrackers. I understood what it was that drew them, the purity and innocence of the children, the hunger to defile and despoil.

I wrenched myself free of my stupor and plunged after them. In the cartoonish manner of dreams, a shotgun appeared in my hand. I aimed and fired at them. Reloaded and fired again.

Suddenly my mother stood behind me. "Bad boy," she whispered. "I know what you're about, what you dream of. I've found the magazines you hid. I know you're a pervert."

I whirled and unloaded both barrels into her chest. She flew backward, as if her dress were caught beneath the wheels of an express train. Meanwhile the gargoyles cavorted and clapped like teenagers at a concert.

I awoke, quivering like one in the throes of a malarial attack. Terrified, and understanding that Vic and Heather had somehow stirred desire in these monsters.

Tormented by the nightmare, I dressed and drove to a pub I'd begun to frequent, thinking, I suppose, to down a pint or two and have another go at sleep.

By the time I arrived, the pub had shut, the only sign of life a boy of no more than fourteen hanging around in the adjacent alley beneath the awning of a pawn shop, taking shelter from the cold drizzle that had begun to fall. Slitted, haunted eyes. A heroin pallor sallowed his skin. Sizing me up as just another punter, I could tell. "Well?" he said, "I don't read minds. You got to tell me what you fancy."

The question, in its brazen bluntness, took me aback.

"That isn't what I want," I said. "I'm not that sort."

He sneered. "You're out this time of night passing out religious pamphlets."

"Do you have parents?"

"No, I was hatched. 'Course I got parents."

"Where are they?"

"Why you want to know? You going to ring them up?" He thrust his hips at me and patted between his legs.

"Your parents, do they know what you're doing?"

"Know? The old man bloody well buggered me, he did. Mum was sick a lot the past years and me, I had a swishy way a' walkin'. So what's a man supposed to do, when his wife's of no use and his son's got a tight bum like a virgin girl? 'Keep it in the family's,' what he said." He made a languid up-down motion at his crotch and grinned the gargoyle's grin.

"I told you I'm not that way," I said.

"No, you're from Rentboy's Anonymous and you want to introduce me to my Higher Power who'll save me from a life of squalor, sin, and sex addiction."

"Stop wanking!"

"Bugger off, you old—"

"I said stop!"

I don't think the boy was dead when I left him, merely unconscious, but there was a lot of blood. I rang the police from a telephone box and informed them a young man had been badly hurt, and told them where he was.

Then, not wanting to wait any longer, I drove to St. Cuthbert's to deal with the creatures that tormented me.

There was a thumbnail moon by the time I arrived at the garden, but almost at once thick clouds plucked it from view like an insect under a wadded hanky. The rain began in earnest. I took a claw hammer from the selection of tools in the boot of my car and plodded into the darkness. The going was slow. I reached the gargoyles just as the rain became a downpour, pelting my face and hands with stinging force.

I attacked the priapic one first, bringing the claw end of the hammer down on its lewd dome.

I know what you're about. I'm not deceived. Evil creatures. Coveting the kids.

In the dark and rain, I couldn't see the extent of the damage I'd done, but I heard the chip of stone, the dull thud of the hammer. I swung again, but the wet granite seemed to writhe into thrashing life. It bunched like a flexed muscle and twisted in my grasp. The claw end of the hammer slammed into my left wrist with stupefying pain. A tree of lightning crucified the sky. Black blood poured from my wrist.

Leaving the hammer where it fell, I staggered back to the main road, thinking to drive myself to the hospital. But the pain left me foggy and numb. I couldn't find my car and the darkness had grown thick as tar, the rain felt like chunks of ice shot from an air rifle.

The last I recall was seeing Vic and Heather romping toward me, naked in the pouring rain and, God help me—they were mimicking the gargoyles. Their mouths were opened and, as they approached, seemed to unhinge like the jaws of a python, offering a darkness more vast and solid than any I have known as I screamed myself unconscious.

The day after the incident, I begged a paper from a nurse and found a brief paragraph on page two, something about an act of hooliganism on a local church. Police called in. No witnesses. No competition with the brutal beating of a street boy and the pub brawl on page one.

That was a week ago. This morning I left the hospital and returned to St. Cuthbert's to finish what I'd begun.

Dressed like a laborer, I carry a pickaxe with me to the spot where the gargoyles are, but my jaw falls open in disbelief when I see they've gone. I search the garden for the vicar and find him in a secluded nook, worshipping devoutly at the flask.

"The statues that were here. What's become of them?"

The old lush favors me with a conspiratory grimace which I assume at first to be a grin, until I realize it's more a baring of teeth. "Vandals, louts attacked the statues. We had to crate them off to the Victoria and Albert for their own protection. Damned foul luck, they're unique, a bloody bawdy pair." He stroked a palm across his beaded brow. "I'll miss those sweet thorns to the prudes, the *sheela* and her brother."

I should feel vindicated, I suppose. After all, the obscene figures are removed. Or are they? For though the gargoyles may be gone, the fantasies they inspired remain. Their foul sewage taints me still.

We know what you're about, Harry. You can't fool us. We are not deceived.

"You all right, lad?" the vicar says. "You look as though you could use a shot of whiskey."

Suddenly I realize how I've been tricked. The gargoyles

may be gone, yet the true monsters linger still. They didn't leave the church grounds when their likenesses were carted off. No, something else has occurred, something worse.

I gaze down upon the schoolyard, watch the kids trot out onto the playyard. I listen to their squeals and titters. Heather and Vic are among them. Sybil, as well. Heather's eyes are bugged and wild, and Vic, when he thinks no one is looking, dips a grimy hand inside his zipper. And the others, no better—broad inhuman grins, mouths opening like loose sphincters, murmuring vile promises and filthy incantations.

I know then what I must do. After the vicar is dealt with, everything progresses quickly.

I hoist the pickaxe with its crimson tip, step over the old geezer's body, and head down the hill at an easy lope.

Several of the kids see me coming. At once they hide their gargoyle leers, their faces disguise themselves again as sweet, innocent children, but it's too late now, for I know better, yes, I do. I chase them down, swinging the pickaxe again and again and again. I neither flinch nor hesitate, for this time I am not deceived.

BRIAN HODGE

Cenotaph

AFTER MORE THAN HALF a year since their debut tumble into bed, this was their first genuine trip together. But a whole month across an ocean was overdoing it. A month either cemented the bond or drove the wedge, and barely a week after debarking at Heathrow, Kate found herself warming to the idea of scrapping their return tickets in lieu of seats on the Concorde. Financial cretinism, but it would halve the hours next to Alain and his perfect face.

A few days in London, then southwest, until they'd nearly run out of England altogether in rocky, windswept Cornwall: "My gran came from here," Kate had told him. "Left when she was a girl, but the place never left *her*."

"Yeah?" Alain had said. "I guess everybody's from somewhere, aren't they?"

He'd not even meant it as a slight. It simply hadn't occurred to him that he should be interested, even if it did mean a bit of diplomatic faking.

When feeling lazy or scapegoatish she was tempted to blame the bad days on the gap between their ages, her eight-year jump. Sometimes a crack, sometimes a chasm. Look at them thirteen years ago, where they'd been in the world. She'd awakened one morning after sleeping in her car, and shot the photo that won her a Pulitzer. Twenty-three years old at the time. Alain, on the other hand, would've been flunking driver's ed and drowning in hormones.

Thirteen years later Alain Carreras still exuded the petulant charm of a scruffy teenager. This, she decided, was the problem: It was more appealing on paper. At least there you could furnish your own depth. Alain walked through real life as though having stepped fresh from one of his Gap ads, longish hair mussed so artfully it must've taken hours, and really *didn't* have anything else going on beneath the surface. In some people—rarer than you might think—surface went all the way through.

Cornwall was the better part of a day behind them, the county of Shropshire ahead on the A49, when he could no longer take the weather.

"And they call this a climate? I thought climates *changed*." Too bored by it to sound good and annoyed. "How long does monsoon season last in England, anyway?"

Mist. It was a heavy mist. Barely needed the wipers.

"Look on the bright side," Kate told him. "Does wonders for your complexion. No sun? Might as well not even have packed your moisturizers. You'll go home looking like a milkmaid."

There. That made him happy. She was looking pretty peaches and cream herself, while the damp had fluffed her hair, not quite shoulder length, just enough to make her want to grow it again, renew the wild black mass it used to be before she got practical.

But shoot Alain in the same frame as some of the millennium-old carvings strewn about the region, and the contrasts between skin and stone would never be any more pronounced. Along with the other big difference: Some of those graven faces actually smiled, without fear of giving themselves wrinkles.

Between the two, she was already anticipating which would be better company the next few days.

• • •

The thing about England was, you could scarcely throw a mossy stone without hitting something to remind you of how vastly *old* the place was. Back home, Kate Haskins had snapped her cameras across a country that had been given birth by this one, but had lost its mother's stately sense of time. A century just didn't mean as much to one as it did the other.

Kate's grandmother had cherished the antiquity of her birth country, and the history, myths, and legends left behind. Normans, Vikings, Angles, Saxons, Romans, Celts . . . from Bronze Age on, each had left its imprint on both land and psyche. The island absorbed them all, wasting nothing.

The Church of St. John the Baptist was just such a reservoir of essence. Buildings from the Middle Ages could today be found in total ruin or as well-preserved as last week's corpse, and here stood one of the more fortunate. Stood as paradox—both monument to time, and entirely divorced from it.

West of the motorway, it was shielded from passing sight by hills, and by sufficient oaks and ash to retain just enough of the fourteenth century to send most people seeking a warm hearth the moment the sun began to blend into the Welsh border.

It had been her gran who'd discovered it to be something of a legacy from the earliest known roots of their family.

St. John the Baptist came from the second phase of English Gothic architecture known as Decorated, while still showing clear Norman roots, from the semi-circular arches of its walls, to the square bell-tower whose parapet looked better suited to archers than priests. The leaded glass of the rose window would catch the morning sun, when it shone at all. Rain or shine, though, the stone walls emitted an earthier feel. Once brownish-gray, they were now mottled green with lichen, as though having come to peaceful coexistence with the land on which they stood—a part of it, rather than its conqueror.

"So this is it?" Alain said. "This is all there is to it?"

"This may surprise you, but there's also an *in*side."

They were still in the car, parked. Alain was starting early today. If he was *too* bored, their bed-and-breakfast down in Craven Arms wasn't out of hiking distance. Two mirrors, too; those would keep him entertained awhile.

"Well, the way you were talking, I was expecting, like, Notre Dame." He shrugged. "Color me underwhelmed."

"If we were at Notre Dame, you'd be underwhelmed because it wasn't the Taj Mahal. Anyway, what can *your* family lay claim to creating?"

He turned toward her with lifted eyebrows and an up-turning of the corners of his mouth that passed for a smile without actually creasing anything. "Well . . . *me*."

"See if *you're* still standing in six hundred years," she said. "Then we'll talk."

They began circling the outside of the church. The closer she got, the greater the hand-me-down pride in one remote ancestor and his hammers and chisels.

The place was a well-kept wonder, a menagerie of impossible life seeming to burst from inert stone. The downspout carvings themselves were only the most obvious, jutting from the roofline as though in that instant before springing free. Here, a lion-faced dragon with fangs bared. There, a gigantic snake with its coils bunched against the eaves, mouth yawning wide. Next, a pensive creature with an ape's face and feathered wings, perhaps stymied by its own contradictions.

"Hey, look at this!" Glancing at each once and getting it over with, Alain was ahead of her, around the southwest corner. When she caught up to him, he pointed with delight.

The figure overhead was entirely human, enviably limber. Its feet and face were flush with the stone, while it bent double, thrusting a naked rump toward Wales. Undeniably male—a plump scrotum bulged down between its legs—his hands reached back to grip both buttocks and wrench them wide apart. On rainy days . . . well, no imagination needed.

"There's a rumor going around that's how Fabio got his big break," Alain said. "I might've been the one who started it, too. I can't remember."

She stared without comment. This was the first one that

she suddenly remembered, the first thread between now and nearly three decades ago. Her parents had brought her on vacation—seven, eight years old, had she been?—and it made sense that nudity would've made the biggest impression. At that age, fanciful beasts were one thing, but genitalia quite another. Each inspired its own terror, curiosity, and awe; but for staying power it was no contest.

Kate remembered her mother's hand on the back of her head, trying to redirect her attention. More than once. Inside and out, icons of fertility and sexuality abounded here, to the chagrin of parents of precocious children: a man sporting ram's horns and a proud erection; a hag stretching open her oversized vagina. And every few minutes, Mom's hand and an exclamation of wonder at some more benign thing invariably in the opposite direction. Must've thought she was being subtle about it, as subtle as the carvings weren't, but the *real* message had been quite clear.

Their circuit brought them back around to the front, where serpents twined up the columns on either side of the wooden double-doors. Every overlapping scale was distinct, while together the serpents made a weave of Celtic knotwork too intricate for her eye to unravel. Each column was crowned with a fearsome head whose toothy mouth chomped down over its top with grim relish.

The bas-relief arch above the doorway showed a row of bearded Celtic heads, smooth-faced and oval-eyed. Below them, a row of ravens whose beaks pecked and tore at less placid faces. And below those, the centerpiece: a huge, robust face grinning defiantly from out of a nest of oak leaves. Between face and hair and leaf there was no distinction. All were one and the same.

"The Green Man," Kate murmured.

Alain blinked up at him. "You mean one of these ugly things really has a name?"

"He's a kind of forest spirit. Growth, regeneration, renewal, like that," she said. "It's all coming back now. My gran used to tell me about some of this ancient imagery. And they're *not* ugly."

"Between me or him, now, really: Whose tongue *would* you rather suck on?"

"You never know. Maybe I wouldn't mind a mouthful of sap."

"I think you may be as kinked as your"—Alain rolled his eyes up at the carvings—"whatever he was to you."

"Grandfather, a few dozen times removed. And he had a name. Geoffrey Blackburn."

And here he'd stood. Shaped that stone, breathed life into it as surely as those he'd chiseled it for believed God had breathed life into Adam. She wished she could see with gargoyles' eyes, back through time, see him as these sculptures would've seen the face of their maker. What Geoffrey had looked like, if after six and a half centuries there was still some family resemblance.

Had he used himself as a model? Left his face slyly wrought somewhere in these stone tapestries? You'd think so, that there'd have to be enough ego to strive for whatever immortality it could. Maybe right above these doors, in the Green Man himself.

Sacred? This place was that, all right. But it was becoming harder and harder to think of it as a site that would've had any connection with Rome.

Certainly Rome—as well as the Anglicans—had nothing to do with it now. The Church of St. John the Baptist was time's relic, administered by English Heritage. That they charged her a fee to get past the door seemed a minor slight; but how would they know?

Inside, more of everything . . . more faces, more beasts, more fabulous hybrids. If there'd ever been so much as one crucifix here, it'd been carried away, rather than anchored in rock.

Besides the woman posted at the door, there were only three others here. The man she took for the curator was serving as guide to a pair of elderly women who clutched ghastly handbags and hung on his every word.

"Oh yes, quite the risqué rogue, was our Geoffrey," he was saying. "Didn't waste many opportunities to raise an eyebrow."

"Filthy, just *dreadfully* filthy," one of the ladies said. "I can scarcely bring myself to even look at some of them."

"You must put yourself in the medieval mind." The curator was all tweeds and patience. "Had a belief, they did, that the forces of darkness and evil were all around, but one good look beneath a pair of dropped knickers was enough to send them running."

"Why, good lord. Whatever for?" said the other woman. "No. Don't tell me. I don't wish to know."

"Shame, maybe," Alain muttered to Kate, but by some prank of acoustics the other three heard him plainly as well. An audience was irresistible, so he elaborated: "I mean, you always think of demons as being well-hung, don't you? But what if they're not? What if that's part of their punishment?"

They simply stared, all three, with their mortified British faces. One of the women lingered on Kate's photographer's vest and its bulging pockets as though they must've held weapons.

Don't mind us, she wanted to tell them. *Just the barbarians from America.*

"No?" Alain said to their silence. "Just a thought."

"First one today?" Kate whispered through clenched teeth.

So much for a genteel homecoming.

After she'd tried her best to salvage first impressions, the curator, Nigel Crenshaw, began to thaw. The old women wasted no time in retreating, trailing wisps of lavender in their wake, but Crenshaw seemed to study her and Alain as if they were as exotic as anything chipped out of limestone here.

"A Pulitzer, how very interesting," Crenshaw said. "Yes, I remember that photo quite well. Not often that one sees so much historical nastiness summed up so . . . succinctly."

Nastiness. Typical British understatement. Her famous photo had been taken during a protest siege laid to government land in South Dakota's Black Hills by militants who'd broken away from the American Indian Movement. She'd been clicking away on one of their leaders, on an observation deck, the instant he'd been shot by a sniper with the U.S. Marshals Service. By a fluke of perspective, a streamer of the man's blood looked as though it might spatter the four gargantuan witnesses behind him: the sixty-foot granite heads of Mt. Rushmore.

Everyone remembered that photo. She'd met a few who hated her for it, but only in her own country. Crenshaw wasn't one of them.

He was, in fact, delighted by the documentation showing her to be a lineal descendant of Geoffrey Blackburn. Her grandmother had spent a quarter-century tracing the family tree to learn this, finding Blackburn and his works quite the pot of gold at the end of the rainbow.

Maybe it would pass, but Kate had been bitten by the notion that there might be a photo book in him. If Hildegard von Bingen could become fashionable, why not Geoffrey Blackburn?

On the spot, Crenshaw began bursting with fact, hearsay, and legend—his, the zeal of a man who'd devoted his life to something without having found nearly enough ears to share it with.

"You know what they called him, don't you? 'The Michelangelo of the Gargoyles.'"

She'd heard that much, at least.

"Predated Michelangelo by a century, so not in Geoffrey's time, of course. But what a testament to the man's genius, that *that's* the artistic standard future generations measured him by. Some of the work he did, why, stand it next to 'David,' I say."

"Wouldn't you have to break it loose of the church first?"

Crenshaw sighed. "Thereby hangs the pity."

The makers of most ecclesiastical sculpture had labored in anonymity, he told her, but even in his own lifetime Blackburn had enjoyed renown, although some would've said infamy was the better word. Wherever he employed his craft, there soon followed claims of people seeing movement in his creations.

"Not just the rabble, either," Crenshaw said. "Plenty of priests, too. Bishops, cardinals. Even a pope or two. People have been claiming it for centuries. Still do, but it wouldn't be force of suggestion. I daresay most have never even heard of Geoffrey Blackburn or his reputation."

"And this followed him everywhere he worked?" she asked.

"More or less. Although—and mind, I've never undertaken a formal study—it would *seem* that the later in Geoffrey's life he worked on a church, the more instances you have of people claiming to see movement in the carvings he did there. Makes sense, though. He continually refines his skills, his works appear progressively more lifelike."

"And the Church of St. John the Baptist is . . . ?" Kate said. "My grandmother told us . . ."

Crenshaw nodded proudly. "The last and greatest jewel in our Geoffrey's formidable crown."

"So most of those reported movements, they've come from here, then," she said. "Have you ever—?"

"Oh heavens no. Perhaps I stare at them too directly for them to ever get the better of me."

He filled in the sketchy background. Blackburn had supposedly apprenticed under the master sculptor hired for the Octagon at Ely Cathedral, built to replace a tower that had collapsed in 1322.

"Surviving records indicate he worked on the roof bosses." Crenshaw pointed to a face leering from a junction of two ceiling beams. "Same thing, only in stone, and much higher. Where the ribs of the vaults meet. Gossip had it that his master was more than a bit consumed with jealousy by the end of his apprenticeship."

After Ely, he'd worked on other churches, abbeys, and priories in East Anglia, and within a decade his reputation had taken him even to France, to supervise the sculpture workshop at the cathedral nearing completion in Chutreaux.

It was this aspect of construction that gave her pause. That Geoffrey had been the master sculptor of record someplace—or one of many, on a two-century project like Chutreaux—didn't mean any particular piece had come from his chisel. In fact, most couldn't have. A few, maybe, but the rest only done under his tutelage.

"When comparing, one can tell," said Crenshaw. "I've been to Chutreaux. Been to most of the others. And everywhere, it's two different classes of work: Geoffrey's. And everyone else's."

"But here, though. My gran said he—"

"Did very nearly the whole thing. Yes. You'll find the odd bit here and there that doesn't seem up to his standards, so he must've had an apprentice from time to time. But overall? If you see it, chances are *he* did it. Evidently the last two decades of his life to just this one building."

"Wouldn't that have been a little atypical?"

"Too right. Perhaps a bit mad, considering the ah, well . . . subject matter."

"Are there any records saying *why*?"

"Nothing ever found from the time, no. References in a couple of late-sixteenth-century histories, now, yes, claiming all sorts of deviltry had been got up to here, but one must consider intent. They'd just had the Reformation, so such accounts do tend to smack of appalled Puritans tarnishing the repute of Catholic leftovers." He broke with an unexpectedly mirthful smile. "Rather like what those two lavender-scented lovelies will be telling whomever will listen about your gentleman friend."

Alain. She'd forgotten about him, and glanced around until Crenshaw pointed him out, dozing on a seat while slumped against the outer wall of one of the congregational stalls.

"Except," Kate went on, "I don't see anything here that's patently Catholic."

"Precisely why the Calvinists and their ilk were convinced that Catholics were idolaters, if not outright devil-worshippers. Quite the inharmonious—"

Abruptly, Crenshaw cut himself off in mid-sentence, glaring across the church at something behind her. Kate's first thought was that Alain had roused, and what was he desecrating?

"You there!" Crenshaw shouted. "Get out of here! Right now!"

She turned. Not Alain—he was blinking drowsily at the

ruckus. Instead, it was somebody past him, lingering beside one of the carved pillars. Kate couldn't see him well; he was backlit by the light coming in through a lancet window.

"Out of here this minute, or I'll have the police down, this is the last time, do you hear me?"

He was a sturdy sort, she could tell that much, with broad, heavy shoulders, and hair that in silhouette appeared shaggy and unkempt. When he moved out of the direct light, she saw that he wore a topcoat that might've once been pricey, but had more likely been salvaged from a wealthier man's trash, and beneath it, a dark cableknit sweater, tattered here, unraveling there. His beard hadn't fully grown in, a few weeks' worth. Age? Hard to determine. Old enough to have earned a few lines. More than she had.

"He's only annoyed he didn't collect his fee." It took Kate a moment to realize the man was addressing her. He then turned his bemusement on Crenshaw. "Oh, I *have* it. All you need do is come take it from me. Fair enough, innit?"

Crenshaw didn't move, seething at the man, who held his own ground. Alain glanced back and forth between them as though having awakened in the middle of the wrong movie. Finally the man relented, but with an air of having once more proved a point he'd proven many times before. He strolled toward the narthex and Crenshaw followed, marching a consistent dozen paces behind, until the man was out the door, leaving behind his own distinctive odor.

"Bloody vagabond," Crenshaw said. "How it is he gets in here I'll never know."

"There aren't any other entrances?"

"None we've found in six hundred years. Slips in when both Mrs. Webster and I are distracted, then hides, is my guess, but I'll give him this: He's a first-rank sneak. Been doing it for years, on and off, and we've never caught him."

"Do you even know who he is?"

Alain was walking up, wrinkling his nose in distaste. "Somebody who's never learned why God invented Calvin Klein."

"Must live around here somewhere," said Crenshaw. "I'm sure the locals know him, but Mrs. Webster and I motor up from Ludlow, so these are hardly our people." He shook his head. "Never harms anything, it's just the . . . *idea*. But should you encounter him while taking your pictures, I'd keep my distance if I were you."

Kate nodded, more to pacify than agree, then registered with a shock what she'd missed until now. Surely she'd have seen it as a child, but the recollection wasn't there. Today, for all intents and purposes, was the first time.

It stood upon the wide platform above the doors, a life-size effigy whose heavy-lidded eyes stared the length of the nave, toward the rose window where he would greet each rising sun. In shadows now, his mystery was heightened tenfold, hunching with muscled body and sinewed limbs, balanced on wide-stanced cloven feet. His magnificent head was ever-so-slightly inclined downward, as though deigning to acknowledge whoever paused to stare. Alain, she knew, would kill for his cheekbones, while shunning the wild serpentine beard. And he'd have no use at all for the goat horns, sprouting robustly from either side of the forehead, curving back and to each side. A long tongue wagged from between parted lips with a grin of lascivious delight.

Here was the face that had given medieval churchmen all the devil they'd ever needed.

"Pan, right?" she said.

"Or Cernunnos. Call him what you will."

"I can't believe I didn't notice him before now."

"You'd be amazed how many don't, until they leave," Crenshaw said. "One could be excused for thinking he enjoys it that way."

She was a betting woman all right, but knew no one here well enough to make the bet in the first place. It was nothing to be proud of, anyway: She was giving the relationship another week at most, after which Alain would find an excuse to go home early.

It'd been entirely physical anyway, had just run its course sooner than expected. With his mussed raven hair and caramel skin and long-lashed eyes, he'd never been less than beautiful, always a willing model for her artier, more indulgent shots. Most were admittedly Mapplethorpe-influenced, somewhere between deifying and fetishizing. She'd strip him down and zoom in for the kill, the shadowy, side-lit curves of his arm or ass like a blown-glass vase, then devour everything the camera had left. By now, it didn't amount to much.

After early enthusiasm, Alain now hated England, she deduced, because nobody recognized him. Maybe two dozen ads and dialogue-free parts in three music videos meant he didn't have to walk *too* far back home before inspiring double-takes, but fame apparently ended in U.S. territorial waters and it was eating him alive.

He sulked. He was depressed by British television—only four channels?—and claimed he couldn't find anything but snooker tournaments and sheepdog trials. He ran up a huge bill calling home to reassure himself his world still existed. She'd thrust the keys to the rental car at him—"Take it, go, go find something you are interested in"—but he wouldn't hear of it. Steering from the right on the wrong side of the road? It was no way to drive, not on these twisty, narrow lanes.

Meanwhile, Kate settled day by day into this green and misty autumn sojourn, realizing, Alain's kvetching aside, she'd not been this content in . . . she couldn't remember.

Nigel Crenshaw entrusted her with a spare key to the church so she could come early or stay late if she pleased. He loaned her books about the region, which she eagerly browsed at the bed-and-breakfast in Craven Arms and in the area pubs. Little, if anything, was said about Geoffrey Blackburn, but they did help her lift him farther out of the vacuum of dry intellect and make him into a fuller person, in the context of a real time and place.

With every day, with each roll of film she filled with his labors, the more Kate wondered about him: What had driven him to such excellence instead of settling for being a merely competent artisan? Why had he so thoroughly committed himself to rendering the grotesque instead of threatless, tranquil beauty?

She thought she understood after a few days, understood

as one can only after admitting to infatuation with someone not only never met, but who never could be.

Perhaps, despite the institution behind his commissions, he had seen enough of the world to harbor no illusions of any divine goodness, and spent a lifetime chipping its cruelty into something more manageable. Or making intimate friends of its harsher faces. Or telling everyone else what he knew in metaphor they understood.

She could identify. So maybe Geoffrey Blackburn wasn't so much ancestor as mirror.

Despite everything it had brought her, she often felt that winning the Pulitzer for that hateful photo had been the worst thing that could've happened to her, at least at such a young age. Not that recognition itself was harmful, more that she'd been left with the inevitable what-next syndrome. The odds against her ever again being in such a right time and place were astronomical.

And she doubted she would have the stomach to again witness anything comparable. Even the first time, she'd shot the picture like a pro, but later cried for a day and a half.

She'd shot news only for another thirteen months.

Commercial photography paid better, after all, and nobody died in front of the lens.

At least once per day, while working outside the church, she caught him watching from varying distances and differing vantages: the man Crenshaw seemed to believe he'd run off.

Some days he stood in the meadows, others near the treeline. Never any threat, hardly a movement at all out of him, he'd stand with hands in his pockets while autumn's bluster flapped his coat about his knees; stand there like a displaced and rough-hewn Heathcliff.

At first she ignored him, turning away nearly as soon as she saw him; he'd be gone the next time she checked. Day by day she grew bolder, returning his gaze unphased, and finally snapping his picture, then crossing arms over chest, determined to outstare him. He threw his head back with a hearty laugh, then walked into the trees until trunks and leaves swallowed him up.

She inquired about him of the locals—as long as there were pubs, there was no shortage of opinion on anything—finding that no one knew much about him, only that if he made his home nearby, none could tell you how to get there.

"Jack" was the best anyone could do for a name—this from a man who swore his good friend's cousin had been drunk with the fellow. Popular opinion pegged him as a full-time wanderer—maybe a refugee from one of those rolling communes that motored up and down Britain—most certainly on the dole, and that the area around the Church of St. Johnny B was the crossroads of his travels.

"Fixate on an area, some of 'em, they do," she was told amid the warm, rugged timbers of the Rose & Thistle. It boasted more Jack-sightings than anywhere else, until the next pub. "Get it in their heads it's a holy place, from back before God had whiskers, and next thing you know, you're up to your bollocks in Druids."

"Bollocks is right," countered another. "You wouldn't know a Druid if he hoisted his robe and showed you his own two."

She joined in the beery laughter, but still, this could've been close to the truth. Many of these medieval churches had been built on the ruins of far more ancient sites. Some contended it symbolized a firm triumph over pre-Christian beliefs, others that it was a way of coaxing stubborn pagans toward conversion.

If this was Jack's interest in the place, she approved, even found something endearing about it, the romanticism of clinging to what time had rendered obsolete before you ever had a chance to call it yours. Longing to reclaim it despite the world's derision.

Kate thought of Jack from that first day inside the church, however brief the encounter. Recalling his smell, of all things, a not-unpleasant musk of maleness and the outdoors, as though he'd slept beneath a blanket of decaying leaves, on a pillow of moss.

Alain's liberal dousing with cologne seemed more ridiculous every day, and the nights when they made what passed for love, in a kind of energized mutual loathing, she won-

dered how he'd react if she came to bed with that green and
woody scent on her. If he'd recoil in disgust, accuse her of
going native. If his rejection would be her own rite of passage, an emancipation to proclaim: *I'm sick of you, sick of
your kind altogether, finally, ready for real human beings
again, real passions instead of plastic.*

The next day there was no good reason to waste film on
more exterior shots, but she did it anyway, working until he
was simply there, Jack on the crest of a green-domed rise.
She took a chance.

"I'll bet you know things about this church," she called to
him, "that even Crenshaw doesn't."

"Not much challenge in that," he called back. "But don't
get me started on what you won't want me to finish."

She waved him forward, and he came, in nearly every
way the antithesis of Alain. Quick to smile, with the crinkles
to prove it, and probably just as quick to show anger. If he
gave one thought to his appearance you'd never know it.
And that wafting scent, as earthy as Alain's was bottled.

"So let's have one of them," she said. "Crenshaw's blind
spots."

Jack stroked and scratched at his days of beard. Threads
of gray she hadn't noticed before were obvious now, in the
sun.

"Didn't happen to tell you anything about the money running out, did he? During construction? And how they reme-
died that?"

"Not a word."

"I didn't think he knew of that one. Well, then. It was the
early 1350s when the coffers scraped empty, and they had to
close down. Stonemasons, carpenters, mortar makers . . .
nothing to pay them with. How you going to raise the rest, if
you've half a church?"

"I don't know. Fleece the flock?"

"Good start, but you'll need more than what you can tap
them for. So, for the next two years, they displayed their
relic. It's to be St. John the Baptist's, right? If you remember
your church schooling, maybe you'll remember the way he
ended up."

"His head on a platter, right," she said. "For Salome."

"The very same." Jack grinned. "Got themselves a stray head, then, put it in a box, called it John's own noggin, and charged by the peek. Did a fine pilgrimage business with it, too. Enough to finish what you see here."

"How do you know this and Crenshaw doesn't?"

"Well, now, that you'd have to ask him." Jack shook his great shaggy head. "Not to be too hard on the old boy. It's good he cares as much as he does about the place. Just that he's too much of a Presbyterian to *really* understand it."

"No such obstacles with me," she said. "Agnostic, reformed."

"Oh, better than that. This place was in your blood from the start."

"I didn't realize you knew. About my ancestry."

"Got ears, haven't I? They work just fine." When he smiled, his weathered face became a splendid interplay of crease and hair and twinkle. Such pictures he'd take, in his natural element; for her, an antidote, maybe, to the vapidity that came out of her studio, every blemish erased by airbrush or microchip.

It occurred to her Jack could've wrought a thousand delusions about this place and believed every one of them. Sometimes the mad did speak with the most conviction. He could've left a dozen bodies buried along his wanderings, for that matter.

"They worshipped heads, you know, back when," he said, with a nod toward the church, as if reading her mind and deciding to play with any misapprehension rather than assuage it. "The Celts. The reverence outlasted the actual headhunting itself. Still, you have to know that before you can ever understand this place."

It made sense. This region, she'd already learned, had seen a tenacious holding to Celtic tradition from the murkiest antiquity, surviving well past Saxon times. That much was clear enough from the edifice itself. The gods of old religions become the devils of the ones that follow, and the Christian hell was full of them, but here in this particular stone they straddled two worlds in uneasy collusion.

"Then the dedication to John the Baptist," she said, "wasn't just coincidence."

"Now you follow. What you had here were people who found this headless saint a lot more interesting than the main character. You should count the heads carved here. Inside, out. Forget anything with a body, just heads. Come up short of a hundred, I say you're not trying very hard."

Kate looked above, found two within paces of where she stood; one was clutched in the hands of a giant who was stuffing it into his maw.

"Geoffrey, they hardly knew ye," she said, and wasn't it the truth. Inside, in less obvious nooks and crannies, she'd found the editorial imprints of a man clearly antagonistic to Rome. One bas-relief depicted a fox in bishop's robes preaching to a flock of geese. Another, a bloated pig in a papal miter guarding a horde of coins.

"That two-year down spell they had?" Jack said. "Didn't apply to him. Geoffrey Blackburn never stopped work."

"Meaning they paid him on the sly, or . . . ?"

Jack shook his head. "Meaning he thought it more important this place be finished before he died. Never went hungry or cold, him nor his family, though. Always some dressed venison or fowl showing up at the door, baskets of vegetables. Wood pile never ran low." A broad grin. "There's instant karma for you."

She looked into his eyes, green and merry, for any hint he'd been pulling her leg for minutes and was about to slap his thigh and howl. But no.

"What *is* your story, Jack?" she asked.

"Mine?" He looked taken aback. "Now, how can I tell you that? It's got no end yet."

She took him by the arm, steering him toward the west end. "Come on. We're going inside. To count heads. My treat. They can't throw you out then, can they?"

"You're missing the point of all the fun."

"Like hell," she said. "Wait'll you see Crenshaw's face when he sees you have every right to be there."

• • •

When he did it, Alain took the easy way out, the time-honored tactic of cads and cowards: told her in a public place so she'd be less likely to cause a scene.

Showed how much he'd been paying attention. Opinion on them at the Rose & Thistle was neatly divided. She was liked, he wasn't. It wouldn't be difficult to make his strategy backfire. Making two ways the joke was on him.

"I didn't think you'd last *this* long," she said. "I had a bet with myself you'd crack by day before yesterday."

Alain masked every emotion well but surprise. She knew he was thinking it wasn't supposed to be this way, she was supposed to be devastated. To plead. How could any woman in her right mind not? Especially her—older by nearly a decade, and getting no younger.

The truth? His youth and beauty really had been good for her ego. What she hadn't expected was how great the boost discovering she could wave goodbye to all that as easily as she could a pigeon who'd eaten popcorn at her feet. Now that he'd seen that departure alone wasn't going to ruin her, he progressed to petty jealousy.

"I thought I'd hang in London for a couple days first." All nonchalance, holding up his cellular phone. "Guess who's in for a shoot. Andi Wexler. I called my agent earlier and got her number, so she's . . . expecting me."

Kate nodded. "When you kiss her, make sure it's before she disappears to stick a finger down her throat. Otherwise, she might not've rinsed well. You . . . *knew* about the bulemia, didn't you? No? Forget it, then. Just try not to think about it."

Low, but the only kind of parry he'd understand.

She could've told him of the past few nights: *Sixteen hours ago, in bed? In my mind it wasn't even you. I replaced you with a stranger whose last name I don't know and it was better that way, and it was just as better the night before when I dreamed of him, when I pulled him deeper into me than I ever did you on your best day. I did it because he smells of an earth you don't even like to touch. I did it because he's real. More real in a dream than you are in the flesh.* Could've told him, but didn't, because Alain's comprehension stretched only so far.

As easily as that, they were done. He got a few steps away, then turned as if he wanted to say more but had no idea how it was done. As emotions went, he handled bewilderment well, too.

Amid stone and timber, fire and ale, she wished for misery but felt only relief. Misery would be proof of something, that she had risked and cared enough to want to die for a day or two. That she'd been *alive.* That for the next few hours she was entitled to drink with strangers until she was stupid, and listen to their advice, their comforts, cry if she wanted.

Instead, she couldn't even imagine tearing up his pictures after she got home because they were technically flawless. Good God, had it always been this bland? Sometimes she thought herself cut from denser stuff than Geoffrey Blackburn had ever worked on.

She ordered a shot of Welsh single-malt anyway, and they all laughed when she told them that his name wasn't even Alain, but Albert. He'd been held in low regard ever since loudly observing that most of the local faces seemed modeled on the potato.

She drank for an hour, then another. The fire had warmed her body, the whiskey her belly, the company her soul, and she allowed how much better this trip would've been if she could've shared it with someone who appreciated such modest provincialities.

She was achieving her latest annual drunken epiphany that it was time to change her life, when a regular came in shrugging the October chill off himself and telling of the wreck he'd passed a few miles down the road. Police already on the scene, but what a mess, some idiot driving too fast for the curves, looked like, slamming head-on into a stone fence and through the windscreen he went, straight at the curled-up edge of the smashed bonnet.

That son of a bitch, was the first thing she thought. *Doesn't drive one mile since we came here and now he takes the car? Thinks he'll drive it to London?*

For the rest of the night, the mood in the Rose & Thistle

was glum. She remained by the fireside, listening to talk and awkward condolences, clutching her thick pullover sweater tightly about her, and fearing if she left the fire she'd freeze.

And by last orders, word had it that, peculiarly enough, the authorities still hadn't recovered Alain's head.

Late in the night, unable to sleep, Kate left the bed-and-breakfast before its walls grew more claustrophobic. Earth and sky and stone seemed the only things lasting enough tonight, so she walked in their company. Around her the town lay in stillness so deep it felt as though her heartbeat might wake it.

She was more than a mile along to the church before she even knew she was going there, and quickened her pace once she did. The town behind her, meadow and pasture rolling away to either side of the lane, she felt the deep age of the land as she rarely had during the day. Now and again, something would rustle, out of sight, on the other side of hedgerows and stone fences. Foxes, maybe. Once, a vigilant border collie.

Near the church she spotted a sheep, strayed from its fold, thick-shagged and four-horned, a breed she'd never seen back home. She knew in her heart that a sheep was all it was, but as it stood against the fence, munching vigorously on grass with the moonlight glinting off eyes like wet glass, it seemed less beast and more facade for an intelligence that lurked and watched, biding its time with inhuman patience.

The church's bell tower and faces rose black against a few moonlit gray clouds as she ascended the hill. Below the eternally grinning visage of the Green Man, she used the key entrusted to her by Crenshaw. This was the first time she'd entered without a camera dangling from her neck.

Kate turned on only as much light as needed to prevent collision with anything; would've brought candles had she known the night would end here.

Step back, look up, and there he was, Pan in bestial glory. "Go on. Move," she commanded. As its maker's descen-

dant, who was more entitled to see this happen? "*Move.*
Prove it. What are you waiting for?"

Nothing. Neither shift of cloven hoof, nor waggle of
tongue.

Down the aisle, to the altar, to her knees. It seemed that at
some point tonight she should offer a small prayer for Alain,
but no time or place had seemed right earlier. Now that they
were, she couldn't think of what to say, or where to send it.

"Why are you crying?"

She thought she'd heard someone enter. Suspecting who
it was before his voice confirmed it. "Is that what I'm
doing?"

Jack allowed her her space, coming no closer than the
first congregational stall and sitting inside. "Saw you from
the trees. Thought I'd pop in."

"Don't you ever sleep in a bed? Or anyplace with a
roof?"

"Not if I can avoid it."

"Well, you can't for much longer. In another month
you'll freeze to death out there."

"Won't I just," he said, with his broad merry grin—
vagabond, madman, whatever he was. "But, death . . . its
longevity? Exaggerated a bit, you ask me."

"Not in my experience." She wiped her nose on her
sleeve. What a sight she must've presented, no longer feeling capable of even seducing the village hobo.

"Why are you here, Kate?" he wondered. "Not tonight, I
don't mean tonight. Not even asking *you*, really. Just . . .
Blackburn's granddaughter: why her, why here, why now?"

If there were reasons they were beyond her, beyond Jack
too, but the faith he held in their being was touching. He left
the oaken stall to wander, hands trailing over wood and
stone, caressing each surface as though an immortal
beloved.

"I've seen a lot of Britain," he said. "Seen it thrive, seen
it fall. Rise, fall again. One group taking it from another, 'til
they lose it themselves. What it is now? Sad ghost of someone's old dead ideas of glory. But no matter who's mucking

about on top, it's always been the land itself that holds the magic. Can't kill a thing like that, now, can you?"

He'd done it so smoothly, she nearly missed the way Jack had begun talking as someone who'd witnessed more history than was one person's due.

"Don't know much of America. I know it's *there*," he said. "I've wondered if any of you ever look this way and realize it's your own future, too. Are you that far along yet?"

"Yeah," she said. "We just pretend we don't notice."

"Doesn't matter." He began moving closer. "Let me tell you a story. Used to be an island, there did. Full of forests so deep and thick, you could drop in something big as London is now, never find it again. Not everything that lived there stuck with either four legs or two. Good days, those. But nothing stays the same forever. People come in, they bring their own ideas along, chase out the old if they don't murder it first.

"What you had here over six centuries ago were amongst the last people to remember the forests as they'd been. Put yourself in their place. Got no use for any pale dead god all the rest are only too eager to kill you for, if you don't convert. Not when the forests gave you all the gods you'd ever need. Gods that were old before that pale dead one was even born. So what do you do?"

Was he insane? Or merely eccentric?

"Hide in plain sight?" she said.

"*Now* you're thinking like a wily pagan. If the Church steals the faces of your gods and turns them to devils, who's to say you can't steal them back, and right under the Pope's nose.

"But they didn't stop there. When time came to build, they found themselves a likeminded man who knew stone so well it was said he could talk it into making room for a soul. So that's where the old gods went." He lifted his hands as if to seize the church and wrap it around him. "Geoffrey Blackburn sealed them in, on every side."

It made a fine story. Now, if only it were true.

"Why bother with that?" she asked, because it was fun to

play along, and meant she didn't have to think of Alain. "Why couldn't the gods take care of themselves?"

"Because their time was up. For a while, at least." Jack's furrowed brow creased deeply. Was it only poor lighting that he looked worse than he did before? "The other day, told you of the Celts, their reverence for the severed head? One of the women from those final days, she could work a real magic with heads. They'd talk to her. Sing for her. See where she couldn't—even into the future. They saw what was coming. Had two hundred years of bloody Crusades by then, and they'd already come home to the west. Wasn't a time to be clinging to gods that would get you killed, and the gods of the woods loved their followers too much to let that keep happening to them. Rather sleep than see it happen. So sleep they did. Waiting for a better time to wake again."

It was such an Arthurian notion, she thought, the once and future king become once and future gods. Again, if only it could be true.

Kate was about to excuse herself, time to go back to the B&B, when Jack straightened to his full bearish height and smiled down at her, such a peculiar smile, protective and courtly and wistful.

"I should be saying goodbye to you now, Kate Black-burn. I'm glad I have the chance. Didn't expect I would. You don't mind if I call you by that name instead?"

She told him of course not, asked where he was off to. Jack turned at the waist to gaze toward the narthex and doors.

"Autumn, nearly over. Winter, nearly here. Said it yourself already, Kate. Time for me to find someplace to freeze."

She went to him, near tears again, gripping him by shoulders stout as oak boughs. For one night, for one lifetime, she'd seen enough of delusions and death. She hit him, cursed him, trying to beat sense into him, then he pulled her close to still her arms, like a child, and stroked her hair. She breathed in the scent of him, so rich and green and woody it had to come from someplace far deeper than the shabby fibers of his clothes.

"I watched you from those same trees, when you were a

wee girl," Jack whispered. "'She'll be back,' I told myself. 'She'll be back one day.'"

Then his mouth was upon hers, with a kiss that tasted of time and seasons, loss and renewal, and if her intellect yet resisted, her body knew, and her blood. These obeyed the cycles of the moon already, didn't they? They knew that if she plunged into him, and he into her, there awaited for her wonders of which she could scarcely conceive. And conceive she would, if the time was right.

But not tonight. When he pulled his mouth away it broke her heart.

"No," he said. "Not as I am now. Not half-dead."

Half-dead? Even then he was more alive than most she knew. "Then when?"

"Come spring. When I live again."

So easy for him to say. He'd be the one for whom those months meant nothing. What a long, terrible, cold winter hers would be.

"I've one more thing needs doing," he said. "You won't like it. I'd rather you not watch."

She wouldn't be dissuaded. He could do no worse than she'd seen already.

Solemn, Jack left the church a moment. When he returned she understood his concern, and despite all she'd said, still had to avert her eyes. Mangled by glass and steel, yes, it was, but the head was recognizably Alain's.

"I know what you're thinking. You'd be a fool not to," Jack said. "But he *did* lose it by accident, nothing more. I'll not be a fool, then, and waste it."

The head was bled clean by now, and he set it aside while grappling with the altar. He struggled, strained, and with a deep grinding of stone it shifted, tilting up and to the side. If doubts still lingered, this did them in. No one man could lift this hollowed limestone block.

Beneath the altar was concealed a round cavity, a shallow well. When he dropped the head inside, she winced at the rattling of its moist heft against dried old ivory domes and mandibles. Jack heaved the altar back, the shadow of its base sliding slowly across Alain's upturned face like the fall of his final night.

Jack nodded out over the menagerie of spirits. "To give them dreams," he said. "To strengthen them against the winter, 'til I see them again."

In the narthex, as the doors swung wide into the moonlit dark beyond, she wanted to cling to him, possess him, to know more and listen to everything he could tell her about . . . well, where she had come from wouldn't be a bad start.

"Why you?" she asked instead. "Why did you get the job of staying up to watch so much of it die around you?"

While it seemed a hideously lonely vigil, if he regarded it that way, you'd never know it. Could he even feel such a thing as loneliness?

"Who better, love?" he said. "Who else tracks time the way it was meant to be measured?"

Just past the doors, he stared up at the pattern of leaf and hair and face carved above them centuries before, by bone of her bone, flesh of her flesh.

"Not a very good likeness, really. I'm much better looking." He laughed with her, and in that moment she knew that, no, even a god was not beyond loneliness. Else why had he told her any of this, and who else could he have told?

"Called me Jack-o'-the-Green, too, they did. And I think, deep in his heart, Crenshaw knows exactly who I am . . . and that's what scares him so."

He drew his pitiful coat about him, looking to the sky, to the vast ocean of stars. Above them, Orion, the Hunter. It was his season. She could always find Orion.

"Best go, love," he said. "Not nearly as much forest as there was once. And I have to go deep, where I'll not be disturbed."

She imagined him in sacred hibernation, fetally curled or regally prone, beneath a blanket of brittle leaves, hair and beard dusted white with frost, snowflakes clinging to his eyelashes. Waiting for warmth.

He drew a huge breath, held it, let it out in a noisy gust and broad grin. "I've a splendid sense of smell, Kate. And I smell a great wildness coming. Maybe not next spring. Nor the spring past that. But it's coming. The land always takes back its own."

He left her soon after, a bulking shape made smaller, darker, with every stride toward the treeline. She lost sight of him even before he entered. Heard the crack and crunch of his passage, then even that was gone.

She returned inside the church, intending to lock up, and got as far as turning out the lights before she knew its floor was all the bed she needed tonight.

And swaddled by spirits, she did not sleep alone that night, dreaming of longer days and the fall of empires, while warmed by the breath of goats.

HARLAN ELLISON

Bleeding Stones

ALCHEMY HIGH ABOVE THE crowds.

Over one hundred years of the Industrial Revolution had spewed chemical magic into the air. The aerosols known as smog. Coal and petroleum fractions containing sulfur, their combustion producing sulfur dioxide, oxidized by atmospheric oxygen to form sulfur trioxide, hydrated by water vapor in the air to sulfuric acid. Alchemical magic that weathers limestone. Particles of soot, particles of ash. Unburned hydrocarbons. Oxides of nitrogen. The magic of ultraviolet radiation, photochemical reactions, photochemical smog: it magically cracks rubber. Unsaturated hydrocarbons, ozone, nitrogen dioxide, formaldehyde, acetone. Magic. Carbon monoxide, carcinogenic hydrocarbons, days and nights of thermal inversion in the atmosphere. Carbon particles, metallic dusts, silicates, fluorides, resins, tars, pollen, fungi, solid oxides, aromatics, even the smells of magic. Catalysis. Carriers of electrostatic charges. *To the extent that they are radioactive,* says page 184 of volume 18 of the 1972 ENCYCLOPAEDIA BRITANNICA, *they increase the nor-*

mal radiation dosage and may be cancer- or mutation-producing factors.

Finally, it goes on, *as plain dust, they soil clothing, buildings, and bodies, and are a general nuisance.*

Alchemical magical nuisance, high above the crowds.

Jammed, thronged, packed, overspilling, flowing and shuddering . . . forty thousand people drawn like iron filings to the magnet of St. Patrick's Cathedral, filling the sidewalks and overflowing into Fifth Avenue . . . the mass bulging outward, human yeast, filling the intersections of 51st Street and Fifth Avenue, 50th and Fifth, 52nd and Fifth . . . rolling to find space along the sidewalks and doorways and garden walks of Rockefeller Center . . .

Hallelujah! The Jesus People have come to the holy summit of organized religion in the land that is the very apotheosis of the Industrial Revolution. St. Patrick's Cathedral, built between 1858 and 1879, puffed out mightily like the pigeons roosting there for over one hundred years as the magic took its time performing its alchemical wonders, the nuisances of cracking rubber, weathering stone, pitting metal, mutating and inverting thermals. Hallelujah!

They are recognized. The Jesus People. One way, united in the worship of Jesus Christ, the Savior, the Son of God; here, at last, at this greatest repository of the faith in the land of ultraviolet radiation, they have come to spread their potency at the altar of organized power.

While above them, on the spires of the city and the parapets of St. Patrick's, the nuisance bears fruit and the stones begin to bleed.

The Cardinal steps out through the massive front doors. The Archdiocese in person, recognizing them. They raise index fingers, thousands of index fingers raised in homage to the One Way.

The Cardinal lifts his arms slowly, his gorgeous robes resplendent in the sunlight glancing off a thousand automobiles spewing out alchemical magic; his arms lift and he is a human crucifix for a moment before his arms rise up above his head and he lifts his index fingers. The crowd trills and sighs with joy. They are known!

The Cardinal feels moisture on his left hand and looks up at his flesh emerging from his sleeve. There is a drop of blood running down through the fold of skin between his thumb and index finger. A fat, globular drop of blood that glistens in the magic air. It bulges and runs in a line down his palm. He is alarmed for a moment: has he cut himself? Then a second drop falls and he realizes the blood is dropping from above.

He looks up.

On the tallest spires of St. Patrick's Cathedral, there is movement.

For over one hundred years the stones of the Cathedral have been silent, still, solid and unwanting. Now the stones begin to bleed as the gargoyles come to life.

His eyes widen and see only movement. . . .

But above, up here where the winds of the city carry alchemical magic, the stone gargoyles tremble, their rock bodies begin to moisten, and blood stands out in humid beads.

The first of the many shudders and its eyes open slowly. Color comes to its stone flesh. Its taloned hands rise from its knees and flex. Corded muscles bunched for a hundred years slide and move. Its belly heaves as it draws in life. Its bat wings twitch and suddenly unfurl. It drinks of the sunlight and the air, drinks deep and sucks the carcinogens deep into its bellows lungs; the nuisance mutation is complete. Come to life after a hundred years is the race that will inherit the Earth; hardly meek, the race made to breathe this new air. The gargoyle throws back its head and its stone fangs catch the sunlight and throw it back brighter than the hides of the vehicles below.

The clarion call blasts against the noonday tumult of the Jesus People. And they fall silent. And they look up. And all around them, on a hundred spires of a hundred skyscrapers the inheritors rise from their crouched positions, their shapes black and firm-edged against the gray and deadly sky.

Then, like the fighting kites of Brazil, they dive into the crowd and begin the ritual slaughter.

The first of the many swoops down in a screaming fall that sends the Jesus People scattering. At the final instant the gray death-kite flattens and sails across the crowd, its talons extended, arms dangling. The razor-nails embed themselves in a skull and rip backward as its flight carries gargoyle and victim forward. It skims skyward again and great muscled arms throw the limp meat against the walls of a building, the body ripped open from occipital ridge to buttocks, entrails bulging, spilling from the sprung carcass. The body slides down the wall leaving a red fluorescent smear.

Another, with a hundred isinglass-thin lids over its lizard eyes, dives straight down at a young girl wearing a halter top and blue jeans with cloth patches of butterflies, flowers and elaborate crosses appliquéd to the fabric. It extends the extraordinarily long and pencilthin first finger of each four-taloned hand, and drives them deep into her eye sockets. Then, hooking the fingers, it lifts her, shrieking, into the sky. It drops her from twenty stories.

Two demi-devils with the heads of gryphons and the bodies of hunchbacked dwarves land with simultaneous crashes on the roof of a Fifth Avenue bus, slash it open with their clawed feet and throw themselves inside. Screams fill the air as the bus fills with bloody pulp. A window is smashed as an old man tries to escape and one of the demi-devils saws his neck across the ragged glass, spraying the street outside with a geyser from the carotid artery. The body continues to kick. The windows of the bus smear and darken over with pulped flesh and viscera. The demi-devils wallow like two babies in a bathtub, drinking and splashing.

A gargoyle with a ring of spikes circling its forehead hurtles into a knot of Jesus People on their knees and hysterically singing *Jesus is a Soul Man*. It rips off the arms of a bearded young man and, flailing about, crushes the skulls of the group. One boy tries to crawl away, his head bleeding, and the gargoyle kicks aside bodies to reach him, grabbing him by the heavy silver chain around his neck. The chain supports a silver crucifix. The gargoyle twists the chain till it sinks into the flesh of the boy's neck. Screaming, the boy tries to struggle erect, clawing at the garrote with both hands, eyes bulging, face darkening to blue-black as the blood gushes from his ears and mouth. The gargoyle flaps its wings, lifts into the air dangling the struggling boy at the end of the silver chain and, swinging him violently, batters the crowd till the body is dismembered.

A gargoyle has ripped the arms from an old woman and peeled the skin and muscle from the bones, sharpening them with its fangs. It charges up the front steps of St. Patrick's Cathedral and impales the Cardinal through the chest and stomach. The Cardinal, spasming in pain, is carried aloft by two other gargoyles who drop him with titters and giggles onto the topmost spire of the Cathedral. He slides down the spire, the point protruding from his stomach, and the gargoyles spin him like the propeller on a child's wind toy.

A gargoyle crouches on a mound of bodies, eating hearts and livers it has ripped from the not-quite-dead casualties. Another sucks the meat off fingers. Another chews eyeballs, savoring the corneal fluid.

A gargoyle has backed a dozen Jesus People and elegant Avenue shoppers into a doorway and jabs at them with bloody talons, taunting them till they howl with dismay. The gargoyle scrapes its talons across the stones of the building till sparks fly . . . and somehow catch fire as they shower the shrieking victims. The fire washes over them and they run screaming into the fangs and talons of the marauder. They die, smoldering, and pile up in the doorway.

A gargoyle with a belly huge and round flies up and around, crouching and defecating on the hordes as they trample each other, running in all directions to escape the slaughter. The voiding is diarrheic and rains down in a thick green and brown curtain that splashes in heavy spattering pools and begins eating into cement asphalt. It is acid; where it strikes human flesh it eats its way through to bone leaving burning edges and smoking pits. Hundreds fall and are crushed by stampeding pedestrians with no exit.

A gargoyle alights atop the bronze statue of Atlas holding the world on his shoulders that dominates the entrance to 630 Fifth Avenue, kicks loose the great bronze globe and sends it hammering into the crowd. Dozens are crushed at the impact and the gargoyle, laughing hysterically, boots it again and again. The globe thunders through the street flattening cars and people, leaving in its wake a trail of twisted bodies and a gutter-wash of blood and pulp that clogs drain basins with human refuse.

Three gargoyles have found a nun. Two have lifted her above their heads, and wrenching her legs apart like a wishbone, they are splitting her in half as the third creature breaks off a bus stop sign and punches the jagged end of the pole up her vagina, shrieking *Regnum dei in vobis est,* the kingdom of God is within you.

The slaughter goes on and on for hours. The screams of the dying rise up to meet the automated chiming of the Cathedral bells. Darkness falls and the hellfire of demon flames and human beings used as torches illuminates the expanse of Fifth Avenue.

All through the night it goes on as the gargoyles range out and around, widening their circles of destruction. Nothing can stop them. The weapons of humankind are useless against them. They are intent upon inheriting the Earth all on the first day and night of their birth.

Finally, nothing moves in the city but the creatures that were once stone; and they fly up, circling the stainless steel and glass towers of industrial magic. They look down with the hungry eyes of those who have slept too long and now, rested, seek exercise.

Then, laughing triumphantly, they flap bat wings and soar upward, flying off toward the east, toward the Vatican.

THE GALLERY
(Contributors' Notes)

JO CLAYTON's many books included the *Diadem* series (*Diadem from the Stars, Star Hunters, The Nowhere Hunt, Quester's Endgame,* etc.) and the *Shadith's Quest* series (*Shadowplay, Shadowspeer, Shadowkill*).

DON D'AMMASSA is the author of the novel *Blood Beast,* and has had short stories published in *Shock Rock,* the *Hot Blood* series, *Blood Muse, Adventures in the Twilight Zone, Peter Straub's Ghosts, Deathport,* and other anthologies and magazines. He reviews horror and science fiction for *SF Chronicle,* and *D'Ammassa's Guide to Modern Horror* is available from Borgo Press.

CHARLES DE LINT is a full-time writer and musician who presently makes his home in Ottawa, Canada, with his wife MaryAnn Harris, an artist and musician. His most recent book is *Moonlight and Vines*, a third collection of Newford stories (Tor Books, 1999). Other recent publications include the mass-market edition of *Someplace to Be Flying* (Tor

Books, 1999) and reprints of his classic novels, *Greenmantle* (Orb/Tor Books, 1998) and *Jack of Kinrowan* (Orb/Tor Books, 1999). For more information about his work, visit his website at http://www.cyberus.ca/~cdl.

The incomparable HARLAN ELLISON is one of the world's most celebrated authors of imaginative fiction in any language, and is also a widely-published and respected essayist and reviewer. His many awards include the Lifetime Achievement awards of both the Horror Writers Association and the World Fantasy Convention, and multiple Hugo, Nebula, Bram Stoker, and Edgar Allan Poe awards. Among his 74 books are *Slippage, Mind Fields, Deathbird Stories, I Have No Mouth and I Must Scream, Shatterday, Stalking the Nightmare, Angry Candy,* and the current Edgeworks series of 31 titles in 20 volumes.

CHRISTA FAUST'S short fiction has appeared in anthologies such as *Love in Vein, Hot Blood: Stranger By Night,* and *Millennium* (with Poppy Z. Brite). Her image can be found in publications ranging from *Tattoo Savage* magazine to *The New York Times.* She lives in Hollywood with husband David J. Schow. For more info, visit Pandora Station: http://www.negia.net/ ~pandora/

Born on the 10th of November, 1960, NEIL GAIMAN is best known as the author of the World Fantasy Award–winning adult comic *Sandman,* a story about dreams and stories, available in ten volumes beginning with *Preludes and Nocturnes* and finishing with *The Wake.* He also wrote *Neverwhere,* a TV series and novel about a strange world underneath London, and the International Horror Critics Guild winning *Angels and Visitations.* He is currently writing three films and a novella. His recent works are the short story collection *Smoke and Mirrors* and the novel *Stardust.* His hobbies include sleeping and eating.

CHARLES L. GRANT has written over one hundred books in many genres. His more than 140 short stories have appeared in many major genre magazines and anthologies, with translations appearing in most European markets. He was the editor of the long-running and widely acclaimed *Shadows* anthology series. In 1987 he received the British Fantasy Society Award for Life Achievement. He has also received two Nebula and three World Fantasy Awards for writing and editing. He is married to writer and editor Kathryn Ptacek and lives in New Jersey.

ROBERT J. HARRIS has several stories published in anthologies and with his novelist wife, Deborah Turner Harris, works on constructing the worlds for her fiction. He is the author of several well-known role-playing games. Harris lives with his wife and three small sons in St. Andrews, Scotland.

BRIAN HODGE has published seven novels, most recently *Wild Horses,* a major 1999 hardcover release from William Morrow & Company. He has also written upwards of seventy-five short stories and novellas, several of which have been chained like galley slaves into the highly acclaimed collections *The Convulsion Factory* and *Falling Idols.* He also pens book and music reviews, and other nonfiction as the voices command. He lives in Boulder, Colorado, where at this very moment he is likely to be sawing away at his next novel, or hammering together music in his cramped but functional collective of recording gear dubbed Green Man Studio. Visit the mandatory web site: http://www.para-net.com/~brian_hodge

NANCY HOLDER has sold thirty-eight books and over two hundred short stories, articles, and essays. She has received four Bram Stoker awards from the Horror Writers Association, three for Short Fiction and one for her novel *Dead in the Water.* She has been translated into over two dozen languages. Solo and with her frequent coauthor, Christopher Golden, she has sold thirteen *Buffy the Vampire Slayer* projects, and she also writes fiction based on *Sabrina, the Teenage Witch.* She lives in San Diego with her husband, Wayne, their daughter, Belle, and their pack of Border collies, Mr. Ron, Maggie, and Dot.

CAITLÔN R. KIERNAN's first novel, *Silk,* has received both the International Horror Guild and the Barnes & Noble Maiden Voyage Award for best first novel, as well as a nomination in the same category for the '99 Bram Stoker Award. Her goth and gothnoir short fiction has appeared in such anthologies as *Dark Terrors 2* and *3, Love in Vein II, The Year's Best Fantasy and Horror Eleven,* and *The Mammoth Book of Best New Horror 9* and *10.* Her 1998 chapbook, *Candles for Elizabeth,* will be followed in 2000 by two full-length collections—*Tales of Pain and Wonder* and *From Weird and Distant Shores.* Caitlín also scripts *The Dreaming* and other projects for DC Comics/Vertigo and studies vertebrate paleontology in her spare time.

KATHERINE KURTZ is best known for her *Deryni* Saga, now comprising 12 novels and several companion works, and also the Adept series, co-authored with Deborah Turner Harris, and several "crypto-historical" novels. A resident of Ireland for the past decade, she and her husband, fellow-author Scott MacMillan, share their gothic revival house just outside Dublin with their son, three cats, and at least two resident ghosts.

MARC LEVINTHAL is a musician and writer who has lived in Los Angeles since 1980. He co-wrote the score for the film *Valley Girl* and the hit single "Three Little Pigs" for *Green Jello.* Marc composed the music for cartoonist Krystine Kryttre's "Anemia and Iodine," a segment on the *Kablaam* show on Nickelodeon. He has played in way too many bands, including The Torture Chamber Ensemble. Marc recently released his first CD, a collection of atmospheric/ambient music under the moniker *Dimetrodon Collective Volume One.* Past collaborations with John Mason Skipp include "The Punchline" (*Dark Destiny II*) and "On a Big Night in Monster History" (*Dark Destiny III*). A novel is in the works. Marc currently lives in ultra-groovy Silverlake with his fiancée and five moderately evil cats.

Initially inspired by Lovecraft, BRIAN LUMLEY has gone on to carve his own niche in horror. The bestselling author of the *Necroscope* series, winner of the 1998 World Horror Convention's Grand Master Award, and the former president of the Horror Writer's Association, he is a frequent visitor to the U.S.A. but makes his home in Devon, England, with an American wife and Jasper the cat. Brian's web site at http://www.brianlumley.com is among the very best of its kind, and all visitors are made welcome.

ALAN RODGERS is the author of *Bone Music, Pandora, Fire, Night, Blood of the Children, The Bear Who Found Christmas*, and *New Life for the Dead*. *Blood of the Children* was a nominee for the Horror Writers of America Bram Stoker Award; his first story (actually a novelette), "The Boy Who Came Back from the Dead," won a Stoker and lost a World Fantasy Award. During the mideighties he edited the fondly remembered horror digest, *Night Cry*. He lives in the San Fernando Valley.

Writer/director/musician/et cetera JOHN MASON SKIPP has spent the last seven years preparing *PEEKABOO*, his feature filmmaking debut. "I call it my 'Decapathon,'" he says, "because it features more severed heads per square inch than anything since *Apocalypse Now*." On the literary front, upcoming books include *The Emerald Burrito* (with Marc Levinthal); *PEEKABOO* (THE NOVEL) and *Mondo Zombie*, an anthology that picks up where Skipp and Spector's *Books of the Dead* left off.

LUCY TAYLOR is a full-time writer whose short story collections include *Close to the Bone, The Flesh Artist*, and *Unnatural Acts and Other Stories*. Her first novel, *The Safety of Unknown Cities*, was awarded the Bram Stoker Award from the Horror Writers Association for superior achievement in a first novel. Her second novel is *Dancing with Demons* (Obsidian Press, 1999), and she contributed a novella to the book *Triptych*, available from Sideshow Press in late 1999. Her third novel, *Eternal Hearts*, will be available in the fall from White Wolf. She and her partner share a home in Mead, Colorado, with six wonderful cats.

Among MELANIE TEM'S novels are *Revenant, Desmodus, Wilding, Witchlight* (in collaboration with Nancy Holder), and *The Tides* (Leisure, August, 1999). Her short fiction has recently appeared in the *Hot Blood* series and *Cemetery Dance*. A former social worker, she lives in Denver with her husband, writer and editor Steve Rasnic Tem. They have four children and two granddaughters.

WENDY WEBB'S short fiction has appeared in many anthologies. She has coedited three anthologies, including the recent *Gothic Ghosts* with Charles Grant. A playwright when not working on stories and novels, she has staged a professional production of her children's play, "The Dark Under the Bed," as well as readings of multiple works. Her collection of gargoyles continues to adorn her office, and her lastest novel-length work features the stoic creatures in locations around the world.

JANE YOLEN is the author of over 170 books for children and adults. Her stories and books have won the World Fantasy Award, the Caldecott Medal, the Mythopoeic Society Award, the Daedelus Award, and the Skylark Award. She has been a finalist for both the Nebula and the National Book Award. She lives with her husband in Hatfield, Massachusetts, and St. Andrews, Scotland.

ABOUT THE EDITORS

NANCY KILPATRICK has edited seven anthologies, published thirteen novels and over a hundred short stories. She won the Arthur Ellis Award for Best Short Fiction. Currently she is working on her third collection of short fiction, *The Vampire Stories of Nancy Kilpatrick*, to be published in 2000. She lives in Montreal, Quebec, with her cat, Bella, and loves to travel the world searching for grotesqueries with her companion. Visit her website: http://www.sff.net/people/nancyk.

THOMAS S. ROCHE is a staff writer at the online culture magazine www.GettingIt.com, as well as a freelance music journalist, a humorist, and a writer of fantasy, horror, and crime fiction. His articles have appeared in such music magazines as *Carp Noctem* and *Experience: The Jimi Hendrix Magazine*, and his short stories have appeared in numerous anthologies. He lives in San Francisco, where he has recently completed his first novel.

PENGUIN PUTNAM INC.
Online

Your Internet gateway to a virtual environment with
hundreds of entertaining and enlightening books from
Penguin Putnam Inc.

*While you're there, get the latest buzz on
the best authors and books around—*

Tom Clancy, Patricia Cornwell, W.E.B. Griffin,
Nora Roberts, William Gibson, Robin Cook,
Brian Jacques, Catherine Coulter, Stephen King,
Jacquelyn Mitchard, and many more!

Penguin Putnam Online is located at
http://www.penguinputnam.com

PENGUIN PUTNAM NEWS

Every month you'll get an inside look at our upcoming
books and new features on our site. This is an ongoing
effort to provide you with the most up-to-date
information about our books and authors.

Subscribe to Penguin Putnam News at
http://www.penguinputnam.com/ClubPPI